(continued on next page…)

"[Perrotta] draws the title of his novel from Dave's band, a collection of tuxedo-wearing, competent musicians who dig Black Sabbath but pay the bills with Village People covers and the Electric Slide . . . Their Cheez Whiz and cheap-beer lives give Perrotta the landscape for some good comedy."

—*Boston Sunday Herald*

"Perrotta lays out Dave's difficulties with an expert sense of pacing and revelatory incident, combining moments of unassuming poignancy with an offhand humor that occasionally rises to the hilarious."

—*The New York Times Book Review*

"Tom Perrotta has an amazing sense of humor, and *The Wishbones* is an intensely funny book."

—Wayne Koestenbaum, author of *Jackie under My Skin*

PRAISE FOR TOM PERROTTA'S
Bad Haircut:

"More powerful than any coming-of-age novel I've read recently . . . These stories of the '70s deserve to be read by everyone who grew up in that blighted decade."

—*Washington Post*

"Somewhere between Bruce Springsteen's 'Thunder Road' and Princeton's tennis courts lies the New Jersey of these darkly tender, simply written tales about growing up in the Garden State in the 1970s."

—*The New York Times Book Review*

"Funny and ingenious . . . It's tempting to call *Bad Haircut* an 'auspicious' book, but that doesn't say enough; in fact Perrotta has already delivered the goods."

—*Los Angeles Times*

Berkley Books by Tom Perrotta

BAD HAIRCUT: STORIES OF THE SEVENTIES
THE WISHBONES
ELECTION

The Wishbones

TOM PERROTTA

B
BERKLEY BOOKS, NEW YORK

THE WISHBONES

A Berkley Book / published by arrangement with
the author

PRINTING HISTORY
G. P. Putnam's Sons edition / May 1997
Berkley trade paperback edition / April 1998
Berkley mass market edition / July 1999

The Penguin Putnam Inc. World Wide Web site address is
http://www.penguinputnam.com

ISBN: 0-425-16971-5

BERKLEY®
Berkley Books are published by The Berkley Publishing Group,
a division of Penguin Putnam Inc.,
375 Hudson Street, New York, New York 10014.
BERKLEY and the "B" logo
are trademarks belonging to Penguin Putnam Inc.

PRINTED IN THE UNITED STATES OF AMERICA

10 9 8 7 6 5 4 3 2 1

I'd like to thank John Talbot and Maria Massie for their help in making this book a reality. I'm grateful to Mike Perrotta and all the members of R.S.V.P., one of New Jersey's finest wedding bands, for letting me watch them in action. Special thanks to Mary and Nina for too many gifts to enumerate.

For my parents

This must be the death of rock 'n roll. . . .
—Todd Rundgren

The
Wishbones

Tom Perrotta

May

The Wednesday-night Showcase

Buzzy, the bass player, had a suspended license, so Dave swung by his house on the way to the Wednesday-night showcase. Buzzy did quality control for a company that manufactured prosthetic devices, and lived with his wife and two kids on a street of more or less identical split-levels that must have seemed like an exciting place in the days before the British Invasion, back when Kennedy was President and Elvis was King. Buzzy was the only member of the wedding band who was married, a fact whose irony did not escape the notice of his fellow musicians. Artie, the sax player and manager, had just broken up with a girl who danced at Jiggles. Stan, the drummer and sometime accordionist, was sleepwalking through a painful divorce. Ian, the singer/keyboardist and all-around showman, was living at home with his parents, as was Dave, who handled rhythm guitar and background vocals.

Buzzy was waiting by the curb, a scrawny, ponytailed guy in a tuxedo and Yankees cap, with a beer in one hand

and a guitar case in the other. He stowed his bass in the backseat, on top of Dave's Les Paul, and climbed in.

"Daverino," he said, tilting the beer can in salute.

"Buzzmaster."

Dave shifted into gear and headed for Central Avenue. The silence in the car was mellow, uncomplicated. Buzzy took a swig from the can and smacked his lips.

"Yup. Another Wednesday-night showcase."

"You ready? The people are counting on you."

Buzzy thought it over for a couple of seconds, then nodded.

"Coach," he said, "I'm gonna play my heart out."

Dave snorted his appreciation. The guys in the band liked to joke about the showcase, but they were careful not to complain—bookings had doubled since Artie found them the slot. And besides, goofy as it was, the showcase turned out to be a real time-saver: instead of scheduling separate auditions for every interested couple, the Wishbones could just tell prospective customers to come to the Ramada every third Wednesday of the month.

"You going out afterward?" Buzzy crushed the can in his hand and dropped it on the floor. "I'm in the mood for a few beers."

"I can't. I'm supposed to go over to Julie's."

"Hey." Buzzy didn't bother to conceal his surprise. "You guys really getting back together?"

Dave didn't feel like going into the details. He had made a mistake telling the guys what had happened in the first place. He should have known he'd never hear the end of it. Now the incident had become part of band lore, like the night Ian got propositioned by the mother-of-the-bride, and that time Artie got his lights punched out by a Puerto Rican DJ.

"We've been talking on the phone. She says her parents aren't so upset anymore."

Dave kept his eyes on the road. He didn't have to look to know that Buzzy was smirking.

"I wish I'd been there, man. Just to see the look on their faces."

Dave grimaced. The look on their faces was the last thing he wanted to think about.

"We've been going out for a long time. I guess it was bound to happen sooner or later."

"A long time?" Buzzy seemed to be deriving great pleasure from the conversation. "Fifteen years, Dave. You've been going out with the woman for fifteen years. Since your sophomore year of high school."

$5.99 BUFFET, proclaimed the marquee outside the Cranwood Ramada. SHOWCASE OF MUSICAL TALENT. Dave pulled into the sparsely occupied lot, glad for the opportunity to change the subject.

"Looks like a slow night." He put the car into park and shut off the ignition.

Buzzy wasn't about to give up so easily. "What are you going to say to her parents?"

Dave undid his seat belt and opened the door. It was a lovely spring night. Leaving the guitars for Buzzy, he stepped out of the car and started walking at a brisk pace toward the entrance of the Sundown Lounge. Buzzy had to run to catch up with him, the hardshell cases banging like luggage against the outside of his legs.

"Bring flowers," he advised, panting a little from the exertion. "You'll need all the help you can get."

Sparkle was nearing the end of their set when Dave and Buzzy entered the lounge. Their lead singer, Alan Zelack, was strutting across the stage in his red sequined tux, belting out "My Girl" in the heavy-metal falsetto he'd perfected during years of touring with the Misty Mountain Revue, a wildly successful Led Zeppelin tribute show. Now everything he touched came out sounding like Zeppelin, from Sinatra to the Hokey Pokey.

Artie and Ian were sitting at a table in the corner, looking like a couple trapped in a bad marriage. Both of them seemed relieved by the arrival of some new blood.

"Guess what?" Buzzy said, before they'd even had a chance to settle into their chairs. "Dave's going over to Julie's later on."

"No way," said Ian.

"Bull*shit*," said Artie.

Dave held up both hands in a futile plea for restraint.

"Don't ask. It's none of your fucking business."

But it was already too late. The story had moved into the public domain. Artie turned to Ian, smiling nervously.

"Mr. Muller, sir? I'm not sure if you remember me. I'm Dave . . . Dave Raymond?"

Ian inhaled through his teeth, looking puzzled. "Sorry, Dave. The name doesn't ring a bell."

"You know," Artie added helpfully, "the guy you caught poking your daughter?"

Ian clapped himself in the forehead. "Oh, *that* Dave. How could I have forgotten. Come on in. Honey, guess who's here?"

Even Dave had to laugh at that. All day long he'd been dreading the thought of having to face Julie's parents. He'd run through a number of scenarios in his head, but none of them included the possibility that he'd have to jog their memories about the circumstances of their last meeting.

"If they don't recognize you," Buzzy suggested, "you can always try pulling your pants down."

Dave's bandmates traded high fives as Sparkle launched into "Stairway to Heaven," their final song of every showcase performance. It was the secret of their immense popularity, the ultimate sales pitch to a generation that couldn't imagine a special occasion that wouldn't be made even more special by a faithful live version of what radio station after radio station had determined to be "the most popular song of all-time."

"Fuckin' Stairway," mumbled Artie.

Ian glanced at the stage. "Look at that fool."

Zelack was sparkling in the spotlight, eyes closed, mouth pressed lovingly to the mike as he crooned the immortal gibberish about hedgerows and spring cleaning. Dave pushed his chair away from the table.

"I can't listen to this shit," he said, to no one in particular.

It was better outside. The night was quiet and the air seemed reasonably fresh for this part of the world. Dave sat down on the curb by the fire lane and stared at the lopped-off moon glowing dully above the Parkway overpass. He liked being part of the Wishbones, and he liked the other guys in the group, but sometimes the showcase got to him. It was more the atmosphere than anything else, the unmistakable odor of mediocrity that seemed to be as much a part of the Sundown Lounge as the paper tablecloths and the green leatherette menus.

Alan Zelack pissed him off too, and it wasn't just the sequined tuxedo or his idiotic falsetto. Four years earlier, Dave had auditioned for the Misty Mountain Revue. He wasn't a huge Zeppelin fan, but he was unemployed at the time and would've killed for a chance to make some money playing rock 'n roll on a regular basis. He kicked ass at the audition, nailing the "Heartbreaker" solo note for note, every bend, hammer, and blast of feedback accounted for. But he didn't get the job.

"You've got the chops," Zelack told him afterward. "There's no doubt about that. But this is show business. You've got to look the part."

The sad thing was, Dave knew he was right. Zelack looked like a rock star. He was tall and whip thin, with high cheekbones and the mutant jaw of a born singer. Dave, on the other hand, just looked like a regular guy. He was an inch or two shorter than average, maybe a bit on the stocky side. Once, out of curiosity, he'd squeezed

himself into a pair of leather pants, and it hadn't been a
pretty sight.

Tonight, though, he had bigger things to worry about
than his inability to pass for Jimmy Page. The guys could
laugh all they wanted; Dave was the one who was going
to have to walk into the Mullers' house and try to conduct
some sort of halfway civil chitchat with people who
wouldn't have to use their imagination to picture him hop-
ping from foot to foot, naked except for a hot pink condom.

It was ironic in a way. He and Julie had been having
sex since they were sixteen. They had been reckless back
then—no self-restraint, no birth control, no common
sense. They used to screw in the basement rec room with
her parents right upstairs, snoring in dreamland. If they
were going to be caught, they should have been caught
back then, at the height of their passion, back when they
used to stare at each other's bodies in stupefied amazement, and compete to see who could say "I love you"
more times in a single night. It didn't make any sense to
be caught now, when they'd already been through an
abortion, four different breakups, mutual infidelities, and
so many bitter discussions about the future that they didn't
bother to talk about it anymore. Not now, when Julie suf-
fered from a more or less chronic yeast infection that had
turned their lovemaking into a polite and tentative activity, full of murmured questions and apologies. Not now,
when it was embarrassing enough just to *be* over thirty
and still fucking in the rec room.

But Mr. and Mrs. Muller didn't care about any of that.
They were supposed to have been in Atlantic City that
afternoon, but Mr. Muller had forgotten his wallet, and
hadn't realized it until two hours into the drive. So they'd
just turned around and come on home—what else was
there to do?—only to find their youngest daughter on her
hands and knees on the rec room floor, and Dave kneeling
behind her, singing along with the unbearably loud music

blasting from the stereo (John Mellencamp, Julie's favorite), the volume of which had apparently concealed the noise of their arrival.

What transpired after that remained mercifully fuzzy in Dave's memory. All he really remembered was the bloodless shock on Julie's mother's face as he scrambled to his feet, his penis shrinking rapidly inside the neon condom (a random selection from a novelty assortment he'd purchased in Greenwich Village), only to discover that his right foot had fallen asleep.

"Mrs. Muller," he'd assured her, reaching down like Adam to conceal his shame while unsuccessfully trying to balance on his left foot, "this isn't what you think."

A car door slammed. Dave looked up and saw a bulky, apparently perturbed man come jogging across the parking lot in a tuxedo. As he drew closer, Dave heard him mumbling to himself as he fumbled with the hooks of his cummerbund.

"Slow down," he called out. "You're not late."

Stan stopped running and peered in the direction of the voice, shading his eyes with one hand as though it were daytime.

"Dave?"

"Yeah."

"What are you doing out here?"

"You got any better ideas?"

Stan's only response was to trudge over to the curb and sit down. After a couple of seconds he exhaled wearily and stretched his legs out in front of him, revealing a pair of battered work boots protruding like loaves from the cuffs of his black trousers.

"Artie's not going to like that," Dave pointed out.

"I lost my good shoes," Stan explained. "I turned the damn house upside down trying to find them. That's why I'm late."

"Don't sweat it. It's only the showcase."

"I looked everywhere," Stan continued, an edge of desperation creeping into his voice. "I mean, what did they do? Get up and take a walk without me?"

Stan had been a wreck for the past couple of months, ever since his wife announced that she was leaving him for her boss, a fifty-five-year-old lawyer with strange puffy hair who appeared in his own TV commercials, encouraging viewers to consider legal remedies for a host of everyday mishaps and conditions. Never the most reliable guy to begin with, Stan had lately been screwing up on a scale that was beginning to jeopardize his situation with Artie, who insisted on running the Wishbones like a business. He'd been late for two gigs in the past month (once because he'd locked his keys in his car, and once because he'd driven all the way to the Royal Oak before remembering that the reception was actually at the Blue Spruce); on a third occasion he'd shown up on time, but without drumsticks.

"I don't try to fuck up," he explained, as if Dave had inquired about this possibility. "I've just got a lot on my mind right now."

"No problem." Dave patted him on the shoulder blade. "It happens to everyone."

Stan nodded for a long time, as though the secrets of the universe were being revealed to him one by one.

"Do me a favor," he said. "Tell that to Artie."

Phil Hart and His Heartstring Orchestra were tuning up on stage #2 when Dave returned to the lounge with Stan's hi-hat in one hand and drum stand in the other. Sparkle was breaking down their equipment on stage #1, and when they were finished, the Wishbones would begin setting up. The two stages—one at either end of the lounge—were the key to the smooth operation of the showcase.

As always, Phil and the boys opened with a surprisingly spunky version of "Celebration," by Kool and the Gang—surprising, because with the exception of the drummer (Phil's grandson, a pockmarked recovering drug addict named Joey), everyone in the combo had more or less vivid memories of the Hoover administration. Walter, the piano player, whose hands shook terribly when he was doing anything but tickling the ivories, was rumored to be eighty-two years old.

Despite their age, powder blue uniforms, and schizoid repertoire, the Heartstring Orchestra was made up of real musicians, old pros from the Big Band era (the reed player's twin brother had apparently toured for a couple of years with Tommy Dorsey). When they shifted away from disco standards to songs that were better suited to their talents—"Chattanooga Choo-Choo," "Paper Doll," "Boogie-Woogie Bugle Boy"—you couldn't help but notice a change of weather inside the Sundown Lounge. Fingers started snapping; heads began to bob. It wasn't unusual to see a natty-looking older couple—the Orchestra specialized in second and third marriages—put down their drinks and take a graceful turn around the dance floor.

Phil Hart himself wasn't the greatest singer in the world, but he was a true showman. The man had style. Dave always took a moment to admire his distinctive way of moving onstage, a high-elbowed liquidy sway that was the essence of geriatric cool. If you asked, Phil would happily reveal the secret of his remarkable vitality.

"Artificial hips!" he'd exclaim, shaking his head at the marvels of modern technology. "I can wiggle again!"

One of the things Dave liked best about the wedding band was its efficiency. They could set up in twenty minutes and break down even faster than that. Some of the rock bands he'd played in had been weighed down by so much equipment that he'd felt more like a roadie than a musician. Löckjaw was the worst offender. He remembered an outdoor Battle of the Bands where they'd taken four hours to set up for a forty-five-minute performance marred by such earsplitting shrieks of feedback that even the die-hard headbangers in the audience were squeezing their ears, begging for mercy. (Löckjaw came in fifth out of five bands and dissolved a few months later.)

The Wishbones made music on a more human scale. Dave had joined the band with a number of reservations—the uniforms, the cheesy tunes, Artie's reputation as a ballbuster—but he quickly came to realize that the rewards went far beyond the two hundred dollars he got for playing a four-hour gig.

It turned out, amazingly enough, to be a blast. People drank at weddings. They danced like maniacs. They clapped and hooted and made requests. Every now and then, when the chemistry was right, things got raucous. And when that happened, the Wishbones knew how to crank up the volume and rock, with no apologies to anyone.

Dave had friends who were still chasing their dreams, playing in dingy clubs to audiences of twelve bored drunks, splitting thirty-nine dollars among four guys at the end of the night, then dragging themselves home at three o'clock in the morning. He saw the best of them growing exhausted and bitter, endlessly chewing over the thankless question of why the world still didn't give a shit.

Dave himself still hadn't completely surrendered his dream of the Big Time, but he had moved it to the back burner. Someday, maybe, the perfect band would come along, a band so good that no one would be able to say no to them. Until then, though, Dave was a Wishbone, and it was a helluva lot better than nothing.

Afterwards, because the event came to seem so signifi-
cant in retrospect, he sometimes found himself trying to
reconstruct it in his memory, as though the smallest detail
might hold the key to some larger mystery.

The Wishbones had just finished setting up when the
Heartstring Orchestra broke into "Like a Virgin," their
next-to-last tune of the night. If Madonna had happened
to wander into the Sundown to check out the showcase,
Dave thought she would have approved. Phil Hart gave
the song a hilarious deadpan interpretation, as though it
had never entered his mind that some people might find
it amusing to see a seventy-three-year-old man with artificial hips doing a dignified shimmy at the mike stand as
he sang about being touched for the very first time.

Dave leaned his guitar against his amp and stepped
down from the rickety wooden platform that served as
stage #1. He waved to the waitress, a brassy-haired
woman of indeterminate age named Hilda, and mimed the
act of bringing a glass to his mouth. Hilda nodded, but
moved across the lounge in the opposite direction to wait
on some paying customers, a young couple holding hands
across the table and gazing at each other with that blissful
prenewlywed intensity that would somehow evolve over
the next two decades into the vacant stares of the long-
married. It wasn't until Ian sidled up to him a few seconds
later that Dave realized he'd been frozen in place, the
invisible empty glass still tilted to his lips.

"Mick Box," said Ian.

"Shit," said Dave.

At every Wishbone function, Ian tried to stump Dave
with a piece of rock trivia. He specialized in obscure British musicians from second-rate bands of the early seventies.

"Take your time," Ian taunted. "It'll come to you."

"Mick Box," Dave chanted. "Mick Box . . . Mick Box
. . . Mick Box . . ."

"You probably haven't thought about this band for fifteen years."

A face began to take shape in Dave's mind. Narrow, ferrety features. The obligatory hair.

"I'm seeing a mustache," he said.

"If it's a Fu Manchu, you're definitely getting warmer."

"I want to say Mott the Hoople, but that's Mick Ronson."

Dave's eyes strayed around the lounge as he attempted to place the mustachioed Mick in a band he hadn't thought about for fifteen years. Up on stage #2, Phil Hart was twisting his way through a musical interlude in "Like a Virgin." On stage #1, Artie was lecturing Stan about proper Wishbone attire, frowning and jabbing his finger in the direction of the offending work boots. Stan kept nodding like a kid, mouthing the words, "Okay, okay," over and over again.

"I give up," said Dave. "Is it Slade?"

"Close," groaned Ian. He winced as though pained on Dave's behalf. "Mick Box was in Uriah Heep."

"Damn. I used to love Uriah Heep."

"Easy Livin'," agreed Ian. "One of the great tunes of all time."

"Mick Box," laughed Dave. "What the fuck kind of name is that?"

In the middle of the lounge, the gazers were still enraptured with one another while Hilda stood by, pencil in hand, looking bored. At a nearby table, Alan Zelack touched wineglasses with a ridiculously beautiful woman in a slinky black dress who appeared to have materialized out of nowhere. With the sixth sense of a complete asshole, Zelack turned slowly, grinning with triumphant smugness, and raised his glass in greeting. Dave pretended not to notice.

"What the fuck kind of name is Uriah Heep?" Ian wondered.

That was when it happened. Dave looked up just in time to watch Phil Hart stop singing in the middle of the final chorus. A look of mild surprise passed across his face—*recognition,* Dave would later decide—as he turned slightly to the left. He wobbled—there was no other word for it—and the microphone slipped through his fingers, bouncing off the stage with a percussive cough of static.

Joey stopped drumming and looked around in alarm. Phil remained upright for a moment, empty-handed and wonder stricken, before sinking, almost gently, to his knees. Walter kept pounding his electric piano, oblivious to everything but the final measures of the song. Phil's eyes got big. He flung his arms wide like Al Jolson, as if to embrace his fate, and then pitched suddenly forward, landing facedown on the stage in a position he never would have chosen if he'd been offered even the slightest amount of choice in the matter.

Two hours later, drained and without flowers, Dave pulled up in front of Julie's house. He sat in the car for a few minutes listening to the engine tick, trying to work up the energy to open the door.

For the first time in his life, he had actually watched someone die—a man he liked and admired—and for the moment, at least, everything else seemed insubstantial, not fully serious. The thought of facing Julie's parents no longer disturbed him. Instead he felt a strange tenderness, as though he were preparing to visit them in the hospital.

It hadn't taken Phil Hart a long time to die, but an eternity seemed to have passed between the moment of his collapse and the arrival of medical assistance. At first the whole room seemed paralyzed, as though everyone were simply waiting for Phil to leap up and finish the song. Finally, Mel, the arthritic sax player, bent down with visible difficulty and retrieved the fallen microphone.

"Phil's hurt," he announced, in a voice too calm for

the circumstances. "Would someone be kind enough to call an ambulance?"

The Sundown burst into a hectic flurry of motion, with people scattering in several different directions at once, shouting for a telephone. Dave and Ian rushed across the lounge to check on Phil.

"Is there a doctor in the house?" Mel inquired. "How about a nurse?"

By the time Dave reached the edge of stage #2, Joey had already emerged from behind his drum kit, rolled Phil onto his back, and begun loosening the buttons of his ruffled shirt. Phil submitted patiently to these ministrations, his awestruck face turned to the ceiling. Even then, from a distance of about ten feet, Dave could see that he was gone.

"Grampa," Joey implored him. "Grampa, *please.*"

"Is there a doctor in the house?" Mel repeated. "Does anyone know CPR?"

Dave hunched his shoulders and took a step back from the stage, trying to look as inconspicuous as possible. He had taken a CPR class in high school, but all he remembered was that Ralph Vergiliak had pretended to hump the dummy, earning himself a week's detention.

"Grampa." Joey's voice was stern now, as though he were scolding the dead man for his lack of cooperation. He grabbed hold of Phil's shoulders and gave them a hard shake. "Come on now, Grampa."

From the corner of his eye, Dave caught a brilliant flash of red. Before he understood what he was looking at, Alan Zelack had rushed across the stage, shoved Joey out of the way, and begun CPR. The whole sequence came back to Dave as he watched—the head tilt, the sweep of the mouth with one finger, the pinching off of the nostrils. The multiple chest compressions for every breath of air.

Zelack performed these actions with ostentatious competence, his blond hair flying, his red tuxedo shooting off tiny urgent flares. Dave's first, ungenerous impulse was to resent him for hogging the spotlight even in a tragedy, but that quickly passed, replaced by a grudging sense of respect. Like everyone else gathered around the stage, Zelack must have known that Phil was already dead. And yet he kept trying fiercely to bring him back, pumping his chest and filling his lungs, minute after interminable minute, until the ambulance finally arrived, and Phil's body became the property of professionals.

The Wishbones played their set anyway. They thought about canceling, but a couple had traveled all the way from Belvidere with their wedding consultant to check them out, and didn't want to have to make the trek again. As a courtesy to them, Artie decided that the show must go on.

Dave felt a little weird about it, but as soon as he strummed the first chord of "Jailhouse Rock," his reservations vanished. The music jolted him like an electric shock. It seemed to pass through his body on its way from the guitar to the amp, cleansing him, reminding him of how good it felt to be alive.

And it wasn't just Dave, either. Buzzy, who usually stood stone-faced and motionless while he played, was grinning with amazement, rocking from side to side as he plucked out the pulse of the song. Ian had abandoned his usual two-bit Elvis impersonation and was singing like he meant it, while Stan pounded the drums as though exorcising the demons from his life. Even Artie caught the wave. The solo jumped out of his horn, every note of it a fresh squawk of pleasure. It seemed to Dave that the song had never existed before, that they'd invented it on the spot.

Somehow they kept the momentum for ten more tunes, finding something real in even the tiredest old standards. When they had run the gamut of their repertoire, from disco to pop, from polka to R&B, Ian surprised them all by breaking into one last song on his piano, something the Wishbones had never done before.

"This is for Phil," he said. "Rest in peace, brother."

The chords were simple, and Dave recognized them right away. He hadn't played "Knockin' on Heaven's Door" since high school, back when he was lead guitarist in a band called Exit 36. Listening to the words now, colored as they were by death, Dave wondered what they could have meant to a bunch of teenagers in a suburban garage in 1979, kids whose idea of heaven was half an ounce of Colombian Gold and a girl with big tits to smoke it with.

But then he stopped wondering and gave himself up to the song. He closed his eyes and sang the chorus with every ounce of strength in his body. It was a blessing. *Rest in peace, brother.*

Julie answered the door in gray sweatpants and a baggy orange T-shirt. In her hand was a fat paperback with a tortilla chip marking the page.

"You lucked out," she whispered, jerking her thumb in the direction of upstairs. "They went to bed."

As he had on countless nights before this one, Dave followed her down the carpeted stairs to the rec room. As always, Julie left the door open, a somewhat discredited token of good faith to her parents. He pulled off his tuxedo jacket and draped it over the armrest of the brown-and-beige-plaid couch.

"Sorry I'm late. Things got messed up at the showcase."

She shrugged. "It's probably better this way. They still haven't really forgiven you. Or me, for that matter."

"You can't really blame them."

Julie didn't respond one way or the other. She plopped down on the couch and stretched her legs out in front of her, resting them on the coffee table next to the bowl of chips that had supplied her bookmark. One leg of her sweatpants was pushed all the way up past her knee, while the other one extended down to her ankle. She put her hands behind her head and smiled up at him.

"So what happened at the showcase?"

Dave opened his mouth to tell her about Phil Hart, but something went haywire in his brain. He looked at her and thought how pretty she was, smiling up at him, rubbing her heel over her bare shin, waiting for his answer. He thought of how much they'd been through together, and how crazy he was to imagine that he would ever want more from life than she'd be able to give him. He spoke without intending to, and didn't really gauge the significance of his words until it was too late, until she was already off the couch and in his arms.

"Let's get married," is what he'd told her.

We're Soooo Thrilled

He woke the next morning with a consciousness—
it felt something like a hangover—of having made a terrible mistake. He couldn't figure out how it had happened,
how he'd allowed years of resolve to crumble in a single
moment of weakness. In the half darkness of his bedroom,
he fantasized about calling and rescinding the offer.

"I'm not ready," he'd explain. "I don't have a steady
job or any money in the bank. You deserve someone more
reliable, a husband you can count on." He figured he'd
leave out the part about not believing himself capable of
a lifetime of sexual fidelity.

"So why'd you do it?" she'd ask, more curious than
upset. "Why'd you propose if you didn't mean it?"

"I—I really don't know. I was just in a weird mood
or something." He could hear the lameness of his excuse.
"I love you, but I'm just not prepared for this."

The imaginary Julie listened carefully, her brow knit-
ting into wavy lines of concentration. "I understand,
Dave. It would be crazy for us to get married right now.

But I do want to continue having sex with you.'' Her voice dipped into a more sultry register. "In fact, I want to have sex with you right now."

He threw off the covers and forced himself to get out of bed. This was no time to get sidetracked. He really did have to figure out a way to tell her that he hadn't actually meant to pop the question (though it wasn't even a question, now that he thought about it), but had somehow taken leave of his senses as a result of Phil's sudden death and that pushed-up leg of her sweatpants . . .

It wasn't going to be easy, he could see that. But maybe he wouldn't have to convince her. Maybe Julie was having second thoughts, too. Maybe she'd opened her eyes that morning and had the same realization as Dave—that they were acting rashly, that this was precisely the wrong time to be making such a momentous decision. He resolved to go downstairs, have a cup of coffee, and call her at the office. It was entirely possible that they could straighten out this mess in a matter of minutes, and maybe even laugh about it afterwards.

As usual, he had the house to himself. His mother left at seven to catch the train to Newark, and his father left at eight for his part-time retirement gig as a deliveryman for a local printer who called himself "Mr. Speedy." Dave did the same sort of work, driving on a freelance basis for a courier service owned by Artie's brother, Rick. Mostly he worked afternoons, but his schedule was erratic. Some days he drove for three hours, some for twelve. It all depended. Some days he didn't work at all.

He should have been used to it by now, but being alone in the house on a weekday still made him feel like he was back in high school and had just put one over on his parents. All sorts of exciting and illicit behaviors offered themselves up for consideration. He could smoke a joint, phone an escort service, fry up a whole box of breakfast sausages. In the end, though, all he ever did was sit down in front of the muted TV and strum his acoustic guitar.

On the way to the coffeemaker, he stopped to read the note his mother had left on the kitchen table. She never failed to dream up an errand or two to fill his morning, as though she couldn't bear the thought of a grown man alone for a few hours with absolutely nothing to do. But today's message was completely errand-free.

"CONGRATULATIONS!!" it said. "We're soooo thrilled. Julie's a wonderful girl." Then, at the bottom of the page, in tiny letters: "P.S.—It's about time."

His mother answered on the second ring. "Mr. Nordberg's office." There was a singsong lilt in her voice, a sunny, professional note that still caught him off guard after all these years of calling her at the office.

"It's me," he said.

"HELL-loo," she cooed, shifting to a more maternal, but equally cheerful tone. "I was just about to call. Your father and I are so happy, honey."

"How'd you find out?"

"Dolores called this morning, right before I left. Didn't you hear the phone?"

"I must have slept right through it."

"Have you picked a date?"

"Not yet."

"September's a good month."

"*This* September?"

"August is too hot. And lots of people are away. I think you should hold off till September."

"You mean four months from now?"

"It's May now, so let's see . . . June, July, August . . . Four months sounds about right."

"That's a little soon, don't you think?"

His mother laughed. "When you've been dating the girl for fifteen years, honey, you don't need a long engagement."

"Mom," he said, making an effort to control his exasperation, "we haven't been going out for fifteen years. Everybody says that, but it's just not true."

"On and off," his mother said, correcting her error. "Fifteen years on and off."

"Okay, whatever. It's really not worth arguing about."

"Anyway, for what it's worth, I still think September is a good month."

"I'll keep that in mind."

A brief silence ensued. When his mother spoke, her voice had dwindled into a worried, confidential whisper. "She's not . . . in trouble, is she?"

"In trouble?" Dave teased. "You mean with the law?"

"Ha ha," she replied.

"Not that I know of."

"Good." Another phone rang at her end of the line. "I have to grab that, honey. Bye."

"Okay," he told the hum that had replaced his mother. "Talk to you later."

Julie called before he'd swallowed his second sip of coffee.

"Hey, sleepyhead."

"Oh, hi."

"What's wrong?" she asked quickly. He caught the barely perceptible note of fear in her voice.

"Nothing."

"You don't sound too good."

"I'm fine."

"Are you sure?"

He saw the opening, but couldn't bring himself to take it. The kind of talk they needed to have, you couldn't do over the phone, he realized, especially during business hours.

"I didn't get to tell you last night. Phil Hart died at the showcase. He collapsed right onstage."

"Phil Hart?"

"You know," Dave told her. "Phil Hart and His Heart-string Orchestra. The guy with the artificial hips?"

"He collapsed onstage?"

"Right in the middle of 'Like a Virgin.' I'm not sure if it was a stroke or coronary or what."

"God, Dave. That must have been awful. Why didn't you tell me?"

"I don't know. I guess I didn't want to spoil the mood."

"That was sweet of you." She sounded vaguely perplexed.

Dave didn't answer. He just sat there, staring at the nutritional information on the side panel of a box of Cheerios, marveling at his own cowardice.

"I love you," she said.

"Yeah." He massaged an eyelid with two fingers. "Same here."

"Oh, by the way," she said. "You're invited for supper tonight. My parents want to celebrate."

He forced himself not to groan. "What time?"

"Seven?"

"Okay."

"There's so much planning to do," she said happily. "I'm overwhelmed just thinking about it."

"Yeah, me too."

"By the way," she added, "what do you think of September?"

Dave had two courier runs that afternoon—a quick in-and-out to Wall Street, followed by a trip to Morristown to drop off some X rays at a doctor's office. He liked driving for a living, especially since it meant he got paid for time spent listening to tunes on his car stereo. There was no better way to experience music, cranking the volume as high as it could go in an enclosed space, singing at the top of his lungs as he zigzagged like a stuntman through slow-moving traffic on the Pulaski Skyway. He could never understand how people managed to survive entire days cooped up in an office, with nothing to listen to but ringing phones and hushed voices. Even worse, a few of the places he visited had piped-in Muzak, the sound track of living death. Just thinking about it gave him the willies.

Another cool thing about his job was that it brought him into the city two or three times a week. Manhattan was always a jolt of crazy energy, a reminder that life wasn't meant to be safe or easy, the way it was in the suburbs. Dave even appreciated the stuff that gave most drivers headaches—the insane cabbies and squeegee men, the pedestrians who swarmed around his car at red lights like ants around a piece of candy, the whistle-tooting bike messengers and Rollerbladers who zipped past his windshield in suicidal blurs. Just making it in and out of this mess in one piece qualified as a triumph, an achievement he could carry around for the rest of the day.

Sometimes he wondered if things would have turned out differently if he'd moved into the city after dropping out of college instead of drifting back to his parents' house and the routine of familiar places and faces that had consumed his life ever since. Maybe it would have sharpened him somehow, having to live in a dingy, roach-infested shoe-box apartment, eating canned soup and SpaghettiOs, following in the footsteps of Dylan and Lou Reed and Talking Heads and the zillions of wannabes who'd journeyed to the city to test themselves against the myth Sinatra sang about. It wasn't something he brooded about, just a possibility he turned over in his mind every now and then when he found himself trying to answer the thorny question of how it was he'd ended up a Wishbone instead of a star.

In the car, he was able to consider his predicament more clearly, without the edge of panic that had clouded his morning thoughts. The first thing he realized was that it wasn't the idea of marrying Julie that frightened him; it was the idea of *being married,* of joining this big corny club of middle-aged men that included his father, Julie's father, his uncles, and every scoutmaster, Little League coach, and volunteer fireman he'd ever known. There were some exceptions—Bruce Springsteen and Buzzy came to mind—but in general, marriage seemed to require that a man check his valuables at the door: his dreams, his freedom, all the wildness that had defined the secret part of his life, even if, like Dave, he wasn't all that wild in reality.

It was easier if you were a woman. Women were supposed to *want* to get married, to go through life with a husband and children. A man's job, as far as Dave could see, was simply to resist for as long as possible before surrendering to the inevitable. You didn't have to play guitar in a wedding band to know that there was something at least slightly pathetic about a bridegroom.

Beyond his personal fears, though, he identified a deeper, more philosophical question: Was marriage something you chose, or was it something that happened whether you wanted it to or not, one of those mysterious, transforming events on the order of birth and death? The no-brain answer, of course, was that you chose. You were an adult in a free country; there were no arranged marriages in America. You didn't have to do anything you didn't want to.

He accepted all that, but on another level, it was hard to say that he and Julie had actually chosen each other in some rational, adult way. Fifteen years ago—half their lifetime—she had walked up to him in the hallway of Warren G. Harding Regional High School and told him that Exit 36 had put on a great show at the spring dance and predicted that they would someday be famous. A week later he took her to see *Midnight Express.* Two months after that they split a six-pack purchased by her

older sister's boyfriend and had sex for the first time. It
just *happened,* in some urgent hormonal haze that had
little to do with concepts like choice or intention, and they
hadn't been free of each other since. And now, apparently,
unless he thought of something fast, they were going to
get themselves married.

Dave's father sat at the table in his Mr. Speedy baseball
cap, reading the *Daily News* with the almost religious
thoroughness he devoted to every edition. It seemed to
Dave that he pored over every word of it—the adver-
tisements, the classifieds, the bridge column, all twelve
horoscopes. Reading the newspaper filled most of Al Raymond's spare time; it was his version of a hobby.

"Hey," he said, looking up with a smile that was surprised and satisfied at the same time. "Congratulations.
Your mother told me the good news."

"Word travels fast."

"You had her worried there for a while, Dave. She
didn't think Julie would stick around long enough for you
to make up your mind."

"It wasn't a matter of making up my mind. I just didn't
feel ready."

"No one feels ready. It's the same with having kids.
You just jump in and start treading water. If everybody
waited until they were ready, we wouldn't need express
lines at the supermarket."

Since his retirement, Al had emerged as something of
an armchair philosopher, full of cryptic insights into the
workings of the world. It was a development that surprised the whole family. Dave still came home half expecting to find the old Al lurking behind his paper, the
grumpy exhausted chief of maintenance at the county
courthouse, the human jukebox of grievances.

"So what do you think about marriage?" Dave asked,
sorting through the junk mail on top of the microwave.

"About what?"

"Marriage."

"Julie's great," his father replied. "I hope you'll be happy together."

"I didn't ask about Julie. I asked what you thought about marriage."

"What? The institution in general?"

"Yeah. I mean, you've been married for thirty-six years. I figure you might have formed an opinion by now."

His father studied him for a few seconds, apparently trying to decide if he was serious.

"Come on," he said, chuckling uncomfortably. "Quit pulling my leg."

Until that evening, Dave had never given serious consideration to the matter of in-laws. He'd known Jack and Dolores Muller for a long time—almost as long as he'd known their daughter—and paid them the wary respect due the parents of the girl you're sleeping with, but it hadn't occurred to him, except in the vaguest, most fleeting way, to think of them as *relatives,* people whose lives might one day be intimately and inextricably caught up with his own. In-laws were people you were required to visit on holidays, people whose genes your children would inherit, people who might—it happened all the time, he realized with dismay—end up, for one reason or another, living in your house.

Mrs. Muller answered the door in a ruffled apron, the bib of which was emblazoned with the image of an eggplant. Despite her manufactured smile, the air between them was instantly thick with embarrassment; Dave had to resist an impulse to place his hands over his crotch. Stepping through the awkwardness into the house, he greeted his future mother-in-law with a clever approximation of a hug.

"Congratulations," she said, rallying a little. "We're so pleased."

"Thanks. It's kind of amazing, isn't it?"

"I'll say," Mrs. Muller agreed, her voice suddenly full of conviction.

Julie was in the kitchen, tenderly probing a casserole with a very large fork. She was wearing gingham oven mitts and a gingham apron over a black floral print dress that was one of Dave's favorites (she occasionally "forgot" to wear underwear with it, a lapse that thrilled him beyond words). Still clutching the fork, she rushed across the room to embrace him. Her skin was clammy; she smelled of meat and Obsession.

"You're gonna love this," she said. "We made all your favorites."

Dave had never seen her in an apron before, and the effect was disconcerting, especially with her mother standing so close by, also in an apron. The two of them shared a facial resemblance so strong that you could almost imagine them not as mother and daughter, but as the same person at two different stages of life.

Dave had heard the joke about taking a long hard look at your prospective mother-in-law before deciding to get married, but he'd never given it a second thought. It was one of those pearls of marital wisdom a certain type of middle-aged guy liked to dispense, something Henny Youngman probably said on Johnny Carson back in 1963.

But now he looked at Julie and Dolores and wondered. Was it possible that Mrs. Muller had once possessed a body as curvy and stirring as Julie's? If so, when had it changed? Was it a gradual transformation, or did it happen overnight? He made a mental note to ask Julie to show him the family photo albums. It was never too early to start bracing for the future.

"So," he said, gazing around the kitchen with feigned interest, "anything I can do?"

"I don't think so," said Julie.

"Why don't you go downstairs," Mrs. Muller suggested, in a tone that made it clear he had no choice in the matter. "Jack wants to have a drink with you."

Dave shot a quick, pleading glance at Julie, but she refused to save him. Shrugging an insincere apology, she shooed him out of the kitchen with a puffy, checkered hand.

Downstairs, Mr. Muller was waiting on the couch in a tweed jacket and striped tie. He had a glass of scotch in one hand and a thoughtful expression on his face. Except for the metronomic tapping of his right loafer on the carpeted floor, he seemed utterly calm, as though he would've been pleased to sit for hours dressed up like that in a dim and quiet basement.

"Make yourself a drink," he said, gesturing toward the bar in the corner, on top of which rested an array of bottles, a bowl of lime sections, and an ice bucket that turned out to be empty when Dave lifted the lid.

Grateful for the diversion, he poured himself a stiff vodka tonic. Given that he and Mr. Muller usually made it a point to steer clear of each other, he was somewhat alarmed by the formality of the situation. A roster of unpleasant questions unfurled itself in his mind. What kind of life could he offer Julie? What was the state of his finances? Could he foresee a day when he might be able to afford a house or children? Dave knew all the questions; they were the same ones he'd posed to himself when he'd needed to talk himself out of marriage in the past. Nonetheless, it was galling to have to justify his life to Mr. Muller. He dropped a chunk of lime into his drink and vowed not to apologize for the choices he'd made.

For some reason, the couch was the only piece of furniture in the rec room, so he had no alternative but to sit down a cushion's distance away from Mr. Muller, who was examining Dave's ratty jeans and dirty Converse All

Stars with an expression of careful indifference. Dave wished that Julie had warned him that her family was dressing up; he might've at least shaved and given a little more thought to his wardrobe.

"Cheers," he said, raising his glass in a halfhearted toast.

Mr. Muller returned the gesture without enthusiasm, then pointedly cleared his throat. "I think we need to talk."

"Okay."

Mr. Muller swirled the scotch around in his glass. He looked vaguely pained, as though he were trying hard to remember a name. "You've been hanging around Julie for a long time," he observed, "but I don't feel like I know you. I haven't gotten a handle on . . . How should I say this? Your angle on the world."

"Obtuse," Dave replied, his nerves getting the worst of him.

Mr. Muller cupped one hand around his ear like Ronald Reagan. "Excuse me?"

"Obtuse," Dave repeated, enunciating more clearly. "I was trying to make a joke. It's a kind of angle. More than ninety degrees?" He tried to illustrate the concept with his hands, but ran into some unexpected difficulty.

"I see," Mr. Muller replied, attempting to look amused. "Obtuse, acute."

"Right," said Dave.

"Geometry," Mr. Muller said approvingly, as though the subtleties of Dave's remark had finally fallen into place.

"Exactly."

Mr. Muller polished off his drink and set the glass down on the coffee table with a decisive smack.

"Do you like to fish?"

"Excuse me?" said Dave.

Mr. Muller reformulated the question.

"Fishing," he said. "Do you like it?"

"Not really. I went a couple of times as a kid, but then I got the hook caught on my eyelid one time, and I pretty much lost interest after that."

"That'll do it," Mr. Muller agreed.

"What about you?" Dave ventured after a moment or two of silence. "Do you?"

Mr. Muller gave the matter some thought. For his age, he was a good-looking man, tall and lean, with a boyish shock of gray hair falling over his forehead. He looked senatorial, Dave thought, although his brief entry into the political arena had been a disaster. After losing three close races for a seat on the Darwin school board, he'd bowed to the wishes of the Republican Party and made way for another candidate.

"Never did much for me," he admitted. "It's bad enough watching them die, but then you have to clean them. Grabbing a handful of slimy guts just isn't my idea of R & R." He retrieved his glass from the table. "Mind if I have another?"

"Be my guest," Dave told him.

Mr. Muller got up and poured himself a generous drink. Julie sometimes wondered out loud if her father had a drinking problem, if that was why his career had stalled and he'd ended up as a low-level manager at Prudential instead of the bigwig executive he seemed cut out to be.

"Why did you want to know?" Dave asked.

Mr. Muller eased himself back into his seat. He tasted a mouthful of the scotch as though it were a fine wine. "Know what?"

"Why did you ask me if I liked to fish?"

"Just curious. I was wondering what you do for fun. If you have any hobbies and so forth."

Dave shook his head. "Just the music, but that goes way beyond a hobby. It's the only thing I really care about."

"Julie tells me you're in a wedding band."

"The Wishbones. I've been playing with them for two years."

"Good money in that?"

Here it comes, Dave thought.

"Not bad, actually. About fifty bucks an hour when you break it down."

"Must be interesting," Mr. Muller observed, "going to all those weddings."

Dave nodded. "You learn a lot about people."

"I bet." Mr. Muller shoved one hand into his pants pocket and jingled some change. "What about DJs? Give you much competition?"

"Not really. There's no real substitute for live music."

Mr. Muller gazed contemplatively at his beverage. "A kid I work with is a DJ. He calls himself Rockin' Randy or some such."

Before Dave could reply, Julie opened the door and poked her head into the room.

"Dinner," she told them.

Mr. Muller jumped up from the couch like he'd heard a gunshot.

"Chowtime," he said, looking deeply relieved.

Later, after her parents had gone to bed, Dave and Julie went down to the rec room to watch TV. Dave channel-surfed for a while, stopping to watch an Amy Grant video on VH1. He'd never told anyone, but he thought Amy Grant was the sexiest woman alive. The fact that she was born-again just made fantasizing about her that much more exciting.

Julie snuggled up next to him like they were back in high school. "Well," she said, "that wasn't so bad, was it?"

Amy Grant was dancing against a chaste white background, wearing a succession of cute hats, looking like she was having the time of her life. That was the secret of her appeal, Dave realized. She just seemed so ecstatically happy to be herself, beautiful and dancing on VH1.

"Was it?" Julie asked again.

"The food was great. You outdid yourself."

"My parents were good, too, don't you think?"

"They were fine."

In fact, the evening had been fairly painless, much easier than Dave had expected. Mr. and Mrs. Muller were surprisingly civil with each other, and Julie hadn't snapped at them once. No one made even a veiled reference to the sex incident. Julie slid her index finger between two buttons of Dave's shirt.

"It's amazing how excited they were when I told them. How did your parents take it?"

It had always interested Dave how some artists were able to make videos that captured their sensibility, while others couldn't even come close. As a general rule, the cooler you were, the less likely you were to succeed on video. You couldn't really imagine Chrissie Hynde or Natalie Merchant dancing around in twelve different hats.

"Dave." Julie snatched the remote from his hand, erasing Amy from the screen. "I asked you a question."

"Sorry. I got a little distracted."

"What's wrong? You act like something's bothering you."

He swallowed hard. It was now or never.

"There is," he confessed.

She moved away from him, sitting up straight and watching him with an alertness that was fierce, almost animal.

"What?"

"I feel awful about this."

"Go on," she said. There was the faintest quiver in her voice.

All at once, he knew he couldn't do it. He'd never be able to. They'd live together for fifty years and be buried side by side before he'd be able to explain that it was all just an accident.

"Go on," she repeated.

"It's the ring," he said. "I can't afford to buy you a good one."

The tension drained visibly from her face; she slumped back against the couch and shook her head.

"I don't care about the ring," she told him.

"I do. You deserve a nice one."

"I really don't care, Dave."

"Well, I do."

She terminated the discussion by reaching behind his head, pulling his face against hers, and kissing him in a way that normally would have made him forget everything else.

"Julie," he said, when she finally came up for air, "I was wondering about something."

"Hmm?"

"Do you have any photo albums I could look at?"

"Now?" she asked, kissing him again.

"Yeah," he said. "If it's not too much trouble."

"*Right* now?" she asked, tracing the grooves of his ear with her tongue.

"Uh-huh," he murmured. "As long as it's not a problem."

"This very minute?" she asked, sucking on his earlobe while tugging with gentle efficiency on his belt.

"Whenever," he told her.

You've Got a Friend

On the way to Phil Hart's wake, Dave told Buzzy about his engagement.

"That's great," Buzzy said. He was wearing a black pinstripe suit with a black shirt and a skinny white leather tie, an outfit that made Dave vaguely embarrassed on his behalf. "I'm really happy for you."

"You mean that?"

"Why wouldn't I?"

"I don't know. I'm not sure it's such a great idea myself."

"Why?" Buzzy turned to Dave with an expression of dawning comprehension. "Her old man answer the door with a shotgun?"

"Nothing like that."

A couple of seconds went by. "So how'd it happen? You get down on your knees and all that crap?"

"I don't know."

"You were there," Buzzy reminded him. He looked at Dave more closely. "You *were* there, right?"

"I was," Dave admitted. "I just didn't mean to do it."

"Ah," said Buzzy.

Dave's chest felt constricted, as though he were wrapped from armpit to navel in Ace bandages.

"I'm up the fucking creek," he said. "She's already reserved the church."

Buzzy laughed. "Tell her you have a gig that day." When Dave didn't respond, he rolled his window down and spit a wad of gum into the street. "It was easier for me. JoAnn was pregnant with Zeke. That kind of made the decision for me."

Of all the Wishbones, Buzzy had come closest to the big time. In the mid-eighties he'd been part of Flesh-Wound, a locally popular speed metal band that had been on the verge of signing with one of the major labels when the guy they were negotiating with got fired and the deal collapsed. FleshWound's lead singer and lead guitarist split off to form LasseratoR, which had since become a fixture on the local club circuit, but Buzzy had retired from serious rock 'n roll in favor of marriage and family.

"Jesus," said Dave. "Look at this."

Warneck's Funeral Home looked like the scene of a good party. Cars lined both sides of the street in front of the imposing Victorian mansion; well-dressed people stood in clusters on the porch and lawn, taking advantage of the balmy evening.

Dave parked on a nearby side street. He and Buzzy walked in silence down a sidewalk sprinkled with a confetti of white blossoms already going brown along the edges. There was a greenish fragrance in the air, a soft springtime smell that made him nostalgic for high school, the feeling of endless possibility that stretched out in front of you every time you left your house on a night like this.

"Are you glad you did it?" he asked.

"What? Get married?"

"Yeah."

"I'm forty-one," Buzzy replied, after a brief hesitation.

"I got a house, a wife and kids, and a job that doesn't make me want to buy a gun and go wreak havoc at the mall. I get to play music on the weekends and drink a couple of beers every once in a while. Things could be worse, Daverino. They could be a helluva lot worse."

"I hear you," said Dave.

A couple of teenage girls nearly bumped into them as they rounded the corner to Warneck's. The girls were nothing special, a pair of giggly fifteen-year-olds in baggy jeans and tightly cropped shirts that exposed their navels, but Dave and Buzzy parted like the Red Sea to let them pass, then turned to watch them continue down the street, the air still vibrating from the mysterious power of their bodies.

"Damn," said Dave.

"Sweet Jesus," said Buzzy.

Just then, for no reason at all, the girls turned in unison and waved. They exploded into a fresh round of giggles when Dave and Buzzy waved back. Buzzy tugged on the sleeve of Dave's sport coat.

"Come on, let's go talk to them."

"Okay," said Dave.

Despite their agreement, both men remained motionless as the girls receded into the distance, finally disappearing around a corner. Without further discussion, Dave and Buzzy turned and walked the rest of the way to the funeral home.

•   •   •

Stan knew he was going to be late for the fucking wake, but there was nothing he could do about it. He had to give Susie her goddamn birthday present. That was the important thing. If Artie didn't like it, Artie could take his shiny saxophone and ram it up his managerial ass.

He uncapped the bottle of Jack Daniels between his legs and took a long pull, keeping his eyes trained all the

while on the door of the handsome white clapboard house
with the wraparound porch that doubled as the law offices
of Joel Silverblatt, attorney-at-law.

"I'm Joel Shysterblatt," Stan mumbled, "and if you
suffer from hemorrhoids or tooth decay related to an au-
tomobile accident, I've got important information that you
need to know."

When she first started working for the guy, Susie had
loved it when he did his Joel Shysterblatt imitation.

"That's him," she'd say, covering her mouth to hold
in the laughter. "That's Joel to a T."

Then, all of the sudden, she didn't find it so funny
anymore.

"Joel's a sweet guy," she'd tell him. "He's not like
you think."

"Come on," Stan would say. "The guy's a shyster. He
gets rich off other people's misery."

"You know what?" she'd tell him. "You don't know
the first thing about the contingency fee system. It works
to protect the little guy."

"The guy's a shyster, Susie."

"And stop using that word. It's anti-Semitic."

She was probably already fucking Shysterblatt by the
time she started talking like that, but Stan was living in a
dreamworld. Susie was his wife. They'd been happily
married (at least in Stan's opinion) for eighteen months.
It never occurred to him that she might be even the least
bit attracted to her boss until he came home from a wedding one Saturday night and found an envelope on the
kitchen table with his name on it.

He lifted Susie's unwrapped gift off the passenger seat
and studied it in the failing light. It was a framed enlarge-
ment of a picture taken on their honeymoon in Cancun.
Stan couldn't remember who'd taken the picture, but he

knew it couldn't have been him or Susie, since both of them were in it.

The subject is Susie, standing on the beach in a pink bikini, squeezing water out of her hair with both hands. She's smiling, and her evenly tanned skin glistens with tiny droplets of water. Behind her, the ocean glows a rich shade of turquoise. At the left edge of the image, a man's arm reaches into the frame, offering the woman a towel. The arm belongs to Stan.

He thought the picture captured something important about their relationship, something she needed to think about. If it hadn't been for the restraining order, he would've just walked into the office and laid it on her desk.

"Happy Birthday," he would've said. Nothing else. And then he would've walked out.

He still couldn't believe she'd slapped him with that court order. He hadn't been violent with her except that one time, and even then, he'd only put her in the headlock to try to get her to listen. At the hearing, she'd accused him of stalking her and making death threats. On Joel's advice she'd taped his phone calls and kept a log of the time he spent spying on her from his car. Stan was surprised to learn that he'd called her on fourteen separate occasions on Valentine's Day, each time saying the exact same thing before hanging up: "Till death do us part, Susie. Till death do us part." (He'd been drinking that day, and could only remember calling her five, maybe six times at the most.)

Stan explained that he'd only been reminding her of her wedding vows, but the judge—probably an old law school chum of Shysterblatt's—had ruled in Susie's favor. So now Stan wasn't allowed within a hundred feet of the woman he'd married and still loved with all his heart. That was the fucking legal system for you.

•   •   •

At five after seven, Joel Silverblatt emerged from his office and walked across the street. He tapped on the driver's-side window of Stan's LeBaron. Stan rolled it down.

"Go home," Silverblatt told him. "We just called the police."

"The police can't do anything. I'm more than a hundred feet away."

"You're drunk. You're sitting in your car with a bottle of whiskey. You want to lose your license on top of everything else?"

"Everything else?" Stan repeated incredulously. "You mean like my wife?"

The evening was breezy; Silverblatt reached up with both hands to protect his hairdo from the elements. He was a rubber-faced guy with a fleshy nose and dark circles under his eyes from trying to keep up with a woman half his age.

"Go home, Stan. Go anywhere. Don't you have someplace else to be?"

Stan thought of the wake. He thought of Artie, and of the cops on their way. He thought of Susie in Mexico, ocean water streaming from her hair. Suddenly he felt tired, too tired for any more trouble.

"I'll go," he said. "On one condition."

"What's that?"

Stan poked the picture into Silverblatt's tummy. "Give her this. It's her birthday present."

With obvious reluctance, Silverblatt accepted the photograph. Stan started his car.

"It's our honeymoon," he explained. "That's me holding the towel."

●   ●   ●

"I'm sick of this bullshit." Artie pushed up the sleeve of his double-breasted Armani-style suit to consult his nearly authentic Rolex. He held up his thumb and forefinger, spaced about an inch apart. "Stan's about this fucking close to being an ex-fucking Wishbone."

"Come on," said Dave. "It's a wake. What's the difference if he's here or not?"

"What's the difference?" Artie asked. "I'll tell you what's the difference. A band's only as strong as its weakest member. If one guy is a fuck-up, the whole group's in trouble."

"Did you see *Sid and Nancy?*" Ian cut in. He was dressed like a professor on TV, tweed jacket over a black turtleneck. The jacket even had patches on the elbows. "It's just like what you're talking about."

"Didn't see it," said Artie.

"I did," said Dave.

"*Sid and Nancy?*" Buzzy seemed distressed. "The one about the waitress?"

"Waitress?" Ian went cross-eyed and stuck out his tongue. "What planet are you from?"

"Sid Vicious," Dave explained. "The guy in the Sex Pistols."

"Good flick?" asked Buzzy.

"Excellent," said Ian. "You should rent it sometime."

"I liked *The Doors,*" Buzzy told him. "You were right about that one."

"Oliver Stone." Ian nodded as though the director were a friend of his.

"You liked that?" Artie said. "How could you like that crap?"

"I liked the scene in the elevator," Buzzy said, grinning at the memory. "The one where he gets the blow job."

"The guy was a poet," said Ian. "An honest-to-God fucking poet."

"Big deal." Artie shook his head in disgust. "He writes a few good songs, shows the world his dick, gets fat as a pig, and drinks himself to death. That's the whole movie.''

"He was trying to make a point," Ian countered.

"Oh yeah?" said Artie. "What point is that?"

Ian thought it over for a few seconds, then shrugged.

"Beats me," he said. "I still think it was a pretty cool movie."

Nobody said anything for a while. Artie checked his watch again and muttered something about Stan being a total fucking zero. Ian knelt down and rubbed a spot of dirt off his cowboy boot. Dave watched a teenage boy help a frail old woman up the steps of the funeral home and wondered why a grown man would make himself miserable over something as simple as marrying the woman he loved. Buzzy slapped himself in the forehead.

"Frankie and Johnny," he said, his face lighting up with relief. "That's the movie I was thinking of."

Phil Hart was laid out in the clothes he'd died in, the satin-lapeled, powder blue uniform of the Heartstring Orchestra. On a nearby table, surrounded by elaborate bouquets and floral wreaths, a boom box played a tape of Phil singing "Summer Wind," accompanied by a piano.

Dave had never been to a wake with music before, and he thought it made a real difference. Instead of the grim focus on the casket he'd encountered in the past, there was a relaxed, almost cheerful atmosphere in the viewing room. People were mingling; a low hum of conversation filled the void between the living and the dead. If you closed your eyes, you might have thought you'd wandered into a cocktail party by mistake.

The Wishbones joined the line of people waiting to file past the coffin and offer their condolences to Phil's family, who were gathered along the opposite wall in a wedding-style receiving line. Dave was surprised to see the surviving members of the Heartstring Orchestra, also in uniform, standing shoulder to shoulder with Phil's wife and grown children, as though all of them—not just Joey Franco, but Walter and Mel as well—were blood relatives of the dead man, instead of guys he'd played in a band with.

"Candy Man" followed "Summer Wind." Dave thought it was a peculiar song to be playing at someone's wake—he remembered hearing somewhere that it was actually about a drug dealer—but it seemed to have some sort of special meaning for the people in the receiving line. As soon as it began, the attention in the room shifted to Phil's widow, a tiny, white-haired woman with delicate features and a dazed expression on her face. She dabbed at her eyes with a pale green Kleenex, then whispered something to the overweight man standing next to her. The man, who must have been her son, smiled like he was going to cry and said something in response that sent a ripple of amusement down the line. Ian poked Dave in the ribs.

"Daryl Dragon," he said.

"What?"

"Daryl Dragon." Ian looked smug. "I'll be amazed if you get this one."

Dave was in no mood for trivia, but he didn't want to hurt Ian's feelings. He pretended to think about Daryl Dragon while watching the activity on the other side of the room. Phil's widow began to sob quietly, as did Mel, the sax player in the Heartstring Orchestra. He buried his face in his hands while Joey Franco patted him awkwardly on the arm. Walter, the piano player, reached into his inside coat pocket with one trembling hand and pulled out a crumpled handkerchief. An obscure synapse fired in Dave's brain; two lost faces spiraled up at him from the dark swamp of oblivion.

"The Captain," he said.

Ian's mouth dropped open. Despite his best efforts, Dave felt a smile spreading across his face. Mel blew his nose into Walter's handkerchief; the sound of it was audible across the room.

"Daryl Dragon was the Captain in the Captain and Tennille."

"Son of a bitch." Ian ran his fingers through his hair in a way that expressed his total amazement. "They should put you on *Jeopardy*."

The first thing Dave noticed when he stepped up to the coffin was the microphone someone had tucked between Phil's crossed hands and white shirt, as though he'd been booked for a couple of gigs in heaven and wanted to arrive prepared. The unexpected sight of it—black, sleek, technological—made him wonder if, centuries from now, long after Phil himself had returned to dust, archaeologists from another civilization might dig up his grave and discover a pair of artificial hips and a microphone.

Dave never knew how to behave when confronted with the bodily presence of the dead. He didn't believe in God—at least not in a God who had nothing better to do than eavesdrop—so prayer seemed like a hollow gesture. Touching the corpse didn't strike him as an appealing option, either. So he just stood there, looking down at Phil, listening to his disembodied voice singing "You've Got a Friend," and wondering why it was that the people in charge of these things had decided to use such a thick coating of powder on his face.

It seemed to him that Phil had a lot to be grateful for. He had lived a relatively long, relatively healthy life, and had remained active and clearheaded right up to the end. He had lasted long enough to make music with his grandson, and had died doing the thing he loved best. Everyone should be so lucky.

An image took hold of Dave's mind, a vision so vivid it was almost an out-of-body experience. He saw himself standing by his own coffin, gazing down at his own peaceful face. Julie stood nearby, a brave, still-attractive old woman surrounded by supportive children and the remaining Wishbones. There was music in the room, and a sadness muffled by soft music and conversation.

Ian cleared his throat, signaling Dave to move on, but he didn't feel like moving. If Ian hadn't kicked him in the ankle with the toe of his cowboy boot, he might have lingered there indefinitely, basking in the promise Phil seemed to offer of a long, satisfying life and a sudden, painless death.

• • •

Stan could only think of one thing sadder than a car with the keys locked inside, and that was a car with the keys locked inside and the engine still running.

A car like his own.

At least this time it was parked in front of his own house in the early evening, instead of after midnight in a godforsaken rest area somewhere north of Passaic. That was something to be grateful for.

He put his hands on the hood of the LeBaron and felt the living throb of the engine vibrate up his arms. It was time to pull himself together. Time to stop drinking, stop losing things, stop showing up late all the time.

Mostly, though, it was time to stop obsessing about Susie. Her nice round ass in his hands. Her sweet little tits. The way she clenched her teeth and whimpered like a puppy when she was about to come. The tattoo of a strawberry on her shoulder blade. Her habit, when the mood was right, of calling him "Garbanzo Bean."

Hey, Garbanzo Bean, what's for supper?

Gimme a kiss, Garbanzo Man.

Don't be such a Garbanzo.

Garbanzo Bean. No wonder he locked his keys in the car and forgot what day it was.

He didn't have to walk far to find a decent rock, one that felt cool and substantial in his hand. He aligned himself with the target, wound up, and let fly. The rear driver's-side window exploded with a soft crumpling sound, showering the interior with broken glass.

Stan leaned into the car, reaching around the steering wheel to turn off the engine. Better me than some fucking car thief, he thought, shoving the keys into his pocket and glancing uneasily at the cloudless sky.

Warm water. He held his face in the pulsing stream, remembering the pleasure he'd felt as the rock erased the window. It was the kind of thing he could imagine doing again and again and again.

Climbing out of the shower, he felt alive again, nearly refreshed. The idea of spending his wife's twenty-seventh birthday at an old man's wake no longer seemed like a cruel joke. He thought about asking Dave and Buzzy to go out with him afterward, maybe to a club with music, or to one of those restaurant bars where the pretty secretaries went, hoping to meet a nice guy.

Why not? he thought. I'm a nice guy.

He opened the closet door and looked inside. It seemed so empty in there without Susie's clothes, the multicolored jumble of skirts and blouses, some of them sheathed in filmy plastic from the cleaners. After she left, he tried to rearrange his stuff to fill the available space, but the effect was vaguely disturbing, like a smile full of missing teeth.

He couldn't remember if he was supposed to dress like a Wishbone for the wake or not. Artie had mentioned something about it on the phone, but Stan hadn't really been listening.

Just to be on the safe side, he decided to go for the tux.

Reaching for the hanger, he looked down by reflex and saw his missing dress shoes gleaming on the closet floor, right where they were supposed to be. The sight of them made his mouth taste funny.

Freshly dressed and mostly sober, he swept the glass off the front seat, climbed into his car, and set off into the night. The DJ on K-rock said it was the beginning of a commercial-free hour, one of those everyday events you couldn't help thinking of as a good omen.

He was coming down Central Avenue in West Plains, singing along with Melissa Etheridge, when it occurred to him that he didn't know where he was going. He had a clear memory of Artie saying, "We'll meet at the funeral home around seven," but nothing beyond that. Not a word about which funeral home on what street, or even what town.

An unpleasant chill spread up the back of Stan's neck. He saw himself at that moment—a man in a tuxedo, driving nowhere in a car with a broken window—and was overcome by a feeling worse than simple embarrassment. For a few seconds he toyed with the idea that he was losing his mind.

In his heart, though, he didn't really believe it. He was just going through a bad patch, the kind of situation that took a toll on your day-to-day functioning. What he needed was some understanding, a little encouragement, a few kind words. Most of the guys in the band were sympathetic, especially Buzzy and Dave. Ian was okay too, though Stan hadn't been able to take him seriously for a long time now, ever since he'd learned that his real name was Frank. "Ian" was a stage name, borrowed from the lead singer in Jethro Tull. It was the kind of thing you didn't want to know about a grown man you thought of as a friend.

The problem was Artie. A decent manager would have

patted him on the back and tried to help him through the mess. But Artie wasn't like that—Stan understood that now. Artie was a shark, the kind of guy who'd risk his life crossing a busy highway just for the chance to kick you while you were down.

•   •   •

Phil's widow had stopped crying by the time Dave shook her hand and told her how sorry he was. She introduced herself as Rose Cardini.

"Cardini?" he said. "Phil's last name was Cardini?"

She looked amused. "What did you think it was?"

"Hart," he replied, feeling foolish as soon as he said it.

"Back when he started out, most of the Italian performers changed their names to sound more American. That's how you got Dean Martin, Tony Bennett, people like that."

"Not Sinatra, though."

"That's true," she said. "Sinatra was the exception."

On the boom box, "You've Got a Friend" segued into "Danny Boy," and Mrs. Cardini seemed to lose track of the conversation. Her blue eyes clouded over; she craned her neck as though looking past Dave to a taller person standing behind him. Softly at first, but then with more confidence, she began humming along with her husband's voice, effortlessly harmonizing. After just a few bars, though, she stopped. The alertness returned to her face.

"We were married for fifty-two years," she said, gazing in wonder at her own hands. "Can you imagine that?"

Dave shook his head; he couldn't.

"On long car trips, we used to sing to pass the time. 'Danny Boy' was one of our favorites."

"It's a great song."

"He seemed so healthy," she said. "I thought we had a few more years."

• • •

At the other end of the line, Dave held out his hand to Joey Franco. They'd known each other since they were kids without ever really being friends. Joey had gone to Catholic grammar school and was already deep into drugs by the time he arrived at Harding High.

"I'm sorry," said Dave.

Before the words were out of his mouth, Joey's arms were around him, squeezing hard. Dave grunted in surprise, surrendering to the embrace.

"Dave," said Joey.

"Joey," said Dave.

Dave had always tried to keep his distance from Joey— it was as much his bad skin as the fact that he'd been a junkie—but it felt okay to hug him inside the funeral home. Joey was sobbing now, the muscles in his back jumping beneath the fabric of his suit.

"Dave," he said again.

"Joey."

"Believe me," Artie said, when the Wishbones had reassembled on the lawn outside the funeral home, "the Heartstring Orchestra is history."

"Not necessarily," said Ian. "All they need is a new front man."

"Where they gonna find another seventy-year-old front man?"

"Why does he have to be seventy?" Buzzy inquired.

"Because they're a concept band."

"Concept?" said Ian. "What concept is that?"

Artie stared at him like he was an idiot. "Whaddaya mean, what concept?"

"Whaddaya mean, what do I mean?" Ian shot back. "I asked what concept."

"They're a bunch of old guys," Artie explained. "That's the fucking concept."

"What about Joey?" Dave asked.

"What about him?"

"He's our age."

"That's right," said Artie. "And if Stan doesn't get his shit together, maybe Joey wouldn't mind a chance to play with some guys who don't belong to the American Association of Fucking Retired People."

"That's a good organization," Buzzy told him. "Don't knock the AARP."

"Mel's a pretty hot sax player," Ian pointed out. "Maybe we could use him too."

"Eat me," said Artie.

They were still standing on the lawn ten minutes later when Alan Zelack pulled up in front of the funeral home in his red Mitsubishi Eclipse, which Artie liked to mock as a "poor man's Porsche." In a soft voice, Ian began singing "Stairway to Heaven" as Zelack climbed out of the car, pausing in the street to straighten his tie and run his fingers through his expensive haircut. Dave remembered him breathing into Phil's mouth, pressing on his chest.

"Hey, guys." Zelack seemed delighted by the opportunity to stop and chat. "It's a shame about Phil, huh?"

"You did a good thing the other night," Dave told him. "The mouth-to-mouth and all."

Zelack shrugged. "My father died of a heart attack a couple years ago. Shoveling snow. He died right there on the sidewalk. Nobody in the whole neighborhood knew CPR."

"Shit," said Buzzy.

"What can you do?" said Zelack.

The conversation dropped off a cliff. Zelack's glance

strayed to the front door of the funeral home. He didn't look all that eager to go inside.

"Hey, Alan," Artie said. "Can I ask you something?"

"Sure."

"Who was that fox you were with the other night?"

"Oh." Zelack grinned like a guy who'd just hit the lottery. "That's Monica. I met her at a gig a couple weeks ago. She was the Maid of Honor."

"Monica." Artie shook his head at the injustice of it all. "Figures she'd have a name like that."

Zelack rubbed his chin with the tip of his thumb. "I'm in love, man. I'm so fucking in love I can't believe it."

Dave looked at the ground. He felt a hollowness in his abdomen, a sensation something like a hunger pang. He forgot about it when Buzzy slapped him on the back.

"Speaking of the *L*-word," he said, "our man Dave here has an important announcement."

"No way," said Ian.

"No *fucking* way," said Artie.

"It's true," Buzzy insisted. "Little Daverino's getting married."

Dave nodded to confirm this information, a little uncomfortable about suddenly being made the center of attention. Smiling as graciously as he could, he stood on the plush lawn of the funeral home and accepted the congratulations of his friends and colleagues.

*   *   *

The first funeral home Stan visited was full of grief-stricken uniformed cops. In the second one, all the mourners spoke Spanish. The third happened to be located just a few blocks from Feeney's, a corner bar in Cranwood with one of the best jukeboxes around.

It was early, and the place was nearly empty. He dropped a couple dollars' worth of quarters on Merle Haggard and George Jones, then pulled up a stool and called

for a Jim Beam on the rocks. He could only tolerate country music under certain circumstances, and this was one
of them.

Since joining the Wishbones, Stan had grown accus-
tomed to drawing stares in public places. This time they
came from an older gentleman a few stools down, a dap-
per, pickled-looking guy in a mustard-colored suit.

"What happened?" he asked, eyeing Stan's tux with
sympathetic curiosity. "She leave you at the altar?"

Stan wanted to laugh, but the sound never quite made
it out of his throat.

"She should've," he said, tossing back his drink in a
single gulp. "It would've saved a shitload of time."

He pulled up in front of Warneck's Funeral Home at a
few minutes past nine. Except for a lone figure sitting on
the front steps, the place looked empty, closed for the
night.

Squinting into the darkness, he recognized the guy on
the steps as one of the old farts from Phil Hart's band.
Walter, the piano player, the one he privately thought of
as "Shaky."

He got out of the car and headed up the front walk.
The old man watched him from the steps, a shock of white
hair framing the vague outline of his face.

"Hey," said Stan. "Am I late?"

"Depends for what."

"The wake."

"You missed it. Viewing hours are from six to eight."

"Were the Wishbones here?"

The old man cleared his throat with a violence that
made Stan cringe. "The who?"

"The Wishbones. The band that plays after you at the
showcase. I'm the drummer."

"You guys really call yourselves the Wishbones?"

"Yeah."

Walter whistled through his teeth, as though a pretty girl had just walked by. "Where'd you find a stupid name like that?"

Stan didn't answer. He'd always thought the Wishbones was a perfectly good name for a band. Walter reached into his pocket and pulled out a pack of cigarettes. It was painful to watch him extract one and guide it to his lips. Stan had to look away when Walter brought out his lighter. He didn't turn back until he smelled the smoke.

"Your friends left about an hour ago," Walter reported.

"Figures." Stan shook his head. "I'm having one of those days, I'd forget my dick if it wasn't screwed on."

Walter coughed out a dry chuckle. "My age, I'd be grateful for a day like that."

A sudden image struck Stan like a wave of nausea. Susie drinking champagne in a fancy restaurant. Black dress, bare shoulders. Happy Birthday. He made a noise.

"You okay?" Walter asked.

"Not really. Mind if I sit down?"

He felt a little better once he unhooked his cummerbund. He hated the frigging thing, the way it squeezed all the air out of him. Walter sat beside him, thoughtfully gumming his cigarette.

"This must be a tough time for you," Stan observed.

"How so?"

"You know." He pulled the cummerbund out from under his jacket and laid it on the steps. "This thing with Phil. It must have been awful for you."

Walter worked his cigarette like a baby sucking a bottle. "Phil was an old man. Everybody's got to go sometime."

"Still, watching a friend die in front of you like that . . ."

"We had our differences," Walter said curtly.

"What kind of differences?"

"Creative." Walter ejected the cigarette from between his lips. It landed on the sidewalk in a small shower of sparks. "I thought the band was starting to get a little stale."

"How long were you together?"

"Too fucking long. Thirty-three years I took orders from that sonofabitch. I finally feel like I can breathe again."

Stan didn't bother to pretend he was shocked. He'd been a musician long enough to know how it could come to this. There were nights when he'd lain awake writing Artie's obituary in loving detail, nights when he'd imagined committing murder.

"Can you do me a favor?" Walter asked.

"What's that?"

"Help me find my car."

"Whaddaya mean, find your car?"

Walter gestured at the world spread out in front of them. His voice was small now, a little bit frightened.

"It's around here somewhere," he said.

June

It's Your Wedding

"I think I'm going to ask Tammi to be my Maid of Honor," Julie told him on their way to the mall on Saturday morning. "I'm just worried that Margaret's going to be upset."

"She'll still be in the wedding, right?"

"Of course. But you know how she is. Any little thing could set her off. And the last thing we need is a disgruntled bridesmaid."

She shook her head as though exasperated, but Dave wasn't fooled. He could see how happy she was to be talking about the wedding. Her face glowed with it; she spoke in a bright girlish voice he hadn't heard for a long time. It was gratifying to know that he could be responsible for such a major improvement in her mood, though it made him wonder if he hadn't been equally responsible for the mild depression that had plagued her for the past couple of years. He'd blamed it on the fact that she'd been unable to find a public school teaching job, despite her degree in Elementary Ed, and instead seemed resigned to a career in customer service. But maybe that was only part of her problem, and maybe not even the most important part.

"Do what you want," he told her. "It's your wedding."

She pulled down the sun visor and studied her face in the little mirror, puckering her lips as though preparing to kiss the glass.

"Ever since she got married, all she wants to do when we get together is complain about Paul. I mean, sometimes I just want to say, 'Look, Margaret, if the guy's such a jerk, why don't you just divorce him?' "

Dave punched on the radio and began fiddling with the tuner to dramatize his lack of interest in Margaret and Paul. Julie pretended not to notice.

"He's like from another era. She works longer hours and makes more money than he does, but it never even occurs to him to pitch in around the house."

The radio was a Saturday-morning wasteland. The best song Dave could find was "Movin' On" by Bad Company, a band about whom he had profoundly mixed feelings. As stale and mediocre as they seemed now, he could never forget what it had meant to hear them for the first time in Glenn Stella's bedroom in 1975—like being struck by lightning, visited by some rock 'n roll version of the holy spirit. He'd walked home in a daze and announced to his parents at the supper table that he *needed* a guitar.

"You know what he does? He just sits in front of the TV playing his stupid computer games while she vacuums around his feet."

"You think she should divorce him because of that?"

"That's as good a reason as any, considering that he has no redeeming qualities whatsoever."

"He's not so bad," Dave said, defending the guy out of some vague sense of gender loyalty, even though he despised him even more than Julie did. "He probably does a lot of chores around the house. Mowing the lawn and whatnot. Taking out the garbage.''

"That's not the worst of it.'' Julie lowered her voice, in case people in passing cars might be trying to eavesdrop. "He insists on having sex with her every night, right after the weather report on the eleven o'clock news.''

"Every night?''

"That's what she says.''

"Even when she's sick?''

"I'm sure there are exceptions,'' she conceded. "But the basic pattern is every night.''

Dave gave a small shiver of disgust that was only partly for Julie's benefit. Paul was a 240-pound furniture salesman who collected baseball cards and believed that *Hotel California* was one of the high points in the history of human civilization. Margaret was a formerly pleasant person whose personality had been ruined by constant dieting; Dave couldn't remember the last time he'd seen her when she wasn't carrying around a plastic Baggie full of carrot slivers. The thought of the two of them having sex was almost as difficult to get his mind around as the thought of his parents getting it on in a motel room while vacationing at Colonial Williamsburg.

Julie pulled down her bottom lip and inspected her gum line in the mirror. Then she pulled up her top lip and did the same.

"He claims he can't get to sleep without it. If she says no he whimpers and thrashes around until she finally gives in just to get it over with.''

"Aren't there laws against that?''

"Every night,'' Julie said, her voice touched by wonderment. "Imagine watching the news with that hanging over your head.''

A life-sized cardboard cutout of Mr. Spock greeted them as they entered the mall, the normally expressionless Vulcan smiling enigmatically as he extended the live-long-and-prosper salute to the earthlings who drifted past. "MEET SCOTTY!" said a cardboard poster attached to Leonard Nimoy's cardboard shirt. "2 P.M. TODAY."

It wasn't yet eleven-thirty, but a large contingent of *Star Trek* buffs had already begun forming a line in front of an empty table in the mall's central plaza. The table was surrounded by cardboard cutouts of Captain Kirk, Bones, and Lieutenant Uhura, who looked as sexy as ever in her skintight, probably somewhat itchy polyester uniform.

They had to cut through the line on their way to the escalator, drawing a surprisingly huffy response from a man in a plaid short-sleeved shirt who must have thought they were trying to usurp his position. Most of the people in line were nerdy-looking men, though Dave did notice a sprinkling of obese women and a number of people in wheelchairs, some of them severely disabled. It made sense, now that he thought about it, that *Star Trek,* and especially Scotty, might hold a special appeal for people who found themselves at odds with their own bodies.

They stepped onto the escalator and began their slow, effortless ascent. Julie gazed down at the Trekkies and shook her head.

"It's sad," she whispered.

"What?"

"That," she said, gesturing at the lower level. "All of it."

Dave didn't answer. He had never cared for *Star Trek* and wouldn't have wanted to spend the better part of a beautiful Saturday stuck inside the mall, but he'd stood on enough lines for concert tickets in all kinds of weather—sometimes even camping out for really important shows—to feel an instinctive sympathy for the people below. They didn't seem particularly sad or strange to him. They were just waiting for Scotty.

"With diamonds," Kevin explained, "you got four basic variables to consider. You got size, you got cut, you got color, and you got clarity. Within each of these categories, you got separate variables to consider."

Kevin was a pixieish man in a brown suit, maybe forty years old, with curly gray hair slicked back behind his ears and an orangey tan whose origins could probably be traced to somewhere other than New Jersey. Dave made an effort to look fascinated as he droned on about point size, empire cuts, and the alphabetical grading scale for color, but his mind had already begun to wander. He almost wished he were downstairs, standing in line. At least then he'd have something to look at besides pale pink walls, diamond rings, and Kevin's tropical explosion of a necktie.

"The range is enormous," Kevin said, in response to a question from Julie. "The vast majority of diamonds aren't even precious stones per se. They're used for industrial purposes."

Kevin paused for a reaction, so Dave dutifully pretended to be impressed by this information, though he really didn't give a shit about it one way or the other. The whole concept of engagement rings struck him as an enormous scam perpetrated by the jewelry industry to force you into making the single most expensive useless purchase of your entire lifetime just to avoid looking like a cheapskate to your future wife, her family, friends, and co-workers.

"But let's face it," Kevin said, finally bringing his filibuster to a close, "unless you have a lot of money to spend, most of what I just told you isn't going to be directly relevant to your purchase. You're not going to be in the market for some flawless oval-cut diamond of exceptional luster. You'll be looking for a decent-quality round-cut stone, maybe in the H-I-J range."

"What do you mean by a lot of money?" Julie asked.

This question appeared to cause Kevin a certain amount of difficulty. His face cycled through a number of contortions before settling into its default mode of enthusiastic sincerity.

"It's all relative, you know what I'm saying? I mean, you can get a ring like these here for four, five, maybe six hundred bucks." He caressed the air above the left side of the display case; the rings below were sad-looking specimens with stones that resembled pumped-up grains of salt. His hand drifted to the other end of the case, where rocks the size of molars glittered smugly in elaborate settings. "Or you could spend upwards of five grand on one of these."

"We're somewhere in the middle," Julie told him.

Dave paid closer attention as Kevin removed individual rings from the case—insurance regulations didn't permit him to exhibit more than one at a time—and quoted prices in the range of fifteen hundred dollars. They had entered the store committed to paying no more than a thousand, but their threshold seemed to have risen in the meantime.

"I really like this one," Julie said, referring to a round-cut sixty-pointer that would run in the neighborhood of sixteen hundred transferred to a plainer setting. "There's something about it."

"That's a quality stone," Kevin said quickly. "You have a really good eye."

Julie spun her swivel chair to face Dave, the ring cupped like an offering in the palm of her hand, her expression a complicated blend of excitement and apology.

"What do you think?"

Dave took the ring and held it up to the light. The diamond was small but radiant, shooting off pinprick flares of brilliance.

"I know it's expensive," she said. "Maybe we shouldn't rush into anything."

He could've told her to hold off, to shop around and

compare prices, but that would've just been prolonging the ordeal. She had found a ring she would be proud to show off to her friends, a ring that would reflect well on him as part of the union it symbolized. Compared to that, a few hundred dollars didn't seem worth quibbling over, even if it meant he'd have to kiss good-bye any hope of buying the vintage Telecaster he'd been eyeing over at Riccio's Music.

"Get it," he told her.

"Really?" She seemed almost disappointed by the ease of his surrender. "You mean it?"

She started to smile, but something happened to her face before she got there. She made a sudden gulping noise, and the next thing he knew she was sobbing against his face, her arms wrapped tightly around his neck. Pinned against his chair, Dave realized he was choked up as well. If making her happy were so easy, why had he gone out of his way to disappoint her for so long? Why had they wasted all those years?

"Oh, sweetie," she said. "It's so beautiful."

"Jules." His fist closed around the ring as he rubbed his knuckles up and down the back of her neck.

"Congratulations." Kevin reached across the display case to give him a friendly squeeze on the shoulder. "You made an excellent choice."

"So tell me," Kevin said, making salesman's small talk as he wrote up their order, "how long have you two been going out?"

Dave groaned to himself. This wasn't a subject he felt comfortable discussing with strangers.

"A long time," he said.

"How long is long?"

He shot a quick warning glance at Julie, but it was too late.

"Fifteen years," she said.

Kevin looked up from the paperwork, smirking like a guy who appreciated a little good-natured kidding around.

"Come on," he said.

"It's true," Julie insisted. "We've been going out since our sophomore year of high school."

Kevin turned to Dave for confirmation, looking at him for the first time as though he were an actual human being, rather than a Visa card with legs.

"On and off," Dave told him. "Fifteen years on and off."

"That's amazing," said Kevin.

Julie put her arm around Dave's waist and planted a quick kiss on his cheek.

"We didn't want to rush into anything," she explained.

Dave took Julie's hand as they stepped off the escalator, something he almost never did in public, especially since they'd had a fight about it a few years earlier. ("Would it kill you to hold my hand once in a while?" she'd asked. "Yes," he'd replied, after devoting some serious consideration to the matter. "I think it would.") She seemed so grateful for the gesture that she passed up the opportunity to comment upon his courage in the face of near-certain death.

"I'm really happy about the ring," she told him. "I know you think it's silly, but it means a lot to me."

"I'm happy too," he said, and was pretty sure that he meant it. "You deserve something nice after putting up with me for fifteen years."

"On and off," she said, cheerfully supplying his favorite disclaimer. "Fifteen years on and off."

He never meant for the phrase to sound as grudging and nitpicky as it apparently did; it just seemed important to remind people that they hadn't actually been seeing each other for fifteen years without interruption. Some of the gaps in their relationship were minor and forgettable, but others were of a different order of magnitude—Julie's last two years of college, for example, which she'd spent practically living with this jerk who dumped her when he got accepted to law school, and the ten-month affair Dave had had a few years back with a married woman whose husband traveled a lot. In Dave's mind, these two episodes divided up his history with Julie into three separate eras—in effect, three separate relationships: Young Love, The Post-Brendan Reconciliation, and Everything after Maryanne. That was what he meant by on and off.

They were halfway to the exit when someone called his name. He turned toward the line of Trekkies—it had nearly doubled in size during their time in the jewelry store—unsuccessfully scanning the crowd for a familiar face.

"Over here." A hand waved through the air. "Dave."

Once he spotted Ian, Dave wondered how he'd missed him. Surrounded by people not particularly distinguished by their good looks or the care they'd devoted to choosing their clothes that morning, he stood out like a swan among the pigeons. Tall and always well dressed, Ian had the kind of physical presence that often led strangers to mistake him for some kind of minor celebrity—a bit player on soap operas, or maybe a second-string professional athlete.

"Hey," he said. "Talk about coincidences. What are you guys doing here?"

"Engagement ring," said Dave.

Ian looked at Julie's hand. Julie shook her head.

"We just picked out the stone. The actual ring won't be ready for a week or so."

"Well, congratulations," he told her. "You're marrying one of the finest rock trivia minds in the Tri-State area."

"I know," Julie said. "All the other girls are jealous."

"What about you?" asked Dave. "Since when are you such a big *Star Trek* fan?"

"I'm not. I was just shopping for some summer clothes. But then I saw the line and thought, what the hell? Might as well meet Scotty."

"He's not showing up for another couple of hours," Julie warned him. "That's a long time to wait."

Ian shrugged. "I didn't really have anything planned for this afternoon anyway. It's either this or help my dad clean out the gutters."

"It's a beautiful day," she told him. "We're thinking of having a picnic up at Watchung."

She said this as though extending a tacit, no-pressure invitation for Ian to tag along, but he didn't seem to notice the offer.

"I've got to get out of that house," he said, more to himself than to Dave or Julie. "My parents are driving me nuts."

"Join the club," said Dave.

"Tell me about it," said Julie.

"Yeah," said Ian, "but you guys can at least see the light at the end of the tunnel. I don't even think I'm inside the tunnel yet."

Dave patted him on the arm and said he'd see him at the wedding that night.

"Five o'clock at the Westview, right?"

Dave nodded.

"See you then," said Ian. "Have a good picnic."

"Say hi to Scotty," Julie told him.

On the way out of the mall, Dave saw that Mr. Spock had been knocked over and trampled, probably by some unruly teenagers. He lay flat on his back, still smiling gamely despite the waffles of dirt that covered his face and body with a thoroughness that could only have been intentional. Dave thought about propping him up, but decided it was none of his business.

"Do you think he's gay?" Julie asked, as they exited the parking lot, merging with the traffic on Route 1.

For a split second, he thought she was referring to Leonard Nimoy, who seemed more asexual than anything else, at least on *Star Trek*. But then the fog cleared.

"Who?" he said. "Ian?"

"No." She rolled her eyes. "Leonard Nimoy."

Dave ignored her sarcasm and pondered the question. He wanted to say, "Of course not," but realized the moment he thought about it that he didn't know very much about Ian's personal life. In the two years they'd been Wishbones together, Ian had mentioned a couple of ex-girlfriends. He didn't seem to be actively searching for a new one, though, nor was he more than mildly flattered by the number of women who came on to him at weddings (including the legendary mother-of-the-bride). Dave had always assumed that this was because he was used to the attention and accepted it as his due, the way a beautiful woman got used to being stared at every time she walked down the street. But now he wondered.

"I don't know," he said. "Do you think he might be?"

She shrugged. "He's just so different from the rest of you."

"How so?"

"Well, for one thing, he's really handsome. And he's got such good taste in clothes."

"Thanks a lot."

She patted his knee. "You know what I mean."

Dave didn't argue. He knew exactly what she meant. Ian *was* better-looking than the rest of the Wishbones. That was why he was the front man. Generally speaking, people didn't go for ugly singers. The rest of the band could look like a bunch of space aliens and burn victims for all anyone cared, but the singer had to meet certain minimum standards of attractiveness.

"It doesn't matter to me one way or the other," she assured him, "but if he's not gay and he's not going out with anyone, I'm wondering if he might hit it off with Tammi."

"Ian and Tammi?"

"It's just an idea. She hasn't gone out with anyone for a long time now. I think she's ready for someone new."

Dave liked Tammi a lot, but he couldn't quite see her with Ian. Tammi was funny and cute in a tomboyish sort of way, the kind of person who knew how to make a joke at her own expense. The longer Dave knew her the more attractive she had come to seem to him, but her appeal was subtle, often lost on people meeting her for the first time. Dave figured Ian to go for someone a little more eye-catchingly glamorous, more like Zelack's new girl-friend, Monica.

"It's never a good idea to fix up your friends," he pointed out. "Somebody always ends up with hurt feel-ings."

"We just have to find some natural way to introduce them," she mused. "That's the trick with these things. It can't feel like a blind date or it's doomed from the start."

He pulled up to a tollbooth on the Parkway entrance ramp and tossed in thirty-five cents. The exact-change basket was plastered with decals for local bands he had never heard of—the Eggheads, Screaming Willie, Storm Drain. They just kept popping up, these bands, mush-rooms of suburbia. Everyone and his brother chasing after the same old dream.

"You know what you could do?" She smiled at the beauty of what had just occurred to her. "You could ask him to be your Best Man. Then they'd have to sit at the same table and dance together and all that. They wouldn't even know they were being fixed up."

"I told you," he said, "if I ask anyone in the band to stand up for me, it'll be Buzzy."

"No way." She was adamant. "Buzzy is *not* going to be your Best Man. Not unless he gets a haircut."

"I can't ask him to do that."

"Why not?"

"It's just not done."

"Well, I don't want the first toast of our married life to be delivered by a forty-year-old man with a ponytail. That's not how I envision my wedding."

Dave sighed. "It doesn't matter. I'll probably just ask my brother."

"You and your brother don't even talk to each other."

"We don't have to. We're brothers."

"If I were you, I'd pick Glenn before I picked your brother."

"Me too," he said. "I'd pick Glenn in a minute if I thought he'd be willing to do it."

"He'd do it. He wouldn't say no."

"I know. But he'd probably hate every minute of it."

"Well, you better make up your mind," she advised him. "September's going to be here before you know it."

Dave felt a headache coming on. Faster than he'd ever imagined, the wedding had installed itself as a dominant presence in his life, this giant looming cloud of unmade decisions. It turned out to be far more pressing and complicated than the smaller cloud it had displaced, the one emblazoned with the single, no-longer-eternal question: *Marriage?*

"You know what?" she said. "I bet Leonard Nimoy *is* gay."

"Really?"

"Who knows?" She held her left hand in front of her face, as if trying to imagine the ring onto her finger. "After a few years in a spaceship, we'd probably all start rethinking our options."

Dave couldn't remember the last time they'd spent an afternoon like this—a picnic on a blanket in the shade by a lake, Julie stretched out beside him, eyes closed, maybe sleeping, maybe not, nothing unpleasant hanging over

their heads, no fights or disappointments or lurking grievances. It almost seemed to him that they'd managed to
return to an earlier time in their relationship, as if they
themselves had been rejuvenated.

He sat up on the blanket and looked around. Over in
the parking area, shirtless teenage boys were waxing mus-
cle cars while girls in tight jeans looked on, smoking with
the squinty-eyed concentration of beginners. In a grassy
clearing nearby, three teenage boys with flannel shirts tied
around their waists were showing off with a Frisbee,
catching it between their legs and behind their backs, popping it in the air over and over again with one finger. On
a picnic table to their right, a couple of high-school kids
were making out as though their faces had been stuck
together with Krazy Glue, and they were trying every trick
they could think of to pull them apart. In the lake, a black
lab with a blue bandanna collar swam regally toward shore,
a fat stick jutting from its mouth. Somewhere across the
water, "Sugar Magnolia" was blaring from a radio.

It really could have been 1979, he thought, except that
he and Julie would have been the teenagers with adhesive
faces rather than the adults who had just spent more than
they could afford on an engagement ring. There were days
when a realization like that would have struck him with
sadness, days when he ached to be sixteen again, but today wasn't one of them. Today he felt richer for possessing a past, maybe even a little wiser. They had had their
moment; they hadn't let it pass. That was the most anyone
could say.

He looked down at her, the halo of dark outspread hair
fanned out around her peaceful face. She wasn't seventeen
anymore, but she was still beautiful. He thought about
Phil Hart and his wife, the fact that they'd managed to
stick it out for more than a half century. Did he look at
her on the morning of his death and think, *Well, she's not
sixty-five anymore, but she's still beautiful?* Was that a
way it could happen?

"Heads up, dude!"

Dave turned toward the voice, just in time to see an orange Frisbee slicing toward his face. Reacting with the grace born of self-preservation, he ducked out of the way while simultaneously reaching up with his right hand to snag the errant disc. In a surprisingly fluid motion, he rose to his feet and zipped the Frisbee back to the long-haired Chinese kid who had yelled out the warning, not with the cumbersome cross-body discus hurl of the neophyte, but with the precise, economical flick of the wrist he had perfected during countless lazy spring days like this when he was flunking out of college.

Acknowledging Dave's membership in the elite, wrist-flicking fraternity, the kid jumped up and caught the Frisbee between his outscissored legs, then fired it off to one of his friends before his feet even touched the ground.

"Thanks, dude."

"No problem," said Dave. He felt deeply pleased, as though he'd just proven something important to himself and the world.

Julie was stirring when he sat back down. She yawned and opened her eyes, blinking a few times to readjust to the brightness of the day. Then she rolled easily onto her side and smiled at him.

"Hey," she said.

"Hey."

She poked a finger into his thigh. "You know what I want to do?"

"What?"

She pushed herself up from the ground into sitting position and glanced around to make sure no one was within listening range.

"I want to go to a motel."

"Right now?"

She nodded slowly, biting her bottom lip, her face flushed with color.

"This very minute," she said.

Dave's blood began to celebrate; a giddy torrent of ideas flooded his brain. Aside from a few hurried, mostly clothed interludes on the rec room couch, they hadn't really made love in well over a month, not since her parents' ill-fated jaunt to Atlantic City. He wanted to watch her undress slowly, one article of clothing at a time. He wanted to reacquaint himself with her body.

"It's quarter to three," he said, glancing quickly at his watch. "That gives us almost an hour and a half."

Her expression changed. Her teeth let go of her lip.

"Shit," she said.

"What?"

"You have a wedding." She made it sound like an awful thing—a disease, something to be ashamed of.

"I'm sure I told you."

"I forgot. We were having such a nice day, I guess I pushed it out of my mind."

"An hour and a half is enough. We've done it in a lot less time than that."

"I'm sick of hurrying." To illustrate this point, she reached up with both hands and gathered her loose hair into a ponytail with exquisite, painstaking care. "I just want to have a nice quiet Saturday alone with you for once."

"Sorry. I'm not the one who schedules the gigs."

She grabbed her shoes from the corner of the blanket and slipped them on her feet. Just like that, he realized, their picnic had been canceled. She pulled the laces tight and stared at him.

"How much longer do you plan on doing this?"

"Doing what?"

"The Wishbones."

Dave felt shell-shocked. On the blanket, a black ant was struggling with an enormous bread crumb, bigger than its own head. The ant kept lifting it, staggering forward, dropping it, then lifting it again.

"Are you asking me to quit the band?"

Her voice softened. "Haven't you thought about it?"

"It never even occurred to me."

"Well, I don't feel like spending the rest of my life alone on Saturday night while my husband's out having a good time."

"It's not a good time," he said, still reeling from the suddenness of her attack. "It's a job. A good one. I wouldn't be making a living without it."

"You're not planning on being a courier for the rest of your life, are you?"

"No," he said. "But it's not like I've got lots of other prospects at the moment."

"You should start thinking about it. I'd like to start a family in the next couple of years."

"Me too. What does that have to do with the band?"

She stood up and grabbed two corners of the blanket. "Come on. Help me fold this."

Obediently, Dave rose to his feet, still trying to figure out how they'd moved from talking about checking into a motel to talking about him quitting the band.

"Heads up!"

This time Dave was ready. He turned and poised himself for the catch, waiting with his hands up as the Frisbee drifted toward him at a dreamy velocity, a vibrating curve of neon. At the very last second, though, it took a freak hop, jumping right over his hands and striking him smack in the middle of his forehead, much harder than he'd expected, more like a dinner plate than a flimsy piece of molded plastic. Fireworks of pain exploded on the inside of his eyelids.

"Sorry, dude," the kid called out.

"No problem."

Smiling through his discomfort, Dave bent down and picked up the Frisbee. He flicked his wrist to return it, but something slipped. It wobbled feebly through the air and died like a duck at the kid's feet. He turned sheepishly to Julie, rubbing at the sore spot between his eyebrows.

"I guess I'm a bit rusty."

She ignored the comment, frowning pointedly at the limp blanket. Dave grabbed the two corners on his end and they pulled it taut between them, flapping it up and down to clean it off. He thought about the ant with the bread crumb, all that hard work gone to waste.

"I just want a normal life," she said, almost pleading with him. "Is that too much to ask?"

A Religious Experience

"She what?" Buzzy slurped at the foam erupting like lava from the top of his can. "What did you tell her?"

"Nothing. I was in a state of shock."

"I can imagine."

"I mean, we're just sitting there, having this great afternoon, and *bam!*"

Dave was indignant. She had no right to ask him to quit the band. Playing music wasn't just some stupid sideline; it was what he did with his life. If he'd been a doctor, she wouldn't have asked him to quit performing surgery. She wouldn't have asked a cop to turn in his badge. It signified a lack of respect, not only for his chosen profession, but for him—her future husband—as an individual.

"What was her reasoning?" Buzzy had his head thrown back like Popeye, mouth wide open to receive the last precious drops of Meister Bräu dribbling out of his upended can. He could drain a beer faster than anyone Dave had ever known.

"Saturday night. She doesn't want to be stuck home alone while I'm out playing a gig."

"It's a problem," said Buzzy. "Just ask Stan."

"What am I supposed to do? People don't get married on Tuesday."

Buzzy dropped his can on the floor and produced a full one from the side pocket of his tuxedo jacket. He popped the top and vacuumed off the foam with fishily puckered lips.

"You wanna know the solution?"

"What?"

"Kids."

"Please," said Dave. "Just getting married is scary enough. Don't start tossing kids into the mix."

"I'm serious," Buzzy insisted. "Once you got kids, having fun on Saturday night isn't even an option. The whole argument is moot."

"Kids are a long ways off," Dave assured him. "A vague rumor from a distant galaxy."

Buzzy shrugged. "It worked for us. Before JoAnn got pregnant, she was into that whole death metal thing—the spike bracelets, the white makeup, the whole nine yards. Her idea of a balanced meal was a Diet Coke to wash down her speed. Now she's the only mother in the PTA who can name all the guys in Anthrax."

Dave had only met JoAnn once, but she'd made an impression. She was a skinny, tired-looking woman with stringy, dishwater blond hair and pants so tight—they were some sort of spandex/denim blend that zipped up in the back—you had to worry about her circulation. No matter what anyone said, her expression remained fixed somewhere between boredom and indifference. Dave didn't think she was in danger of being elected president of the PTA anytime soon.

"Did she ever bug you about quitting the band?" he asked.

Buzzy shook his head. "Only thing like that, she made me sell my bike."

"Bicycle bike? Or motorcycle?"

"Motor," Buzzy replied, pausing mid-chug to see if Dave was putting him on. "I had me a beautiful Harley."

"I didn't know that."

"Oh yeah. Jo loved to ride it too. We had matching helmets and everything. Used to ride all over the place with this club I was in, stoned out of our minds. Amazing I'm even here to tell about it."

"So what happened?"

"This guy we knew wiped out in a rainstorm one night. Billy Farell. He was in a coma for three months."

"He came out?"

"Yeah. Seems okay too. He was a little off to begin with, so you can't really tell the difference. After that, though, Jo said she'd leave me if I didn't get rid of the bike."

"You miss it?"

Buzzy polished off the second beer and deposited the empty on the floor, which Dave used as a storage area for cassettes and their boxes, separate entities he kept meaning to reunite. He wanted to ask Buzzy to stop treating his car like a garbage can, but didn't want to come across as one of those neat freaks who act like their vehicle is some sort of sacred space, not to be defiled by evidence of human habitation, burger wrappers, or the odd plastic fork.

"I dream about it," Buzzy said. "Every night. Before I fall asleep."

Dave's car was stopped at a red light. Buzzy grabbed a pair of imaginary handlebars and pulled back on the throttle. Except for the tuxedo, he looked a little like Dennis Hopper. The expression on his face was pure ecstasy, sexual transport.

"Every night," he repeated, as Dave shifted into first and eased up on the clutch of his Metro. "Nothing else even comes close."

The Westview Manor was an enormous, windowless banquet complex on Route 22 that could—and often did—accommodate as many as four different receptions at the same time. Despite the congested feel of the place and the less-than-soundproof dividers that separated bands in adjoining rooms, the Wishbones considered it a decent venue. Unlike some of the snootier halls in the area, which required musicians to enter through the kitchen and generally went out of their way to make them feel like gatecrashers, the Westview treated "the entertainment" with a certain amount of respect. The Wishbones could arrive through the front door like normal human beings, relax in a conference room during their breaks, and grab an occasional beer or soda from the bar without feeling like criminals. One way or another, they usually managed to get themselves fed, an occupational perk once taken for granted by wedding musicians, but currently optional-at-best in the general atmosphere of belt-tightening and stinginess that had overtaken the country.

Dave and Buzzy stopped in the lobby to check the directory. It was a classy touch, removable white letters on a field of black velvet, the kind of thing you might find by the elevator in a building full of doctors.

"There we are," said Buzzy. "Lambrusco-DiNardo. Black Forest Room, Second Floor."

Except for Artie and a couple of waitresses tucking crown-shaped napkins into the water glasses, the Black Forest Room was empty. An expectant hush hung over the dais, the bar, the stage, the dance floor, the twenty or so round tables draped in starched white cloths, loaded down with plates and baskets of bread and water pitchers and floral centerpieces, the whole shebang ready and waiting. Dave wished he could describe for Julie the subtle thrill he felt entering a room like this in his crisply pressed (thanks, Mom) tuxedo, and walking straight over to the bandstand like he owned it.

Artie glanced up from the charts he was writing to acknowledge their arrival. Whatever else people might say about him, Artie was on top of things. In his two years with the band, Dave had yet to arrive at a gig before Artie, or even before Artie had singlehandedly managed to set up the entire sound system—amps, PA, monitors, mikes, soundboard—all of which he stored in his garage and transported in his van to avoid screwups. The individual Wishbones were responsible solely for their uniforms and instruments.

Reverently, Dave lifted his sunburst Les Paul out of its lush, coffinlike case, double-checking to make sure he'd remembered to bring an extra set of strings and half a dozen picks. He plugged into a battery-operated tuning gizmo and tuned up quickly and silently, a vast improvement over the bad old days of loud public tuning. Without turning on his amp, he ran through a few blues scales and jazz progressions to limber up, then unhooked the tooled leather strap Julie had given him for Christmas a couple of years before, and set the Les Paul carefully in its metal tripod stand, stepping back for a moment to admire its classic beauty.

Without a doubt, it was the most versatile, sweetest-sounding guitar he'd ever owned. The Wishbones played a dizzying variety of music—everything from ''Havah Nagilah'' to ''Louie Louie,'' as Artie liked to say—and the Les Paul was the only guitar Dave knew of that could handle the whole range without breaking a sweat. It wouldn't make sense, owning a top-flight instrument like that and not being able to play it loud for an audience. He might as well sell it at a loss and buy some chintzy Hagstrom to plunk in his bedroom like a three-chord teenage amateur.

He checked his watch. It was five-fifteen, forty-five minutes before cocktail hour. Buzzy had wandered off somewhere and Artie was flirting with one of the waitresses. Dave thought he might head downstairs and give Julie a call from the pay phone. Their afternoon had ended on a sour note, and it seemed to him they still had some talking to do.

One of the downstairs weddings was just getting under way. Dave stood at the base of the stairs and watched the guests drift through the lobby, dressed up and smiling, some of them bearing gifts. There were jobs, he thought—dentist, prison guard, clerk at the DMV—that brought you into daily contact with a clientele that was angry, bitter, or scared. It had to take a toll, strain your faith in humanity. But playing in a wedding band exposed you to the other side. It was hard to imagine that the festive crowd in the Westview Manor that Saturday evening had anything to do with the shuffling, muttering malcontents you might see on line at the DMV, though, obviously, there had to be some overlap.

On the way to the phone, he heard the soft strains of cocktail music and ducked his head into the Birnam Wood Room to see who was providing the entertainment. Instead of a bandstand, there was a card table full of stereo equipment set up at the far end of the dais, flanked by two unreasonably large speaker columns. A banner strung across the edge of the table read:

ROCKIN' RANDY PRODUCTIONS
The DJ Who Comes to Play

Presiding over the table was Rockin' Randy himself, a cocky young guy in a sharkskin suit (it was a shade of metallic blue Dave associated with new Toyotas), wearing state-of-the-art square headphones and swaying his head and shoulders to the languid rhythms of Anita Baker. His eyes were closed; his hair looked like it had been marinated in Valvoline. Dave felt irritated and superior at the same time, the way he always did in the presence of DJs. They were a revolting breed, scam artists who'd somehow managed to convince the world that it took talent to remove CDs from a plastic case while simultaneously babbling into a microphone.

Rockin' Randy, he thought. *Why do I know that name?*

As though his earmuffs picked up brainwaves, Randy unlidded his eyes and looked straight at Dave. By way of greeting, he turned his hands into pistols and fired several shots in the direction of the door, using both barrels in rapid succession. Then he blew on his fingertips to cool them off and calmly returned to his dancing, spinning one fist over the other while bobbing his head around in a moronic fashion.

Dave looked away in disgust. Aside from the dense clump of guests bearing down on the bartender, the room was sparsely populated by early birds loading up on hors d'oeuvres. He was startled—but only for a second—to see Buzzy lurking at the edge of the dance floor, beer in hand, reaching out like a friend of the family to snag a cocktail weenie from a passing tray.

He dropped the quarter into the slot and played the abbreviated touch-tone tune that was Julie's number (it sounded like the intro to "Peace Train," the Cat Stevens anthem later covered by 10,000 Maniacs). The pay phone was located right outside the ladies' "lounge," an arrangement that didn't offer a lot of privacy, especially since it seemed like every woman who arrived at the Westview made a beeline for the rest room. The night was young, but already a line had formed and was snaking out the door.

"Yes?" Dolores answered with her customary gasp, as

though she'd been sitting by the phone, awaiting ransom instructions from a kidnapper.

"Hi, Mrs. Muller."

"Oh, hi, Dave."

"Julie around?"

"She's right here. We're making stuffed peppers. I'll put her on."

Several seconds elapsed. Dave listened to nothing while surreptitiously admiring a woman in a daring black dress who was rummaging through her purse while waiting her turn for the bathroom. The dress was sleeveless and defiantly short; its back plunged in a dramatic V held together by a web of crisscrossing laces. She didn't really have the body to carry it off—the dress seemed loose where it was supposed to be tight and vice versa—but Dave appreciated the effort anyway. Risky fashion statements were part of what kept his job interesting week after week.

"Yeah?" Julie's voice was all business.

"Hey." He turned away from the woman, who seemed vaguely puzzled by the contents of her purse. "What's up?"

"Didn't you hear?" Julie's bubbly tone was incomprehensible except as sarcasm. "We're making stuffed peppers."

"Sounds exciting."

"Yeah, and after that, Uncle Danny and Aunt Dot are coming over to play cards. They're bringing a No-Fat cheesecake."

"No-Fat? Is that possible?"

"Apparently. The word on the street is that you can't taste the difference."

Dave wanted to make a joke about Danny and Dottie, both of whom were fatter than ever since their discovery of the brave new world of lite desserts, but this didn't seem like the right time to be poking fun at her relatives.

"So," she said. "Anything else I can help you with?"

"Not really. I just had a little down time and wanted to see how you were doing."

"I'm fine."

"Great."

"You don't sound like you believe me."

"Why wouldn't I believe you?"

"I don't know." Her voice was flat and chilly. "Why don't you tell me."

Dave breathed an inaudible sigh. He felt like apologizing, even though he hadn't done anything wrong. If anything, she owed *him* an apology.

"Listen," he said. "Why don't you go to a movie or something?"

"By myself?"

"You could call Tammi."

"I already did. She's got plans."

"Lots of people go to the movies by themselves."

"Not me," she said. "Not on Saturday night."

"Why not?"

"Because I don't feel like having two hundred couples staring at me, wondering why I can't find a date, okay? That's not my idea of a good time."

"What, you'd rather hang around with Dottie and Danny eating No-Fat cheesecake? That's your idea of a good time?"

Julie didn't answer, and he quickly spotted his blunder. After fifteen years, he should have known better than to make her points for her.

"I have to go," she said sweetly. "It's time to stuff the peppers."

She hung up before he could say good-bye, sealing her victory. Dave listened to the dial tone for a few seconds, then gently set the phone in its cradle. At almost the same moment, he yelped and spun around.

"Whoa!" said Buzzy, his watery eyes dilating with alarm. "Easy, partner."

"Jesus," said Dave. "Don't do that."

''Sorry.'' Buzzy held out the frosty bottle of Molson he'd just pressed against the back of Dave's neck. There was a tiny smudge of mustard by the corner of his mouth. ''Thought you might like a cold one.''

''Thanks,'' said Dave. ''Don't mind if I do.''

''Don't thank me.'' Buzzy fished around in his pocket and pulled out a glossy white matchbook, squinting to read the embossed golden lettering. ''Thank Barb and Larry, Two Hearts Beat as One.''

A study in contrasts greeted Dave as he stepped into the basement men's room. Alan Zelack and a priest stood side by side at the urinals, one tall and blond in garish red sequins, the other short and balding in funereal black. As though they'd rehearsed the maneuver, the two men flushed and whirled simultaneously, capping the routine with a synchronized zip. Dave felt like he'd wandered onto the set of a creepy musical.

''Hey,'' Zelack said, instinctively thrusting his hand in Dave's direction. ''Long time no see.''

Despite a qualm or two on the hygiene front, Dave saw no recourse but to shift the beer to his left hand and shake. It was possible that he shook hands frequently with people who hadn't washed up since last using the bathroom, but rarely was he presented with such irrefutable evidence.

''This is Father Mike,'' Zelack added, draping his arm around the priest's shoulder with a proud grin. ''We went to high school together.''

Father Mike offered his hand as well, but Dave didn't mind shaking it. On some deep, irrational level, he didn't believe that a priest's hands could *really* be dirty.

''Mike and I haven't seen each other in what—thirteen or fourteen years?'' Zelack grimaced as he performed the calculations.

The priest nodded. Despite his pleasantly boyish face,

his wire-rimmed glasses and receding hairline gave him an air of gravity and wisdom.

"My parish is in Arizona," he said. "I just flew up for my sister's wedding."

"Mike and I used to get stoned before gym class," Zelack announced with a laugh. He shook his head at the mysterious workings of the universe. "I still can't believe you're a priest."

Father Mike reddened slightly. "That was a long time ago, Alan. We've both changed a lot since then."

"What happened?" Zelack asked. His curiosity seemed genuine. "Did you have some sort of religious experience?"

Dave found himself curious as well, even though the priesthood ranked near the bottom on his scale of occupations, way down below prison guard and clerk at the DMV. The celibacy thing was a real sticking point.

"I don't know." Father Mike consulted his clunky black shoes, which, to Dave's surprise, turned out to be Doc Martens. "I took this solo hiking trip up to the Adirondacks the summer after my freshman year in college. My last night there was this incredible thunderstorm. Like the sky was breaking open. I took off my clothes, stood outside the tent, and let myself get drenched." Father Mike held his open hands out in front of his chest, as though presenting Dave with an invisible gift. "That was when I realized that my life belonged to God."

"Really?" said Zelack. "You became a priest because of a thunderstorm?"

Father Mike thought it over. He seemed troubled by the question.

"I guess so. That's the closest I can come to explaining it. Nothing was the same for me after that."

The door behind Dave swung open; three college-age guys in suits squeezed into the rest room, creating a severe shortage of space. In the confusion, Zelack and Father Mike slipped out the door without washing their hands.

Dave set his beer down on the sink, stepped up to the urinal, and unzipped. On the porcelain lip below, he saw two red sequins and a pubic hair.

Ian's keyboard was a scary instrument, more computer than piano. It was programmable, possessed extensive memory, and could simulate drums, a horn section, and the Mormon Tabernacle Choir, all at the same time. As a guitarist, Dave wasn't terribly threatened by it—something about the guitar remained resistant to mechanical reproduction—but bass players and drummers looked upon these machines with all the enthusiasm of candlemakers pondering their first lightbulb. Already one- and two-piece wedding bands were sprouting up, promising all the music for a fraction of the price. Luckily for Buzzy and Stan, humanity hadn't yet caught up with technology—most people, if they wanted live music at all, still preferred a full-sized band, the more pieces the better. But it didn't take much imagination to visualize a future in which musicians and DJs melted into a single category of performer, and live wedding entertainment became a kind of glorified karaoke. Dave just hoped he was dead by then.

As it was, Ian and his multitalented keyboard handled the cocktail hour by themselves, while the rest of the Wishbones cooled their heels in some out-of-the-way place, ideally after having secured a plateful of chicken wings, baked ziti, and green beans almondine from the buffet table, which they much preferred to circulating trays of greasy, mysterious, invariably disappointing doodads.

Ian was normally one of the first Wishbones to arrive at a job, but that night he didn't show up until twenty to six. By that point, Artie had worked himself into a serious lather, mainly because Stan was also AWOL, and the stage looked naked without his drum kit.

"See?" Artie said to everyone and no one as Ian unzipped the padded bag that encased his deceptively compact instrument. "What did I tell you? This is what happens when one guy in the band decides to become a fuckup. Everybody else figures it's okay for them to be a fuckup too. It's the Domino Theory of Fucking Up."

"You need a new theory," Ian told him, unfolding the metal stand that supported his keyboard. "The Domino Theory is widely recognized as a crock of shit."

Artie ignored this objection. He had entered the Rant Zone, a place he liked to visit at least once per job.

"I should have fired him last month," he said, feverishly capping and uncapping his pen. "All the warning signs were there. But you guys had to keep defending him. Poor Stan. He's going through a hard time. Poor Stan. His wife left him. Poor Stan my ass. He's not going to show, and we're the ones who are gonna be left holding the bag."

"Why don't you call him?" Buzzy suggested.

Artie's head snapped in Buzzy's direction. His sleepy features only really came alive when invigorated by anger or contempt.

"Gee, Buzzy, why didn't I think of that?" He paused for effect, laying two fingers contemplatively on his chin. "Maybe it's because I've only left six frigging messages on his frigging answering machine in the last ten minutes. Maybe because I *do* happen to be familiar with the miraculous instrument your people call a telephone."

"It *is* miraculous," Buzzy pointed out between sips from a bottle of Sam Adams that had somehow fallen into his possession. "Sometimes we forget."

The lugubrious, exceptionally tall maitre d' stepped into the Black Forest Room and beckoned to Artie, who had no choice but to interrupt his rant and obey the summons. On the Wishbone hierarchy of wedding types, maitre d's generally ranked only slightly higher than DJs. The guys at the Westview weren't bad, though. They looked the other way on questions of food and drink, and sometimes plugged the band to patrons who hadn't yet made a decision on the entertainment. (If Artie paid a kickback for this service, Dave didn't know about it.)

"So what happened?" Dave asked, stepping onto the stage to address Ian. "Did you meet Scotty?"

Ian looked up from his fat briefcase full of fake books and photocopied sheet music.

"He never showed."

"You're kidding."

"Nope. His plane had engine trouble in Pittsburgh."

"That's a good one," said Dave. "Scotty stuck in an airport. Air travel must be a real comedown for him."

Ian nodded. "The Trekkies didn't take it too well. We almost went on a rampage."

Cocktail hour was halfway in the bag by the time Stan finally showed his face. Dave and Buzzy were lounging in the conference room, contentedly sucking on chicken bones, when the drummer suddenly appeared in the doorway, a hulking figure wearing sunglasses and carrying a cymbal under each arm.

"Artie around?" he asked cautiously. His shades weren't quite big enough to hide the discoloration under his right eye.

"Check the pay phone," Buzzy advised. "He's describing you to the hit man."

Stan set the cymbals down on the table; they clanged with a quick metallic huff. "You guys want to help me get unloaded? If we hustle, I can be ready by seven."

"Sorry," Buzzy said, quickly rising from his chair. "I was just about to get seconds."

Stan looked at Dave. Even through the dark glasses, Dave could sense the pleading in his eyes. Stan's drum kit wasn't that elaborate—just a bass drum, floor tom, rack tom, snare, hi-hat, and cymbals—but setting it up in twenty minutes would be a real bitch, especially since he'd have to do it on a crowded stage, without disturbing Ian.

"Okay," Dave said with a sigh, eyeing the last lonely scraps of fettucini plastered to his plate like bandages. "I guess I'm done."

"Thanks," said Stan. "I owe you one."

"You owe me about twelve," Dave corrected him.

They hurried past the Black Forest Room, where Ian was playing "Misty" for the chitchatting friends and family of Staci Lambrusco and P.J. DiNardo, then continued down the stairs and through the lobby. Dave had to shade his eyes from the daylight in the parking lot; the evening breeze made him groan with gratitude.

"I'm parked way the fuck over there," Stan informed him, waving his hand at the western horizon, where the sun was blazing like a fat penny. "I tried to pull up to the door, but that asswipe security guard wouldn't let me."

They trudged past row upon row of more or less well-maintained vehicles until they reached Stan's LeBaron, a beat-up piece of crap that looked like someone had been using it for sledgehammer practice. The body was dented in half a dozen places and the rear bumper hung at a precarious tilt; even the license plate seemed inexplicably battered, as if someone had crumpled it into a ball like a piece of paper, then smoothed it out by hand in an attempt to remove the wrinkles. In a new touch, a piece of green garbage bag filled the space that should have been occupied by the rear driver's-side window.

Stan popped the trunk and handed Dave the bass drum, open side up like a big round box. In the natural light, his eye looked worse than before, not so much black as a repulsive amalgam of green and purple.

"Jesus," said Dave. "Where'd you get that shiner?"

Stan reached into the well and pulled out the pillow he used to muffle vibration inside the bass drum. The pillow was an eyesore, shapeless and sweat-stained, a sack of old feathers and bad dreams. The least he could've done was hide it in a pillowcase.

"You really want to know?"

"I'm not sure."

Stan stuffed the pillow into the drum.

"Walter," he said. "The piano player in Phil Hart's band."

"The old guy with the shakes?"

Stan nodded. In spite of everything, he seemed amused.

"I've been hanging out with him the past couple of weeks. He's a great guy."

"So why'd he slug you?"

Stan grabbed a foot pedal from the trunk and set it down on top of the pillow.

"We had one too many. I said some things I shouldn't have."

"Like what?"

Stan's tongue made a thoughtful tour of his mouth, poking at one cheek, then the other. His expression remained inscrutable behind the glasses.

"Well, for one thing, I said Thelonious Monk could suck my dick."

Dave couldn't help laughing. "He hit you because of that?"

"That was part of it." Stan looked up at the sky. "Then I said something about Brubeck. That was when he popped me."

"What'd you say?"

"I can't repeat it. It's too disgusting."

"Come on," said Dave.

Stan blew a weary raspberry and shook his head.

"I'm serious," he said. "You wouldn't believe me if I told you."

Are You Dave?

"Ladies and gentlemen," Artie said, slipping easily into his MC mode as the band struck up a sprightly Spyro Gyra instrumental, "on behalf of Shelley and Frank Lambrusco and Pat and Dick DiNardo, I'd like to welcome each and every one of you to the Westview Manor on this lovely spring evening. If you're not taking photographs, would you be kind enough to please take your seats and join me in offering a *very* warm welcome to our bridal party."

He paused while the guests drifted back to their tables. An honor guard of amateur photographers formed a wall around the dance floor, which was empty except for the camcorder mounted on a six-foot rolling tripod with a small, white-hot spotlight burning at its summit. The videographer, a nerdy, ubiquitous guy named Lenny, stood beside it with an air of proprietary importance, a battery pack wrapped around his waist like an ammunition belt. The professional still photographer, whom Dave had never seen before, was crouching in front of the three-tiered wedding cake, his camera aimed at the doorway, where a bridesmaid and usher now fidgeted, awaiting their introduction.

"o-KAY," Artie resumed, reading from an index card supplied by the maitre d'. "How about a big round of applause for bridesmaid Antoinette Lambrusco and usher Paul Cross."

Arms locked, Antoinette and Paul strode past the wedding cake and across the dance floor. A bodybuilder with a profusely moussed crewcut, Paul acknowledged the tepid ovation with magisterial nods, while Antoinette clutched a bouquet of spring flowers to her chest and beamed ecstatically, as though she herself were the bride. After they passed the video camera, the maitre d' escorted them off the dance floor, and Artie moved on to the next couple.

Dave always enjoyed this part of the ceremony. It was the moment when the evening began to take shape, to transform itself from a generic wedding reception into a unique occasion with a particular cast of characters. By the time the second couple had been introduced (Lori Lambrusco and Joe Tresh), he already knew that the bride had identical twin sisters (sturdy-looking girls with big hair and toothy smiles) and that the groom's buddies spent a lot of time at the gym.

The bridesmaids' dresses always merited a moment's consideration. Julie had once told him that they were designed ugly to make the bride appear more beautiful by comparison, and he was beginning to believe her. Tonight's weren't the most hideous he'd seen by a long shot, though no one in her right mind would have worn one of her own free will. They were shiny green, with puffy sleeves, a scalloped neckline, and a tight bodice that exploded into a big rustling bell of a skirt, really pretty tasteful as far as these things went, except for the yellow bow in the back, so large that it seemed like some kind of practical joke. None of the Lambrusco women seemed to mind—the third sister's name was Heidi—but the fourth bridesmaid (Gretchen Something-or-Other) gave the impression of being deeply chastened to be seen in public in such an outrageous getup. She was a thin, glum-looking woman with men's eyeglasses and sexily bobbed hair, who didn't even pretend to smile as she shuffled across the dance floor attached to the elbow of the first usher who didn't look like he injected steroids for breakfast. *Lighten up, Gretchen,* Dave thought to himself. *Your secret's safe with us.*

The flower girl and ring bearer were introduced right after the Best Man and Maid of Honor; as usual, they hammed it up shamelessly and got the biggest ovation of the night (Dave made a mental note not to allow any kids in his own wedding party). Then the parents of the groom and the parents of the bride came bounding out, the Lambruscos looking markedly more comfortable than the DiNardos (this was also typical, the bride's family possessing the home-field advantage). Finally, the big moment had arrived. The happy couple appeared in the doorway, staggered slightly on account of the bride's prodigious hoop skirt.

"Ladies and gentlemen, let's hear it for the guests of honor, the brand-new Mr. and Mrs. P.J. DiNardo."

Despite unspecified "gown problems" that had delayed the start of the reception by twenty minutes, the bride was glowing as she made her entrance. She was a tall, broad-shouldered, athletic-looking girl—maybe a basketball player, Dave thought—with a crown of flowers on her head and so much makeup that she didn't look completely human. The groom was a muscle-bound behemoth in white tails, black pants, and a black vest decorated with a pattern of white dots meant to suggest champagne bubbles, currently a popular touch. Like his parents, he appeared a bit perplexed to find himself playing such a large role in this particular ceremony.

Mr. and Mrs. DiNardo stopped in the middle of the

dance floor and waited for the cheering to die down. The groom's friends had climbed onto their chairs and begun shaking their fists and woofing Arsenio-style, apparently unaware that this particular fad had run its course some time ago. The maitre d' kept slitting his throat with one finger to get them to stop, a gesture that just egged them on all the more. They only stopped woofing when the bride began slitting her throat as well. Artie pressed his lips to the mike.

"For their first dance of the evening, Staci and P.J. have chosen the unforgettable 'Unchained Melody,' a ballad originally recorded by the legendary Righteous Brothers and later immortalized in the hit movie *Ghost,* starring the gorgeous Demi Moore and the inimitable Patrick Swayze." Dave had never understood why all this information was necessary, but Artie insisted that people *expected* long-winded introductions, and would be disappointed if the Wishbones didn't provide them.

The song had barely started when Staci stood up on tiptoe, grabbed the back of P.J.'s neck, and kissed him. It wasn't an ordinary first-dance smooch, though; it was long and hard and slow, the kind of kiss that made promises for later, as if the very fact of the wedding weren't promise enough. In the heat of the moment, P.J. forgot himself and grabbed the bride's ass with both hands through the various layers of lace and satin and whatnot. The kiss and grope lasted the entire length of the song and embarrassed pretty much everyone in the room with the possible exception of Buzzy, who kept licking his lips and shooting Dave wide-eyed smirks of prurient approval.

The next phase of the reception followed a fairly rigid script. The bride danced with her father ("Daddy's Little Girl," even though the little girl had at least five inches on Daddy), and then, probably for the sake of symmetry, the groom danced with his mother. It was hard to say what the purpose of this ritual was, except to prove beyond the shadow of a doubt that slow-dancing was a dying art. P.J., in particular, didn't seem to grasp the fact that his feet were supposed to move. He stood rooted to the floor, gazing pensively at nothing, while his tiny mother held on to his waist and smiled gamely, shifting her weight from one leg to another to provide the illusion of movement.

Then the Best Man climbed onto the stage and delivered the toast through Dave's microphone. He was short and blond and surprisingly confident, like a talk-show host or professional toastmaster. You saw this now and again, though the usual Best Man could barely mumble his way through the standard boilerplate about a lifetime of health and happiness, etc.

The Best Man spoke at length about a trip he and P.J. and a couple of other brothers from Alpha Chi Rho had taken to Daytona Beach during spring break of their senior year. He recalled the camaraderie of the nonstop drive, the partying, and a couple of long serious talks on the beach, the kind of talks people he knew no longer seemed to have time for.

"Now I don't remember a whole lot about those talks," he said, "and I don't guess P.J. does either. We were probably hung over and distracted by those Duke girls playing volleyball about ten feet away in their bikinis. But one thing I do remember is that we both agreed that we weren't going to get married for a long time, if ever. At least until we were forty."

The Best Man lifted his glass. "P.J. was twenty-five last summer when he met Staci at a barbecue."

Dave looked out at the crowd. All sorts of people stood with glasses in hand, smiling at the stage. P.J. himself was shaking his head, remembering what a foolish kid he'd been. Staci looked triumphant.

"Here's to you both," the Best Man concluded. "We love you."

All through the room, glass clinked against glass. The Best Man stepped down from the stage. Artie turned around and looked at the band.

" 'Twist and Shout,' " he told them.

Ian seemed depressed. He sat across from Dave during the set break, printing circles on a paper napkin with the wet bottom of a glass. It was just the two of them in the conference room. Artie was in the hallway, having "a little chat" with Stan, and Buzzy had excused himself to investigate the rumored sighting of a dessert cart at the early reception downstairs.

"What's the matter?" Dave asked.

"Nothing." Ian lifted the glass and examined his hand-iwork. "What makes you think something's the matter?"

"I don't know. You just seem kind of down."

"Why should I be down?" Ian fished an ice cube out of his glass and popped it into his mouth. "Here we are at the Westview, playing another wedding."

Dave chuckled, as if the remark had been meant as a joke. Through the floor, he could hear the pulsing bass and tinny-sounding drums of the downstairs band, prob-ably Sparkle. He imagined Father Mike out on the dance floor, shaking his clerical booty, and for some reason was reminded of Julie's curiosity about Ian's sex life.

"Are you seeing anyone?" he asked.

Ian looked up. "Women, you mean?"

Dave tried not to look surprised; maybe Julie was a lot smarter than he was about these things.

"Women . . . whoever," Dave managed to mutter, swiping feebly at the air as if to suggest that it was all the same to him.

Now it was Ian's turn to look alarmed.

"No no no," he said quickly. "I thought maybe you were asking if I was seeing a psychiatrist or something. I've been kind of depressed lately."

"No," Dave assured him. "I was asking about women. Actually, it was Julie who was wondering. She couldn't understand why a guy as good-looking and talented as you didn't have a girlfriend."

Ian combed his fingers through his wavy brown curls. He seemed flattered by the explanation.

"I've been out of circulation for a while, trying to finish up this big project."

Just then the doorknob clicked and a woman's head peeped into the room. It was Gretchen, the bridesmaid with the bobbed hair and glasses. She was prettier up close than she'd been from a distance.

"Sorry," she said. "I didn't realize you were in here. I was just looking for a place to hide out."

"Have a seat," Ian told her. "We're just killing time between sets."

Gretchen considered the offer. She had wide-set eyes and a pouty mouth.

"Thanks anyway. I don't want to intrude."

The door clicked softly into place. Dave and Ian kept staring at her long after she'd gone.

"Nice glasses," said Ian. He sounded like he meant it.

Dave nodded. He felt sorry to see her go. He wanted to ask her what she was hiding from.

"Oh yeah," he said. "You were telling me about a project."

"I've been writing a musical," Ian said proudly. "It's pretty much taken over my life the past year or so. I really haven't had time for anything else."

"I didn't know that."

"There wasn't any point in talking about it. The world is full of bullshitters who don't finish what they start."

"A musical," said Dave. "That's pretty ambitious."

Ian closed his eyes and played some piano chords on the tabletop, a dreamy Stevie Wonderish expression on his face. He was a supremely weird guy, Dave decided. No one wrote musicals anymore except for Andrew Lloyd Webber.

"What's it about?"

Ian's hands flattened out. He opened his eyes and frowned.

"Sorry. State secret."

"Come on."

"I mean it. When I'm done, I'll play you a few of the songs."

"When'll that be?"

"Couple of months." Ian knocked on wood. "This could be my big break. My ticket out of Palookaville."

"Just as long as you still talk to me when you're famous."

"Don't worry. I won't forget the little people."

"Uh, listen," said Dave. "The reason the whole subject came up is that Julie's got this friend she thought you might hit it off with. Her name's Tammi."

Ian shrugged. "Sounds good to me."

"Really?"

"Why not? Is she cute?"

"Yeah. She's a nurse. Great sense of humor."

"Cool," said Ian. "Get me her number. I'm ready to get back in the game."

Dave sat back in his chair, relieved and amazed that the conversation had turned out so well after such a terrible beginning. The door opened again. Stan slipped into the conference room, shut the door behind him, and sat down at the far end of the table.

"So what happened?" asked Ian.

"Not a thing," Stan whispered.

"You're kidding."

Stan shook his head, smirking like a kid who'd gotten away with murder.

"I thought he was going to fire my ass, but he only put me on probation."

"Probation?" said Dave. "What the fuck is that?"

Stan took off his sunglasses and touched two fingers to the bruised, puffy skin below his eye. He looked happier than Dave had seen him in a long time.

"It could have been worse," he admitted. "He could have given me detention."

The second set filled the space between dinner and dessert, when people were ready to get up and work off a few calories. Artie sensed the mood and called for three surefire rockers in quick succession—"Good Lovin'," "Grapevine," and "Hang On, Sloopy." Energized by his reprieve—or maybe just the sunglasses—Stan kicked the tempo up a notch, banging his drums like a teenager trying to irritate the neighbors. At one point, a scowling senior citizen charged past the stage with his index fingers plugged into his ears, but Dave was having too much fun to care. The floor was packed and the dancers were starting to get a little crazy, especially the bride, who kept raising her hands and shaking them like a gospel singer praising Jesus.

Artie eased up a bit, letting Ian impress the crowd with one of the Bryan Adams power ballads that were his specialty, then began to pick up the pace again with crowd-pleasers like "Love Shack" and "Surfin' USA." After a couple of swing tunes tossed like bones to the oldster contingent, it was time for the disco portion of the show.

This began, as usual, with a tried-and-true piece of Wishbone theater. Apparently unable to decide what to play next, Artie, Ian, Dave, and Buzzy huddled together in the middle of the bandstand and pretended to have a heated discussion. No one actually spoke; they just stood there, making faces and waving their arms around like idiots. When they had done this long enough to attract attention, Dave and Ian traded a couple of shoves, as if in preparation for a fistfight, but were quickly restrained by Buzzy and Artie. Then everyone returned to their places.

"Maybe you can help us out," Ian told the crowd. He glanced distastefully at Dave. "Our guitar player doesn't think there are ten people here who know how to do the Electric Slide. I say there have to be at least twenty."

Dave stepped up to his mike. "No way," he scoffed. "Not in this bunch."

Ian waved his arms, as if summoning the audience on-stage.

"Come on," he said. "Get up and show us how it's done."

This invitation sparked a complex round of negotiations throughout the room. A handful of women, including the bride and her three sisters, jumped up and began coaxing others to join them. Some flatly refused, but a fair number allowed themselves to be persuaded, including a few who had to be forcibly escorted to the dance floor, as though they'd been taken into custody. Pretty soon a respectable group of the usual suspects—young women, couples who'd taken dance lessons, fun-loving aunts and grand-mothers, plus several smirking men of various ages, some of them obviously drunk—had been herded into three more or less straight lines. Dave was pleased to see Gretchen in the front row, trapped between the Lambrusco twins, a reluctant conscript in the good-time army.

"All right!" Ian raised his fist in solidarity with the dancers, then turned to Dave, shaking his head in a haughty, what-did-I tell-you sort of way. "Oh ye of little faith. I think you owe these people an apology."

Dave approached the mike, a study in contrition. "Sorry," he mumbled. "I must have been thinking about the losers at our last wedding."

Artie counted to four and the bodies began to move. From the stage, the Electric Slide looked like an easy line dance—a couple steps up, a couple steps back, slide, spin, clap—but Dave knew better. Julie had made him try it at her office Christmas party, and he'd found himself hope-lessly lost within seconds, clapping and spinning when everyone else was still stepping up and stepping back. It was almost as bad as the time he got kicked out of a low-impact aerobics class during Bring-a-Guest-Free Week at Julie's health club.

Tonight's dancers were better than average, almost as if they'd gotten together earlier in the day and practiced. All three rows did a half-decent imitation of unison—even the drunks managed to turn on the beat, usually in the right direction—and a few of the women looked like ringers smuggled in from an MTV dance party. For someone who hadn't wanted to get up at all, Gretchen seemed suspiciously competent, improvising her own private dance around the basic steps of the Electric Slide, her easy grace heightened by the presence of the no-frills Lambrusco twins on either side of her, stomping around like bodyguards. She seemed to sense him watching and looked up quizzically near the end of the song, doing a startled double take at the moment of eye contact. Before he could react she spun away, leaving him to smile at the yellow bow pinned above her butt like an award.

Seamlessly, the band segued into a ten-minute medley that included "I Will Survive," "Boogie-Oogie-Oogie," "Get Down Tonight," and "On the Radio," capped by a full-length version of "Y.M.C.A.," a song that had returned with a vengeance from the land of musical oblivion. The Disco Revival had not been a happy development for the Wishbones, highlighting as it did a number of their weaknesses, the most prominent being the lack of a female vocalist (as hard as Ian tried, "I Will Survive" was not something a man could pull off with any credibility, let alone panache), as well as the band's stylistic discomfort with the entire genre. Dave had to fake the choppy strumming, and Buzzy couldn't quite coax the fat, funky bottom notes out of his usually eloquent bass; Ian had recently begun programming his keyboard drum machine to supplement Stan's none-too-subtle attack. In the end, though, none of this seemed to matter. The dancers waved their arms and sang along as though the Wishbones were just the Village People in black tie.

Artie closed off the set with a couple of Golden Oldies. Gretchen returned to her table during "Under the Boardwalk,'' but was immediately accosted by the Best Man, who seemed eager to drag her back out for a slow dance. She shook her head and dabbed her brow with a napkin, apparently pleading exhaustion, but the cocky little guy persisted. Finally she relented, allowing herself to be led back onto the floor for "The Great Pretender." Watching this minidrama from the stage, Dave found himself seized by a sudden and violent dislike for the Best Man, who looked like a puffed-up pigeon in his tightly buttoned vest and shirtsleeves.

They danced at arm's-length like the strangers (he hoped) they were, drifting closer and closer to the stage as the song progressed. Dave tried to concentrate on his playing, but it gradually became clear that Gretchen wanted to reestablish the eye contact that had been broken off during the Electric Slide. Her gaze was frank and curious rather than flirtatious, but he was flattered nonetheless. He even began to feel a bit sorry for the Best Man, the poor guy dancing in a dreamworld, thinking he was making progress with the most intriguing woman in the room while she was busy flirting over his head with someone else. He smiled at her and she smiled back.

This isn't happening, Dave thought. *This doesn't happen to me.* He'd heard lots of talk about willing bridesmaids and musicians getting lucky at weddings, but he'd quickly learned not to take this sort of thing too seriously, at least as it applied to him. He wasn't the center of attention like an Ian or a Zelack; he was just an anonymous guy in the shadows, Joe Average in a tuxedo. Every now and then he got to sing "shoo-bop" or "la la la."

Spoiling the moment in an effort to preserve it, Lenny rolled his video camera through the middle of the dance floor, his spotlight burning like the midday sun. Gretchen got lost in the glare, but reemerged a few seconds later, her eyes seeking out Dave's as she steered her partner back toward the stage. When she had positioned herself directly in front of him, maybe ten feet away, she mouthed a silent question he couldn't quite decipher. He shrugged and grimaced. She tried again, mouthing the words more distinctly.

"Are you saved?"

Shit, he thought, *is that what this is about?* He felt an urge to laugh, even as he registered the surprisingly sharp sense of disappointment in his gut. She really didn't look like the kind of woman who cared if a man was saved or not. He shook his head no, but the Best Man had already spun her away from him. The little guy's eyes were closed; his face looked lost and happy floating above her shoulder. Gretchen rotated him ninety degrees, looking up and repeating her silent question for the third time.

This time his face lit up with comprehension. She was making a much simpler inquiry than he'd thought, one he'd be happy to answer in the affirmative.

"Are you *Dave?*"

She wasn't too surprised he didn't remember. She'd only been seventeen that summer in Belmar, one of a handful of high-school girls who used to sneak into bars to hear Lost Cause, this Beaver Brown–type band he'd played in during his second, and final, year of college.

"Mark Frechetti's my cousin. That's how we knew about you guys."

"Really? How's Mark doing?"

They were standing near the base of the stage, next to the small rolling cart that held the wedding cake, which turned out not to be a cake at all, but an elaborate cardboard facsimile, complete with three-dimensional bride and groom figurines on top. The rest of the band had slipped off to the conference room, and the Best Man had returned to the head table to confer with the happy couple.

"Okay, I guess. He moved to Seattle about five years ago. He was supposedly friends with Nirvana or something."

"Wow."

"I know." Gretchen's eyes widened behind her glasses; he couldn't decide if she was impressed or amused. "My own cousin."

Mark Frechetti wasn't the most talented singer Dave had ever worked with—he couldn't touch Ian's range, for example—but he was easily the most charismatic. Handsome, seedy, and weirdly intense, he was an orthodontist's kid who wrote incomprehensible lyrics and mumbled them into the microphone long before it became fashionable on the alternative scene. The last time Dave saw him, at an Alex Chilton show in Hoboken, he'd grown these ratty-looking white guy dreadlocks and lost one of his top front teeth. It was easy to imagine him hanging with Cobain during those last grim months, neither one of them uttering a word for hours at a time.

"We were groupies," she told him. "Lost Cause was all we ever talked about. We were sure you guys were going to be famous."

"Groupies? How come I didn't know about this?"

"I tried to talk to you a few times, but you always seemed preoccupied."

More than ten years down the road, Dave could still vividly recall that Lost Cause summer. Seven guys sharing a one-bedroom beach rental, crashing anywhere there was enough floor for a body. Delivering furniture by day, getting stoned and playing music at night. It would have been a great time, except that Julie had just left him for Brendan, and he'd forgotten how to eat or sleep. No wonder he'd seemed preoccupied.

"We thought of you as the Sad One," she continued. "The brooding loner of the group."

"Just my luck. The one time in my life I have groupies, and I don't even know it."

Her hand fell softly on his wrist. "It's so weird seeing you here. It feels like a dream or something."

He studied her face, trying to rescue it from the messy

file cabinet of his memory. Was there a folder up there marked "Frechetti's Little Cousin?" Or "People Named Gretchen?" Or "Girls I Should Have Talked to, but Didn't?" Gretchen didn't mind the scrutiny. She stared right back at him with an odd composure that seemed to say, *Go ahead, look at me all you want.*

Dave wasn't fully aware of the intimacy generated by this silence until it was violated by the Best Man. He barged into their moment without a word of apology, grabbing hold of her wrist as though he had some sort of preestablished claim on her body.

"Hey," he said, "we need you back at the table."

She didn't answer right away. Her gaze moved away from Dave to the fingers on her arm, then traveled without haste up to the Best Man's face.

"Are you touching me?" she asked.

The little guy pulled his hand away, his cheeks flushing with remarkable speed. His voice was reproachful and defensive at the same time.

"They're taking the table picture. Everybody's there but you."

"Okay," she told him. "I'll be there in a minute."

The Best Man didn't know how to take a hint. He crossed his arms on his chest and let out a long, impatient sigh. Gretchen grabbed hold of Dave's wrist as easily as the little guy had taken hold of hers.

"Come on," she said, tugging him toward the door. "I need a cigarette."

He was happy to follow her out the door and down the hall, happy to leave the Best Man fuming on the dance floor and the less-fortunate Wishbones twiddling their thumbs in the conference room while he shared a quiet moment with a woman who somehow managed to pull off the nearly impossible feat of seeming sexy and intelligent in a bridesmaid's dress.

"I don't even know what I'm doing here," she said, pausing at the top of the stairs to gather the front of her dress into two big billowy handfuls. "Staci and I haven't really been friends since we were twelve."

"So how'd it happen?"

"It's complicated." She began her descent, hugging her raised skirt like a grocery bag to keep from tripping. "My mother and her mother were like sisters. My mom died this year and Staci asked me to do this at the funeral. Neither one of us was thinking straight."

"I'm sorry."

"This dress is ridiculous," she muttered. "I can't even see my feet."

"About your mother," he added, in case she hadn't understood him the first time.

Downstairs was a madhouse. Just as they reached level ground, an enormous conga line spilled out of the Birnam Wood Room and began snaking through the lobby. Rockin' Randy led the charge in a wild Hawaiian shirt, waving his cordless mike and shouting "Hot! Hot! Hot!" The bride and groom were right behind him, followed by the wedding party and what appeared to be a never-ending line of women in dresses and men in suits, each one holding on to the person in front and chanting along with Randy. It was like one of those freight trains that just kept on coming, car after car after car. When the caboose finally arrived, it turned out to be Buzzy, who was holding on to an elderly woman's waist with one hand and brandishing an eclair with the other.

"Yo," he called out, beckoning to Dave with the pastry. "Get on board!"

Dave turned hopefully to Gretchen, thinking a conga line might not be the worst way to break the ice with her.

"I need some fresh air," she told him.

"Hot! Hot! Hot!"

Rockin' Randy's freight train ran amok through the lobby in a series of overlapping loops and spirals, temporarily denying them access to the parking lot, the only source of fresh air he could think of.

"Hot! Hot! Hot!"

But then he remembered another possibility. There was a fire door at the opposite end of the building that opened onto what amounted to a little patio enclosed by Dumpsters. Buzzy had shown it to him when he first joined the band, explaining that this was where the dishwashers hung out during their breaks. At the time there were even a couple of lawn chairs out there. It was at least worth a try.

"Come on," he said. "Follow me."

They walked toward the rear of the Manor, past the Sherwood Forest Room—Sparkle was apparently between sets, too—past the pay phone and rest rooms, all the way to the kitchen, which sounded like it was in full swing, bells ringing, dishes clattering, people shouting. An angry-looking waitress burst through the doors, a bottle of champagne in each hand, offering them a momentary glimpse of a sweaty Mexican man in stained white clothes holding a flyswatter above his head and staring intently at a table full of steaming plates.

The hallway took a sharp turn to the right, dead-ending about fifteen feet away in an unmarked gray door with an EXIT sign glowing above it. The door opened easily and they stepped onto the patio. At the same moment he saw the lawn chairs—they were right where he remembered them—the combined smells of fresh air, Dumpster funk, and pot smoke hit him in the face. Someone said, "Shit!"

He turned toward the voice and saw Zelack and Father Mike standing close together by the smaller Dumpster, trying to look casual. Zelack had one hand hidden behind his back, his jacket gleaming eerily in the moonlight. Father Mike looked mortified.

"Don't worry," Dave told them, the half-forgotten code of high school rushing unbidden to his lips. "It's cool."

Father Mike apologized for his choking fit.

"I haven't done this for years," he explained, stamping his foot and coughing out little puffs of smoke along with his words. "I think it's stronger than it used to be."

"No kidding." Zelack produced this doofy little laugh. "I'm pretty fucking bamboozled as it is."

Gretchen held the joint in front of her like a candle, eyeing it with a certain amount of skepticism.

"Where'd you get it?" she asked.

"My brother in Vegas. Every year he sends me a couple of joints taped inside a birthday card. It's kind of a family tradition."

Gretchen took a hit and passed it on to Dave. Father Mike looked at Zelack.

"Your brother Charlie?"

"Steve. Charlie's in Atlantic City."

"What's he do there?"

"Blackjack. Both my brothers are blackjack dealers." Zelack shook his head. "What are the odds against that?"

Father Mike skipped his turn, passing the joint straight to Gretchen.

"Are they identical?" he asked.

"Fraternal," said Zelack. "But it's hard to tell them apart."

Dave tilted his head back and blew smoke at the sky. The moon was round and cheesy, just about full.

Hot! Hot! Hot! he thought.

"Twin blackjack dealers?" said Gretchen.

"Yup." Zelack grinned. "Every mother's dream."

"Charlie's a good guy," Father Mike declared. "I'll never forget the day he broke his leg."

Zelack took the joint from Dave but forgot to smoke it. He looked around the circle and smiled approvingly.

"Cool. Everyone's in uniform."

All four of them traded looks, confirming this observation. The joint made two more circuits before Zelack consulted his watch.

"Shit," he said. "Break's almost over."

"How'd your brother break his leg?" Dave asked.

"He jumped off the Little League field house with an umbrella in his hand. Must have been fifty kids watched him do it."

Father Mike took a box of Tic Tacs out of his pocket and offered some to Gretchen.

"Everyone's always in uniform," she told him, as he shook the little white pebbles into her hand.

"Thought he could fly," Zelack added sadly.

"His leg snapped like a pencil," Father Mike reported. "It was a horrible sound."

"Icarus," said Gretchen.

"Tic Tac?" asked Father Mike.

Gretchen lit up a Parliament and exhaled through her nose, which, in profile at least, seemed a little too long and narrow, vaguely reminiscent of Jughead's. It was her one odd feature, the arresting detail that made him want to keep staring, to commit her face to memory for future contemplation.

This is what Julie's afraid of, he thought. They were alone now, sitting on the dishwashers' lawn chairs, listening to the clamor of the kitchen and the shushing of traffic on Route 22. Break was just about over, but the night felt too soft and peaceful to make going inside seem like a plausible course of action. *This is what she meant by "out having fun."*

"I'm pretty buzzed," Gretchen observed.

"I'm right there with you," he assured her.

Julie seemed far away. He tried to imagine her sitting around the table with her parents and her aunt and uncle, all of them worshiping at the altar of the miraculous cheesecake, but he couldn't quite bring the picture into focus. He felt somehow liberated by this failure, as though it canceled out the fact of their engagement, at least for the moment.

"I never expected to get high with a priest," she said.

"Father Mike's a good guy."

Cigarette clamped between her teeth, she laid one foot on top of her knee, pulled off her green shoe, and dropped it unceremoniously on the ground.

"What's with the other one?" she asked, reaching down with both hands to massage her stockinged foot. "Did he borrow that jacket from Liberace or what?"

"Who? Zelack?" Dave tried to think of something cutting to say, but his fund of hostility seemed to be mysteriously depleted. "He's okay, too."

Gretchen recrossed her legs and pulled off the other shoe, letting it fall beside its companion.

"How'd you end up in a wedding band?" she asked, just making conversation as she went to work on her instep.

Dave thought it over. It was one of those questions that had a dozen different answers.

"They asked me," he said.

"You guys are pretty good. Usually I can't stand wedding bands."

The mix of praise and condescension in her comment called him back to reality. He looked at his watch and grimaced.

"Damn," he said, leaping up from his chair. "We better get back."

She looked up at him with mild interest.

"I think I'll hang out here for a while."

"You sure?"

Gretchen smiled. Inside the kitchen there was a loud crash, like someone had just dropped a whole tray of dishes. *I could have it bad for her,* Dave decided.

"Save me a dance," she told him.

He was late.

The band had already taken the stage when he careened through the door, Artie glaring at him, Buzzy looking mock-scandalized, Ian pretending not to notice, Stan cleaning out his ear with the tip of a drumstick. In an effort to excuse himself, Dave winced and rubbed his stomach, feigning indigestion.

Everything seemed unreal as he snatched his guitar out of its stand and threaded his head through the strap—the room, himself, the bride and groom standing by the fake cake with the bride and groom on top, both of them clutching the handle of what appeared to be a cement trowel and squinting through the glare from Lenny's spotlight.

"Okay," said Ian, glancing quickly at Dave to make sure he was set. "The big moment has arrived. It's time to cut the cake."

In Dave's opinion, one of the major improvements in wedding music in recent years involved the phase-out of the traditional cake-cutting song ("The bride cuts the cake/The bride cuts the cake/Hi-ho the cherrio/The bride cuts the cake") in favor of less idiotic tunes. Unless instructed otherwise, or unless one or both members of the happy couple happened to be approaching retirement age, the Wishbones chose "When I'm Sixty-Four" for this interlude in the ceremony.

Staci and P.J. brought the trowel down on the fake cake and smiled like politicians cutting a ribbon. Even as they did so, waitresses had already begun fanning out across the room, distributing slices of the real thing.

So, thought Dave, *you really can have it and eat it, too.*

The maitre d' presented the bride and groom with their own plates for the completion of the ritual. To Dave's surprise, they played it cool, feeding each other small bites from a fork and smooching discreetly afterward, resisting the temptation to mash the cake in each other's faces or engage in some serious tonsil-licking with their mouths full of mush and frosting.

Its work done, a waitress wheeled the model cake out of the room, back to wherever it was things like that got stored when they weren't in use, some dank basement full of cardboard desserts and artificial flowers. The maitre d' nodded at Artie, who relayed the message to Ian.

"At this time," Ian announced, "I'd like to invite all the single ladies out onto the dance floor. And I do mean *all* the single ladies."

No more than a dozen bachelorettes heeded the call, sheepishly clumping together at the far end of the floor, as if for protection. All the bridesmaids were present except Gretchen. Dave wondered if she was still hiding out on the Dumpster patio, massaging her feet and enjoying the almost-fresh air between drags on her Parliament. She didn't strike him as the type who'd get too upset about missing an opportunity to make a diving leap for a bundle of flowers.

The event went off peacefully, according to what appeared to be a prearranged plan. The moment Staci heaved the bouquet, all the women but one beat a hasty retreat, leaving Heidi Lambrusco wide open for an easy catch. It looked so much like a touchdown pass, Dave half expected Heidi to spike the flowers and bump chests with all three of her sisters.

The "Magic Chair" sequence followed the bouquet toss. Despite its lascivious overtones, the whole rigamarole seemed so tedious and time-consuming—bride sits in "Magic Chair," groom removes bride's garter, groom tosses garter to assembled single men, man who catches garter places it on leg of woman who caught bouquet, who is herself now seated in "Magic Chair"—that Dave wondered how it managed to survive for however long a practice like this had to survive to become a tradition. He tried his best to float above it, playing the inevitable can-can music on auto pilot, tuning out Ian's tired spiel about the bride and groom receiving ten years of happiness for every inch the garter traveled on its journey up the thigh of the woman who caught the bouquet.

When all of that was put to rest, the band, with the exception of Ian, vacated the stage for the breaking of the Ceremonial Wishbone. Dave fled immediately to the downstairs rest room, less out of necessity than a desire to avoid a lecture from Artie on the importance of punctuality. He thought about heading out to the patio to check on Gretchen, but wasn't sure he'd be able to make it there and back before it was time to climb back onstage and play some real music for a change.

The Ceremonial Wishbone was a corny gimmick Artie had cooked up about a year before, much to Ian's dismay. Central to the ritual was the bone itself, which Ian and the bride broke onstage. It looked like something from *The Flintstones,* a three-foot-tall segmented piece of V-shaped plastic, held together by a nearly inconspicuous velcro fastener. The joke was that Ian always got the longer piece and therefore got to make the wish. He made a big show of it, scratching his chin and gazing off into the distance, then asked the bride if she wanted to know what he'd wished for. She always did.

"On behalf of the band," he'd tell her, "I'd like to wish you and your husband a lifetime of health, happiness, and joy. May your marriage always be graced by the music of love."

Ian didn't have a problem with any of that. What he objected to was the second half of the ritual, which called for him to serenade the bride with an a capella rendition of "You Are So Beautiful." Some of them cried, but most just stood there, still clutching the losing end of the wishbone, looking troubled and perplexed by this unexpected turn of events.

Dave splashed some water on his face and checked in with the mirror. He was still more stoned than he wanted to be, but the buzz was quieter now, a little less distracting. He rarely smoked dope anymore, and every time he did reminded him of why he'd stopped in the first place—he'd reached the point where coming down was the best part of the experience.

Artie was waiting at the top of the stairs, arms crossed, a stern expression on his face. Dave cursed under his breath. He was in no mood to bow and scrape to the great leader, begging forgiveness for the two minutes of inconvenience he'd inflicted on the universe. Artie snagged him by the coat sleeve as he tried to hurry past.

"Hold on," he said. "I need to talk to you."

Dave let go of a deep breath, the long day catching up with him all at once. He felt limp, wrung out.

"I had a stomachache," he explained wearily. "I lost track of the time."

Instead of arguing, Artie gave a distracted nod. His mind was elsewhere, his voice more worried than angry.

"What's happening to us?"

"Huh?"

"The band. I think we're falling apart."

"Come on," said Dave. "Don't be ridiculous."

Artie shrugged. "Just look at us. Stan's a wreck, Buzzy's a drunk, Ian's out in left field somewhere, and now you're starting to act up on me, too. Where's it gonna stop?"

Dave shifted his gaze to the floor, then forced himself to look back up.

"You really think Buzzy's a drunk?"

"I think he's got a problem, yeah."

Dave peered down the corridor. Stan and Buzzy waved hello.

"The band seems pretty solid to me."

Artie wiped away the mustache of perspiration that had formed above his upper lip. He was good-looking in a bug-eyed, slightly unsavory sort of way, and believed in smelling nice for the ladies.

"I hope so. It took me four years to put together this lineup. All of us worked too fucking hard to get where we are. I'd hate to see us screw it up now."

Dave couldn't decide if Artie was asking for reassurance or trying to make him feel guilty or trying to do both at once. Whichever it was, his concern for the band seemed genuine.

"We'll be all right," Dave told him.

Artie made a halfhearted stab at smiling and put his hand on Dave's shoulder.

"Help me out, okay?"

Before Dave could reply, Gretchen snuck up from behind and grabbed hold of his elbow, squeezing it in a way that made him forget all about Artie.

"I'm back," she said brightly. "Did I miss anything important?"

By the Way

Cresting the Verrazano, a bridge he'd never crossed at night, Dave was astonished by the beauty of Brooklyn spread out below, a vast carpet of darkness dotted by an infinitude of lights, a galaxy of earthbound stars.

"I had no idea," he muttered.

"Look." She directed his gaze along the serpentine coastline, past a range of high-rise apartment buildings to a Ferris wheel spinning slowly through the night. "You can see all the way to Coney Island."

Dave understood that he was hurtling toward uncharted territory, and this knowledge filled him with exhilaration. His head felt clear; his body hummed with the alertness of a second wind.

"I can't believe I ate the blueberry pie *and* the chocolate mousse cake," she groaned. "I haven't had the munchies like that since high school."

"It's an occupational hazard. Before I started playing weddings, I used to have a washboard stomach," he lied, patting himself sadly on the cummerbund.

The reception had concluded with a dessert buffet of memorable proportions, and the maitre d' kindly invited the Wishbones to partake of the leftovers after they'd played the last dance. Dave was busy assembling his plate of goodies when Gretchen appeared at his side and asked if there was any chance of her bumming a ride to the train station in Elizabeth.

"Now?" Dave knew the Elizabeth station; it wasn't a place you'd expect to see a lone bridesmaid at this time of night.

"Whenever," she said. "No hurry. If you can't do it, I guess I can call a cab or something."

"You live in the city?"

"Brooklyn. Park Slope."

"You're really gonna take the train back to Brooklyn tonight?"

She licked blueberry filling off her fingertip and leaned in close to him. She smelled like a vague, pleasant memory he couldn't quite identify.

"I'm supposed to stay at Heidi's, but the whole wedding party's going back there to watch the video of the ceremony. I think I'd be a lot happier waking up in my own bed tomorrow."

He looked past her to the opposite end of the buffet table, where Buzzy was performing surgery on a whole pineapple with a Swiss army knife. Dave couldn't see any reason why someone else couldn't give him a ride home for a change.

"Forget the train," he told her. "I can drive you to Brooklyn."

He expected her to argue, to say she wouldn't dream of imposing on him like that, but all she did was smile with relief.

"Great. I'll go get my bag."

Gretchen didn't drive much and wasn't sure how to get from the Verrazano to Park Slope, though she was certain it could be done. She was impressed by Dave's ability to negotiate the maze of highways branching off from the bridge and his rudimentary knowledge of Brooklyn geography, which got them close enough to her neighborhood that she was able to direct him the rest of the way.

"That's amazing," she said. "The last time I tried that we ended up in East New York."

"I'm a courier. I do a lot of driving around the city."

"Really? How convenient."

"Convenient?"

"Make a left up here. I'm four blocks up on the right."

He didn't press her. He knew exactly what she meant by "convenient," and would even have agreed with her, if not for the inconvenient fact that he was engaged to be married in three months. Somehow or other, he'd neglected to apprise her of this important biographical note. All through the drive he kept waiting for the right opportunity, and it kept not appearing.

"If you see a space, grab it," she told him.

Park Slope didn't look like Dave's idea of Brooklyn. The streets were lush and tree lined, almost suburban, except that the houses were attached brownstones, set back from the sidewalk, with wrought-iron fences and imposing front stoops. The people walking by looked young and prosperous, able to afford high rents. He found a spot about halfway up the block, on the opposite side of the street. It was a tight squeeze, with maybe two inches to spare on each bumper.

"So what about you?" he asked, yanking on the emergency brake as if trying to rip it out by the roots. "What do you do for a living?"

She rolled up the window and groped blindly for the door handle. He reached across the car to pop it for her, his arm brushing across the staticky fabric of her skirt.

"Freelance copy editor," she said, pushing the door open on its dry, protesting hinge. "By night I'm a poet."

Her third-floor apartment was bigger than Dave expected, and fully furnished. On the stark white walls of the living room hung numerous black-and-white framed photographs of stingray bicycles.

"I used to have one of those," he said.

"My roommate's boyfriend takes them. He calls it his Banana Seat Series. A couple of galleries were interested last year, but nothing really came of it."

"You have a roommate?"

"The perfect kind," said Gretchen. "She's almost never home. She basically lives with Dex in Williamsburg."

She got him a beer, put Shawn Colvin—not one of Dave's favorites—on the CD player, and excused herself to get out of the dress. He wandered around the room, taking a closer look at the photographs. All of the bikes were leaning against the same chain-link fence, with a litter-strewn vacant lot in the background. Most of them were rusty and beat-up, with flat tires or ripped seats or missing pedals, though one was in mint condition, with horse-tail streamers shooting out from the handlebar grips. There was something desolate about the pictures, as though the real subjects weren't the bikes at all, but the kids who'd lost or outgrown or forgotten all about them.

Gretchen emerged from her bedroom wearing a short, silky gray robe, and sat down on the couch. Without thinking, Dave took the chair by the TV, making an effort to appear unfazed by the fact that she'd actually "slipped into something more comfortable," a tactic he'd only witnessed in old movies. He felt himself at a disadvantage, an overdressed suburbanite on alien turf, surrounded by depressing folk music and sad pictures of bicycles.

"So tell me," he said. "What does a copy editor do?"

She lit up a Parliament and exhaled in his direction, as though that were a reply in itself. There seemed to be a lot less of her now that she'd escaped from the puffy dress. She was slender, verging on slight, her body lost inside the shimmery robe.

"Spelling, punctuation, house style," she said with a bored shrug. "All the crap nobody else wants to deal with."

"Pay okay?"

"Compared to what?"

He nodded, as if she'd said something profound. She took a long drag from her cigarette, then leaned forward to stub it out in a saucer resting atop some books on the coffee table.

"You know," she said, sitting up straight and smoothing the robe over her thighs, "it's kind of hard to kiss you from across the room."

Dave was vaguely aware of standing up and moving toward the couch. She stood up, too, holding out her arms as if to catch him. Her body felt warm through the silk, thrillingly unfamiliar. Her mouth reminded him of something.

"I can't believe this," she whispered. Her glasses were crooked on her face; one lens had fogged over. "I don't even know you."

They kissed again. She wrapped one leg around him as if preparing for a judo throw, making throaty murmurs of encouragement as he slipped one hand into the robe and found her breast. Her mouth tasted of tobacco on top of alcohol, a combination he hadn't experienced since Julie quit smoking five years earlier, mainly to get him to stop bugging her about it. She'd done it cold turkey, chewing gum like a demon, biting her nails until they bled, sometimes crying out of sheer desperation. Gretchen did something with her leg, and the next thing Dave knew he was flat on his back. She kneeled over him, straddling his waist as she went to work on the buttons of his ruffled shirt. For the first time in hours, Julie was a vivid presence in his mind.

"I'm engaged," he said, reaching up to grab hold of Gretchen's wrist.

"What?"

"To be married."

She took it pretty well, allowing her face to register only the briefest flicker of surprise before prying his fingers from her arm and undoing the belt of her robe.

"Congratulations," she said, closing her eyes and rubbing against him in a way that interfered with his ability to continue the conversation. "Who's the lucky girl?"

July

Carlos and Stevie Ray

For two and a half weeks he had somehow kept himself from calling her, even during his runs into the city, even when his pockets were filled with quarters and there seemed to be an unoccupied phone booth on every other corner. They'd had their fun and he wasn't sorry about it. But he couldn't allow himself to get tangled up in an affair just a few months before his wedding. He wasn't going to be that stupid.

That evening, though, the phone had rung during dinner. His mother picked it up. Right away, Dave knew who it was.

"Yes he is," she said, handing him the phone across the table, her eyes narrowing with suspicion. He stood up, turned his back on his parents, and moved as close to the hallway as the cord would allow.

"I know you can't talk," she said. "Come to my apartment tomorrow night. There's something I want to show you."

Dave didn't hesitate. "Okay."

"Seven o'clock."

"Okay."

"Pretend this is a solicitation. Say, 'Sorry, I'm not interested.' "

"Sorry, I'm not interested."

"Bye, Dave."

"Bye now."

Both his parents were watching him as he hung up the phone.

"Replacement windows," he reported, shaking his head. "They seem to think I'm head of the household."

His father raised one finger while he finished chewing.

"All they have to do," he said cheerfully, "is take one phone solicitor out to the town square, stand him up in front of a firing squad, and blow his brains out." He looked around, apparently expecting an objection. "You think I'm kidding?"

They returned to their meal, a nameless concoction of egg noodles, ground beef, and cream of mushroom soup that Dave's mother had discovered in a women's magazine in the early eighties and had been serving on a weekly basis ever since. Amazingly, Dave still wasn't tired of it. He stared down at his plate, unable to look up for fear that his face would give everything away—his guilt and excitement, his utter, paralyzing relief.

The silence deepened around him. He moved some noodles around with his fork. He hadn't felt this self-conscious in years, not since the days in high school when he used to come home stoned and had to monitor his every move at the dinner table to make sure he wasn't doing something really strange, like staring at a Brussels sprout for a suspicious length of time, or saying the word "potato" over and over again until he dissolved with laughter.

"I'm going over to Glenn's tonight," he announced, his voice cracking from the strain.

"Take 'em out and shoot 'em," his father repeated.

"Put it on national television. That's when people in this country will finally be able to eat in peace."

Glenn Stella's parents had retired to a planned community in North Carolina with an eighteen-hole golf course and state-of-the-art health facility. Instead of selling their house in Darwin, they allowed Glenn to keep living there on his own, with the stipulation that he pay the property taxes, keep the place in good working order, and not mess with the decor. This arrangement was fine with their son, who made a more-than-adequate living as a computer programmer, had no interest in redecorating, and liked to be left alone.

For the past year or so, Dave had found himself vaguely depressed by his periodic visits with Glenn, even though they did the exact same things they'd been doing since they were twelve—listen to records, talk about music, and play guitar in the basement. There was a static quality to their friendship that had become eerie rather than comforting now that they were over thirty, at least for Dave. Glenn didn't seem to notice, just as he seemed oblivious to the fact that he wasn't going to meet any women if he never left his house, or that a healthy diet included foods other than Campbell's Tomato Rice Soup, Weaver's Zesty Wings, and Mr. Salty Pretzels.

Not long ago, Julie asked Dave if Glenn had ever considered seeing a therapist.

"I don't know. I never asked him."

"He must be so unhappy."

"You'd think so," said Dave. "But actually he seems okay. Not happy. Just okay. Same as always."

"Isn't he lonely?"

"He never complains about it."

"What about women? Does he go on dates?"

"Not that I know of."

"Don't you ask?"

"I figure he'd tell me if anything important came up."

"I don't understand," Julie told him. "How can you guys be friends and not talk about this stuff?"

Looking at it through her eyes, Dave saw that there was something lacking in his interaction with Glenn. But it never really seemed that way when they were together. For the most part, they found enough to talk about without venturing anywhere in the vicinity of dangerous subjects like women or loneliness or maybe going to a therapist. And if words failed them, guitars never did.

Dave walked through a wall of Hendrix into a living room full of needlepoint samplers and the dusty porcelain figurines—milkmaids, shepherds, angels, dogs—that were supposedly Mrs. Stella's prize possessions, though she seemed to be doing just fine without them in her condo overlooking the seventh hole. Glenn lowered the volume on the stereo and turned around, dressed in faded green gym shorts and a pink button-down shirt. He had thinning blond hair and the same gold aviator glasses he'd been wearing since he was twelve.

"Can I get you something to drink?"

"Sure."

"Dr Pepper okay?"

Dave nodded, wishing he'd remembered to bring a six-pack. Glenn was a person with intense food loyalties, and had long ago cast his lot with Dr Pepper. There was never any other beverage in the house except for the obligatory half-empty jar of Sanka moldering away in the cupboard. A smell wafted out of the refrigerator when he opened it and lingered in the air long after it was closed. Dave took a seat at the kitchen table and tried not to think too hard about what had produced the odor. Glenn popped the pop top and slid the can across the table like a bartender.

"So how's it going with the wedding plans?"

"Not bad. There's a lot of stuff to take care of, though."

"I still can't believe you're taking the plunge."

"Me neither."

Glenn saluted Dave with his soda. "You're a lucky guy. I never understood what took you so long."

"Strategy," Dave explained. "I wanted to make her sweat a little."

Glenn shook his head. His expression was thoughtful, a bit melancholy.

"Julie's the best. I mean that."

"She's pretty great," Dave agreed.

"The best," Glenn repeated.

Dave looked past his friend to the trucking company magnets stuck on the refrigerator door. Glenn was right, of course. Any man in his right mind would have been thrilled by the prospect of watching Julie march down the aisle to pledge her lifelong love and kiss him in front of a churchful of people. But Dave, apparently, was not in his right mind. All he seemed to be able to think about was Gretchen. The Verrazano Bridge. Her skin under silk. The taste of her mouth. He forced himself to look back at Glenn.

"Speaking of best," he said, "I wonder if you'd consider being my Best Man."

Glenn looked skeptical. He rolled the Dr Pepper can back and forth across his forehead like a construction worker who'd been laboring for hours in the midday sun. Whatever he was imagining seemed to be giving him a headache.

"Okay," he said finally. "Just don't make me deliver the fucking toast."

Dave nodded. He felt an emotion something like love swell up in his chest. It was right that Glenn would be standing up there next to him.

"You sure about this?" he asked.

Glenn shrugged. "My shrink says it's time for me to start confronting my fears."

"You have a shrink?"

Now it was Glenn's turn to look surprised.

"You didn't know?"

"You never told me."

"A nut like me?" Glenn laughed. "I'd be crazy *not* to have one."

His pale blue Stratocaster tucked under one arm, Glenn called up a directory on his basement computer and skimmed through the contents.

"Let's see," he said. "You want to be Carlos?"

"I'm surprised you even have to ask."

Glenn clicked the mouse a few times and the distinctive sound of Santana began to fill the room like a fine mist. Not the familiar Latin percussion of "Evil Ways," the tune Dave had expected, but something softer and spacier, watery organ chords quivering on a spare background of bass and drums.

" 'Song of the Wind'?" guessed Dave.

"You got it. From *Caravanserai*. Remember that picture of the moon on the album cover?"

Glenn spent a lot of time re-creating his favorite songs on a multitrack synthesizer, laying down all the instruments except lead guitar and vocals so he'd be able to jam with a full band behind him anytime he felt like it. His arranging skills seemed miraculous to Dave, as did his ability to simulate the trademark sounds of individual musicians—Clarence Clemons's sax, say, or Bill Wyman's bass—using only a small electronic keyboard hooked up to a MacIntosh computer.

"Song of the Wind" wasn't so much a song as a five-minute excuse for a guitar solo. Dave hit a note on Glenn's red SG (his second-best guitar) and held it, startled and exhilarated by the raw purity of tone and unflagging sustain that had somehow been programmed into the synthesizer. For a moment, it was possible to believe that he'd gotten his hands not only on Carlos's custom-made ax, but on his mortal soul as well. He milked this illusion for all it was worth, tilting his face toward heaven, grimacing as though it hurt to play such ecstatic music, as though every riff pierced him through the heart. Gretchen came to him as he played, her eyes locked on his as they made love, never blinking, not even when she cried out the same note over and over for what seemed to Dave like an extraordinary length of time, a note he found he could nearly reproduce on the SG in Glenn's basement, in the exquisite and wrenching tone of one of the greatest guitar players of all time.

Hot as it sounded, Dave was careful not to kid himself. He understood all too well the difference between sounding like a genius and actually being one. It wasn't that hard, in 1995, if you set your mind to it and invested in the right gizmos, to fool people for a couple of minutes into thinking you were Eric Clapton or Eddie Van Halen or even Jimi Hendrix. But where did that get you? The real trick was creating your own sound, the mysterious signature that belonged to you and no one else. It wasn't a matter of hardware or even necessarily of technique. It was about taking the instrument and technology you had and making them your own, teaching them to say something no one else had thought to say before, in a voice no one had heard.

Dave wasn't there yet. He didn't think he'd ever be. This knowledge didn't torment him; it was just a fact he lived with: that greatness would always be out of reach, that he was what he was—a pretty good guitar player, another face in the crowd, a guy who could do a mean fucking imitation of Carlos Santana.

Glenn was further along on the path to musical enlightenment. He put his own mark on "The Sky Is Crying," transforming it from an almost exuberant bellow of pain to something more muted and matter-of-fact, as though, in his world, the crying of the sky were the ordinary state of things rather than a strange and sinister change in the weather. His voice was less gruffly expressive than Stevie Ray Vaughan's, his licks more furtive, less self-assured; instead of wild anguish you felt a dull pain motivating the song, an ache that wouldn't go away when the sun came out. Glenn was Stevie Ray without the swagger and the cowboy hat, and these were the blues the dead man might have known if, instead of being a famous guitar hero, he'd been a lonely guy in green gym shorts who hadn't gotten laid in a long time and didn't expect the future to deliver anything better than the shrunken-down life he already had.

Glenn was one of the few guitarists Dave knew who didn't make big faces when he soloed; he just hunched down over his Strat and went to work. Every once in a while he looked up, squinting in mild perplexity, his fingers spider-walking over the fret board as though directed by an entirely separate intelligence. Watching him, Dave thought of "Bobby Jean," Bruce Springsteen's tribute to Steve Van Zandt, his musical soul mate from high school all the way through the glory days of the E Street Band. If things had worked out the way they were supposed to, he and Glenn might have had a similar trajectory, instead of a story that began and ended on a single night.

All through their sophomore year of high school, they had had their sights set on the Talent Show. Anonymous underclassmen, they had plotted a musical ambush, a surprise attack on the three-chord simpletons and heavy-metal posers who dominated Harding's rock scene in the late seventies. They'd spent months learning "In Memory of Elizabeth Reed,'' a jazzy and haunting instrumental by the Allman Brothers, teasing out the intricate lead guitar harmonies, playing the song over and over until it seemed less like a duet than the work of a single four-handed musician. Then they went out, scrounged up a keyboardist and drummer competent enough to back them (no spare bass players were available), and signed up for the Talent Show at the last minute as the Allmost Brothers.

They watched the show from backstage, their confidence growing with each addition to the program, every Barbra Streisand imitator, every nerdy juggler and one-trick magician and hat-waving tap dancer, every out-of-tune garage band hacking its way through ''Locomotive Breath'' and ''Smoke on the Water.'' The Allmost Brothers took the stage late in the evening, believing the show was theirs to lose.

Standing in front of an audience for the first time, guitar in hand, Dave felt a surge of adrenaline unlike anything he'd ever known. This was *it*—the destination he and Glenn had been dreaming about for three years as they'd done the private work of learning their instruments, note by note, chord by chord, song by song. Now that they had arrived, Dave felt loose and ready, almost giddy with power. He turned to Glenn, eager to share the sensation.

The strangeness of what he saw still hadn't faded from his memory. Glenn was frozen. There was no other word for it. He was standing near the edge of the stage, trapped in the blazing glare of the footlights, surveying the darkness with an expression of wide-eyed, openmouthed awe, as if he'd just been offered a glimpse of a horror beyond human understanding. His left hand was where it belonged, wrapped around the neck of his guitar, but his right hand was on top of his head, tugging on a handful of his long, blond, Gregg-Allmanesque hair. Dave walked across the stage and touched him on the shoulder.

''Glenn,'' he said.

''What?''

"Let go of your hair."

"I can't."

"What's that supposed to mean?"

"It means I can't."

"Come on, man. Quit fucking around."

"I'm not."

"We're standing up here in front of five hundred fucking people."

"I realize that."

"Well, let go of your hair then. We've got a song to play."

"I can't move," Glenn said miserably. "I think I'm paralyzed."

Some hecklers started shouting at them to shut up and play some music. The MC, a Spanish teacher named Mr. Garcia, approached the stage to ask if there was some kind of problem. Dave shooed him away, then grabbed hold of Glenn's arm, just above the elbow, digging his fingers into the flesh.

"You gonna play or not?"

"I can't."

"Then get the fuck off the stage. We'll do it without you."

Glenn's face relaxed, as if he'd been granted a reprieve. He let go of his hair and dropped his hand to his side. Then he unplugged his guitar and walked offstage, disappearing behind the velvet curtain. Dave returned to his side of the stage and nodded to the drummer, who clapped his sticks together four times, just like they'd planned.

He was surprised by how good they sounded, how well the song came off with only one guitar. His fingers did exactly what he'd taught them, never stumbling once, not even on the fastest and most complicated section of the song. The drummer and keyboardist were right there with him, pushing him forward, lifting him up. His solo took him into a corner of the tune he hadn't explored before, into the whole mystery of Elizabeth Reed, why a song

dedicated to her memory needed to be so bright and
bouncy in some parts, so slow and moody in others. It
wasn't until after it was over, after the first ovation of his
life had stopped ringing in his ears, that he allowed himself to think about Glenn and what he might do to console
him. But when he got backstage, Glenn was gone.

Despite his absence, the Allmost Brothers took third
prize in the show, behind a band called Sunrise Highway
and the baton-twirling DeRocco Sisters (there were four
of them). A week later, the singer in Sunrise Highway
called and asked Dave if he wanted to be their lead guitarist. Without hesitating, Dave said yes (soon afterward,
Sunrise Highway changed its name to Exit 36). In the
fifteen years that followed, he and Glenn had never
stopped being friends or playing music together. In all that
time, though, except for a brief, muttered exchange of
apologies the next day, they'd never really spoken about
what had happened that night, or where they might have
gone together if it hadn't.

Glenn followed him out to his car. It was after ten and
the world was deathly quiet, as though a curfew were in
effect. Dave looked left and right as he fumbled with his
keys, an outlaw on the deserted street.

"Thanks a lot," Glenn told him. Playing music made
him look the way other people looked after sex or a good
workout—like someone had taken an eraser and rubbed
the tension from his face.

"For what?"

"It's an honor."

Dave picked at his top front teeth with the tip of his
car key. Sincere moments like this made him nervous.

"I'll feel a lot better having you up there next to me."

"Are you scared?"

"Yeah. I'm just not sure of what."

Glenn nodded. "I'm like that all the time."

"I'm glad you're seeing someone," Dave said, addressing this comment to his friend's pale feet on the blacktop. "The shrink, I mean."

Just then a car turned the corner at the near end of the block and began moving toward them at five, maybe ten miles an hour. Dave raised one hand in front of his face to fend off the dazzle of the headlights. He had a bad moment as the car rolled to a stop right in front of him, its windows all the way down, as if in preparation for a drive-by shooting. Four kids were inside, jocky teenage guys in backwards baseball caps, looking strangely subdued.

Without a word to his buddies, one of the kids climbed out of the backseat, shut the door, and trudged up the front walk of the house across the street from Glenn's. Once he was safely inside, the car drove off, maintaining its funereal pace. Dave and Glenn looked at each other and shrugged.

"I was kidding about not making the toast," Glenn informed him. "Just don't expect the Gettysburg Address, okay?"

Dave couldn't help laughing, considering some of the asinine toasts he'd heard over the past couple of years. One guy talked for five minutes about what a stud the groom had been, how he used to pick up women in bars, go home with them, and never call them back. "All that changed when he met Maggie," the Best Man assured the wedding guests. "She was the first one he ever called back."

"Don't worry," Dave said, clapping Glenn on the shoulder. "Just make it short, sweet, and from the heart."

He got in his car and pulled away, tooting softly on the horn. At the corner stop sign he glanced in the rearview mirror and saw a barefoot guy in a pink shirt standing with his arms crossed in the middle of an empty street, his oldest friend in the world.

On the way home he listened to R.E.M.'s *Monster* and
thought about how good he felt. He was excited about
seeing Gretchen again—it had to happen, he realized that
now—as well as deeply pleased by the way things had
gone with Glenn. Dave hadn't expected him to agree so
easily, nor had he expected to feel so proud and grateful
that he did. Glenn *was* his Best Man. Anyone else—his
brother, or even Buzzy—would have been a substitute.

There was an obvious tension between the two things
that were making him happy, but he preferred not to spoil
his good mood by dwelling on it. His strategy for the time
being was to keep his real life in one compartment and
Gretchen in another. She was a fantasy, a stroke of good
luck, an opportunity that had fallen into his lap, something
he had to get out of his system. He could explain her in
any number of ways, but there really wasn't any point in
explaining, not even to himself. There was something she
wanted to show him, and he wanted to find out what it
was.

Michael Stipe would have understood, Dave was pretty
sure of that. If there was one message R.E.M. had sent to
the world, it was that standing still got you nowhere.
They'd never been afraid of changing directions or taking
risks. Even Dave was having trouble getting used to *Monster,* all the raw feedback and distortion, the glaring absence of the sensitivity and subtlety that had been the
band's hallmarks for more than a decade. It was like they
woke up one morning, looked in the mirror, and said,
"Fuck it, man. We're tired of being ourselves. Let's be
someone else for a while." If Stipe had been in the car,
Dave would have told him that he knew the feeling.

There was a note on the kitchen table telling him to call
Julie if he got home before eleven. Dave thought about

letting it slide, but his conscience got the better of him. She was his fiancée; the least he could do was return her phone calls.

"Well?" she said. "What happened?"

Dave blanked out for a second.

"What happened when?" he asked cautiously.

"With Glenn. You went over there tonight, didn't you?"

"Oh yeah. He said yes. I didn't have to bug him or anything. He seems to really want to do it."

"That's great, Dave. I'm really happy for both of you."

"He says he's seeing a shrink now. I guess it's doing him some good."

"It's about time."

"The next step is to find him a girlfriend."

"That reminds me," she said. "Tammi just called. She and Ian are going out to dinner tomorrow night. She sounds really excited."

"That's great. I hope it works out for them."

"God, Dave, I feel like I haven't seen you in ages. Are we still on for the movies on Friday?"

"As far as I know."

"Anything you want to see?"

"Whatever you want," he assured her.

This Sad Gift

From Gretchen's apartment they took the F train to Second Avenue on the Lower East Side, a neighborhood Dave rarely visited on his courier runs. An exhilarating sense of anonymity washed over him as they walked the gritty streets past urine-stinking doorways, fruit stands, and displays of stolen goods set out for sale right on the sidewalks. No one here—not the fierce-looking men in turbans or the girls with pierced eyebrows or the Chinese deliverymen on bicycles or the homeless guys with their matted beards or the emaciated, jittery women with their ravenous eyes—knew that the woman he was holding hands with was not the woman he was engaged to marry, and he had a pretty strong hunch that, had they known, none of them would have mustered the energy or interest to care.

"I love this place," Gretchen said, letting go of his hand to circumnavigate a puddle of pink vomit. "It's so alive. Every time I go home I wonder how people can stand it in the suburbs."

"You get used to it," he explained, forcing himself not to stare at the gay couple who brushed by on the sidewalk, arms circling each other's waists. The man in the tank top had a clean-shaven head and appeared to be tattooed all over his muscular body. His companion was blond and boyishly cute, dressed in a brown business suit. "It seems normal when nothing happens."

"I remember coming here for the first time when I was in college and thinking, *So this is what they've been hiding from me all these years.* It's a feeling that's never really gone away."

Now that he was seeing her on her home turf, Dave had a better idea of how out of place she must have felt at the Westview on Saturday night. She was a hipster, bohemian and severe in her buckle-up pilgrim shoes, her black leggings with the ripped knee, her faded purple top shaped like a dress but too short to be worn as anything but a shirt. She had two golden hoops in her left ear, one in her right, and an armful of silver bangles. She walked fast, head up, scanning the world with a calm vigilance.

"So where are you taking me?" he asked.

"You'll see."

"After all this suspense, it better be good."

"Don't worry. You won't be disappointed."

He nodded, not really caring where they were headed, happy just to be walking through the twilight city with this formidable woman as his guide. The sheepish *I'm-from-New-Jersey* feelings that usually plagued him during his visits to Manhattan were absent, replaced by a buoyant sense of invisibility, a confidence that for once he had managed to blend in with the natives. He wished Julie were here to witness it, or at least someone from home—Glenn, maybe, or even Zelack—just so they'd know there was this other side to him, that he was the kind of guy who could walk through the East Village on a Thursday night and look like he belonged there.

Gretchen stopped outside a storefront on Avenue A,

unmarked except for a small chalkboard set up on an easel outside the front door. A few feet away, an old bum was singing "Volare" in a soulful voice as he sprayed his chest and armpits with an aerosol Dave assumed was deodorant but that turned out, on closer inspection, to be Raid. *Open Mike Poetry Reading*, read the yellow letters on the chalkboard. *All Are Welcome*.

Inside, the place was small and crowded and buzzing with conversation. Dave saved Gretchen a seat at the last available table—a rickety roundtop hardly bigger than a dinner plate—and waited for her to return from the rest room.

It was a scene—serious haircuts, lots of posing, widespread hugging and kissing of new arrivals. Half out of guilt and half out of curiosity, Dave tried to imagine Julie's reaction. Would it have pleased her to be sitting just inches away from a table whose occupants included a regal-looking black woman in a Caribbean-style headdress, and a scowling, potbellied white guy with muttonchop sideburns and a stovepipe hat? Or would the strangeness have caused her to shrink down into herself, lapsing into grim silence, rousing herself only to fan cigarette smoke away from her face as though it were poison gas?

Gretchen didn't look so hot when she returned from the bathroom. The color had drained from her face, and she kept licking her lips and swirling her tongue around the inside of her mouth like something tasted bad in there, so bad it couldn't be ignored. When she reached up to tuck her hair behind her ear, her hand was trembling so badly her bracelets chattered like teeth.

"You okay?"

"Yeah." She forced a laugh. "I always get like this when I read."

"You do it a lot?"

"Pretty often. Maybe once a month."

"What are you reading tonight?"

She stuck her hand into her dirty canvas tote bag and pulled out one of those composition books Dave remembered from grammar school, the ones with the cover designed to look like a slab of marble. She set the book down on the table and rapped at it with her knuckles.

"New stuff," she said. "Love poems."

Dave glanced at the book. In the white box reserved for the owner's name and address he saw the words *Blood Blisters* written in neat block letters.

"Blood Blisters?" he asked.

Just then the room burst into applause. Dave looked up and saw a husky, middle-aged guy with long hair and a Hawaiian shirt standing behind a mike stand, his back to a patch of exposed brick wall between the men's and women's rest rooms. His name must have been Pat, because people kept shouting it until it turned into a kind of chant. Pat just stood there grinning, reeling in the ovation with both hands, egging them on for more. Gretchen leaned across the table, an anxious expression on her face.

"It's a working title," she told him. "You think I should change it?"

•   •   •

Ian hadn't made a joke, but Tammi started laughing anyway.

"You're pretty funny," she said. "Julie forgot to mention that."

"I wasn't trying to be funny. I really do think the Monkees are an underrated band."

"The Monkees Monkees? You mean Mickey, Davey, and the guy with the hat?"

"Mike Nesmith." He decided not to mention the fact that he'd worn a watch cap from kindergarten all the way through second grade in an effort to be like Mike. "He's a big-time movie producer now. I think he was involved with *Repo Man.*"

"Didn't see it."

"You should rent it sometime. Emilio Estevez."

Tammi took a couple of bites of her taco salad, watching him the whole time with her sharp little eyes. Ian wasn't that hungry, but he felt obliged to saw off a piece of his chimichanga. If he just let it sit there, she'd probably take it as a sign that he wasn't enjoying himself.

"So explain this to me," she said. "Tell me what's so great about the Monkees."

"Forget it. It's not that important."

"Come on," she said. "Don't be like that. I really am curious."

"Really?"

"If you don't tell me, I'm never gonna know."

She was teasing him, he could see that, but not in a nasty way. She was flirting, actually. Ian had been out of circulation so long he'd almost forgotten how to play the game. But it was starting to come back to him. The rules, the tone you were supposed to strike. He was having a better time than he'd expected. Tammi wasn't a beauty— she was short and solid and athletic-looking, with an open, freckled face—but she wasn't an airhead, either. It was nice being with a woman he could talk to.

"Well, here's the thing," he began. "The Monkees were a product. Some businessmen came up with an idea for a TV show, and then they went out and invented a band to star in it. They were just supposed to be actors. Figureheads. Studio musicians were going to take care of the music. The whole point was that they were going to be controlled. Because this was happening at that point in the late sixties when rock 'n roll was starting to turn dangerous. The Beatles had gone from being these cute moptops to singing about revolution and LSD, and the powers that be were trying to put a lid on all the crazy energies that were floating through the air. That's what the Monkees were supposed to be about."

"Huh," she said, gazing past him in an attempt to make

eye contact with their waitress. "I had no idea."

"But the great thing is, the Monkees didn't go with the program. They rebelled. They insisted on playing their own music, and even started to write their own tunes."

"Wasn't there a fourth one?" she asked distractedly, still trying to flag down the waitress. "Besides Mickey, Davey, and Mike?"

"Peter," he said. "Peter Tork. Do you know the song 'Pleasant Valley Sunday'?"

She didn't seem to hear him.

"You want some coffee?" she asked, covering her mouth to stifle a little yawn. "I always get sleepy when I eat Mexican."

• • •

Dave had never been to a poetry reading before and found the whole process much more engrossing than he ever would have imagined. It was way better than the musical open mikes he was used to attending, where a parade of earnest, guitar-strumming folkies plopped themselves down on the wooden stool to crank out yet another cover of "Cowgirl in the Sand" or "Fire and Rain" or—God forbid—"Greensleeves."

Here, you never knew what was going to happen next. One person would recite a poem or two—sometimes from memory, sometimes from the page—and then Pat would stand up and call out someone else's name. An odd sort of suspense filled the room as the audience members glanced from table to table, waiting for a poet to heed the summons.

Some of the readers looked like poets and some of them looked like regular people. A handful of them looked like nuts, but Dave found out pretty quickly that it was useless to try to judge sanity, or even talent, from the reader's appearance; all you could do was wait for the words. It was like going to a big party and meeting lots of strangers in quick succession. That was all the reading was as far as Dave could tell—people standing up in front of other people, most of whom they didn't know, and saying, to the best of their ability, "Here I am. This is what I'm all about." Some were great and some were terrible and most fell somewhere in between, but none of them lasted for more than three or four minutes, so you could even convince yourself that the terrible ones were actually sort of interesting.

The guy in the stovepipe hat read something he called "The Ballad of Jack and Charlie," which he described as "a philosophical dialogue between Jack Kerouac and Charles Manson," an idea that sounded good to Dave but that turned out mainly to be an excuse to talk really fast and say the word "man" a lot ("Listen, man, speed is just another word for life, man, and that's what those bastards refused to understand"). A woman of about forty with a beautiful cascade of graying hair stood silently behind the microphone, head down, her hands pressed together as if in prayer. Then, after maybe a minute had passed, she looked up and made a visual sweep of the room, apparently trying to make eye contact with each individual member of the audience. When she finally spoke her voice was calm, the voice of an adult reasoning with children.

"Why do I frighten you?" she asked. "Because I see through your lies, or because I am a woman-loving woman?"

That was her reading. She curtsied sweetly, a little girl who had just finished her piano recital, and scampered back to her seat. The woman in the headdress read a series of what she called "subway poems," brief, vivid portraits of people who happened to sit across from her on the D train—a pregnant Puerto Rican teenager with a leashed ferret sitting on her shoulder, an overweight transit cop sucking on a grape Tootsie Pop, a construction worker reading *Penthouse* right there in front of everyone. A wiry, troubled-looking man in hiking shorts, sandals, and mismatched tube socks read something he called "My Confession," a laundry list of things he'd done to hurt other people:

> I farted and blamed it on you,
> I defaced you with my jism,
> I only pretended to like your dog . . .

Gretchen was twelfth on the roster, and Dave watched her pallor intensify as the big moment approached. The eleventh reader was a skinny, tense-looking, college-age woman with bad skin and angelic red hair. She scuffed her way over to the mike, mumbled a sentence that included the word *puberty,* and began to read.

As soon as she uttered the first line, Dave realized she was the one. It happened sooner or later at every open mike he'd ever been to. Somebody got up and reminded you of what the whole thing was about. In the poem she was a kid at the seashore, lying with her face to the hot sun while her older sister covered her from the neck down with bucket after bucket of wet sand, erasing her body one part at a time. It wasn't the story, though—it was the words she told it with. Dave could almost see them emerging from her mouth, little bubbles of language, the individual letters glowing on the air for a fraction of a second as though written by the hot tip of a sparkler.

> That sweet girl is gone, Jenny
> Lost like those sunburn summers.
> You buried her
> And dug me up instead.

The applause that followed was spontaneous and enthusiastic, and the poet blushed with pride and embarrassment. Dave looked at Gretchen, eager to get her reaction, but her face was pinched, a bit too purposefully blank. He forced himself to stop clapping. When the ovation died down, Pat wandered over to the microphone and said, "Our next reader is Marlene Fragment."

Dave figured he must have counted wrong, until he noticed most of the heads in the room turning in the direction of their table. Gretchen rose unsteadily from her chair, her teeth clenched in a determined smile.

"Marlene Fragment?" he whispered.

She reached down to retrieve her composition book, and answered him with a small, helpless shrug.

• • •

"I gotta tell you," Tammi said, threading her arm easily through his as they left the restaurant, "you are one cute man."

Normally, Ian didn't appreciate it when women referred to him as "cute"—it was a compliment they paid him with annoying regularity—but he decided to let it pass. This date was working out much better than he expected. There were women—perfectly desirable women—who had precisely the opposite effect on him. A half hour in their presence and he'd find himself drained and muddled, tongue thick, head full of cobwebs. All he could do was chalk it up to chemistry.

"You're pretty cute yourself," he said.

"Ha." Her laughter was loud and jarring. "Liar."

"I mean it."

"I used to be cute," she told him. "Then I turned eleven."

She reported this as though it were an amusing biographical fact, but Ian heard the pain beneath the quip. His own good looks had announced themselves early, as had his musical talent, and he'd felt himself throughout his teens and twenties to be a powerful and magnetic presence in the world. Only lately, as he sensed his own luster beginning to dim, had he realized how lucky he'd been not to have grown up with his self-confidence already shattered beyond repair.

"Maybe *cute* isn't the right word," he conceded. "What do you think of *appealing?*"

"I'd prefer *ravishing* if you want to know the truth. But these days I take my compliments where I can find them."

They climbed into his car and looked at each other. Their plans had only gone as far as dinner, and now dinner was over. It wasn't even nine o'clock.

"So," said Ian. "Where to?"

Tammi's hands curled into fists and uncurled into hands again. She seemed suddenly shy, tentative.

"I don't know," she said. "Whatever."

"Your call."

She stared down at her lap, rubbing the hem of her skirt between her thumb and forefinger. Then she looked up.

"You like going to malls?"

"Sure," he said, starting the car.

"I know it's not the most exciting place in the world, but sometimes it's nice just to walk around with someone."

"I like malls," he said, releasing the emergency brake and shifting into reverse.

"Not everyone does," she informed him, in a solemn, almost melancholy voice.

She bought a sleeveless denim top at the Gap. He bought a Van Morrison CD at Sam Goody and a cinnamon bun that they ate together sitting on a bench. Without asking, she took his hand as they browsed the upper level. She told him about her work as a delivery room nurse, the odd privilege of sharing a sacred moment with people who were pretty much complete strangers.

"Most of the time you don't know where they live, what they do, or even if they're nice people. But there you are, wiping the brow of this suffering woman, waiting for this little life to come squirting out.''

Ian stopped in front of a store called Exclusively Shirts that was holding a "3 for $10 Sale!!!" Judging from the merchandise in the window, though, even that didn't qualify as a bargain. He thought about footage he'd seen of babies entering the world, the shocking size of the head, the torrent of fluids that accompanied the birth. It seemed so messy and low-tech, out of synch with the rest of late twentieth-century America.

"You know," he observed, "it's a lot like playing weddings.''

． ． ．

The air inside the Second Avenue station was dank and stuffy. Breathing it, Dave thought, was a lot like inhaling despair, an idea that never would have occurred to him if he hadn't just attended a poetry reading.

"Come on," Gretchen said impatiently. "Could you at least try to be a little more specific?"

"I liked it. You have a way with words."

"A way with words?" she repeated. "Is that the best you can do?"

"I don't know much about poetry, Gretchen. I'm not the best person to judge."

"I'm not asking for an expert opinion. I just want to know if you liked my poems."

Dave rubbed his finger over the thick red paint on the support beam he was leaning against and tried to think of something honest and complimentary to say. It was hard, though, because he hadn't really understood her poems. She had said they were love poems, but they weren't like any love poems he had ever come across. Instead of flowers and moonlight, Gretchen wrote about pus and tumors, warts and organs. In one poem, a woman receives a package in the mail on her thirtieth birthday, a box containing a human liver. In another, a woman pops a blood blister on her finger, only to have her body deflate and crumple to the ground at her lover's feet "like a balloon from yesterday's carnival."

He thought about telling her the truth, saying that her poems baffled him, asking her to explain her purpose in writing them, but he had a feeling that this wasn't the reaction she wanted. She was watching him closely, biting her bottom lip, looking anxious and expectant.

She was beautiful, he thought, lapsing into poetry again, a flower in the subway, and her beauty was only enhanced by her sudden vulnerability. Ever since they'd met, he'd been secretly worried that he didn't really belong in her league, that she'd somehow misjudged him as being smarter, hipper, and more talented than he actually was. But now he saw that he'd done the same thing to her, and this knowledge moved him in an unexpected way. He took her face in his hands and kissed her firmly on the mouth.

"You were the best of the bunch," he said.

"Really?" She stepped away from him, her pleasure diluted by suspicion. "You mean it?"

"It's a matter of taste," he said. "I can only give you my own opinion."

She looked down at the tracks, the rails shining dully. Someone's expensive sneaker floated in a puddle of dirty, trash-speckled water.

"I didn't get much applause, though."

"It sounded like a lot from where I sat."

"As much as the red-haired girl?"

"About the same amount."

The train announced itself as a distant rumble. Dave leaned toward the edge of the platform and peered down the tunnel. A star of light flickered in the darkness, growing larger as it approached.

"Did you like her stuff?" Gretchen asked, raising her voice to compete with the onrushing train.

"Who?"

"The redhead."

By that point the rumble had intensified into a clattering roar, which dissolved into a mind-bending screech of metal on metal as the train jerked to a stop in front of them. Dave unclenched his teeth as the doors slid open, inviting them into the fluorescent brightness of the car. He followed her inside, sat down beside her on an orange plastic seat.

"She was okay," he said, rotating his hand in a way that suggested he could take her or leave her. "A little predictable."

•   •   •

Ian tucked the cassette into the tape deck and looked at Tammi, overcome by a sudden wave of doubt. She sat cross-legged on the maroon carpeting, her back to the beige corduroy couch, the only piece of furniture in the basement music room that had become his primary living space over the past couple of years. *She's a stranger,* he thought. *I hardly even know her.*

"You look tired," he said.

"Not at all," she said, trying to smile and swallow a yawn at the same time. "I just got my second wind."

"We don't have to do this, you know. We could just sit and talk for a while. Or I could take you home. I know you've had a long day."

"I'm fine," she insisted. "Really."

He thought about kissing her, trying to distract her that way. He knew she would let him. And he did want to kiss her. But right now they had this other thing to get beyond.

"You sure?"

She rolled her eyes. "Play the tape, Ian."

"I will. But let me explain a few things first."

Ian took a deep breath. With a profound and demoralizing certainty, he understood that he was about to make a terrible mistake. The tape wasn't ready. Half the songs needed to be remixed. One of them needed to be scrapped entirely. He'd worked too hard on the musical to unveil it now, before it was finished.

"Okay," she said. "Start explaining."

Something in her voice steadied his nerves. She was a sweet and generous and intelligent woman. For a long time now—though he hadn't really admitted it to himself—he'd been waiting to meet someone like her. Even if the tape wasn't perfect, he had a feeling she'd understand what he was trying to do.

And besides, he'd been in hiding too long. It was time to crawl out into the light, even if that meant risking injury to his self-esteem. Art was about risk. It was one of those things he had to keep telling himself. Not taking risks was how he'd ended up in a wedding band, singing "You Are So Beautiful" to half the female population of New Jersey.

"What this is," he said, "is a musical I've been working on for the past year and a half. It's called *The Grassy Knoll.* It's about the Kennedy assassination."

"A musical?" she said.

"Yeah."

She smiled slyly, as though they were sharing an inside joke.

"Come on."

"I'm serious," he assured her.

"A musical about the Kennedy assassination?"

"The musical's a more serious form than people give it credit for. I mean, *Jesus Christ Superstar,* for God's sake. You can't get more serious than that. *Miss Saigon. 1776.* Even *Oklahoma!* was about politics, when you think about it."

"Still," she said. "A musical about the Kennedy assassination. It's kind of a downer."

"Listen to it first," he said. "You might change your mind."

Her eyes narrowed. "You're not putting me on?"

"No," he said, trying to conceal the hurt in his voice. He'd expected to encounter some resistance about the subject, but he hadn't expected her to treat it like a joke. "I'm dead serious about this. The Kennedy assassination is the most important event in twentieth-century American history, and the musical is a completely indigenous twentieth-century American art form. It's a natural combination."

She bobbed her head from side to side, looking thoughtful.

"Okay," she said. "Maybe you've got a point."

"You're going to have to use your imagination," he warned her. "The show opens with JFK and Jackie waking up in the White House on the morning of November 22, 1963. Jackie gets out of bed, pulls open the curtains, and sunlight comes streaming into the bedroom. Then she turns to Jack and starts singing the first song, 'Let's Not Go to Dallas.' It's this sweet romantic fantasy about being normal people for once, rather than the president and First Lady. 'Let's not go to Dallas/Let's stay home instead/ Let's dispense with Texas/How 'bout breakfast in bed?' At first Jack protests, but then he gets into the spirit. They sing the last chorus together, dancing around the bedroom in their pajamas. Then they share this long, passionate kiss, which is interrupted when a valet knocks on the door. 'Mr. President,' he says. 'Time to go to Dallas.' "

"Okay," said Tammi, still looking a little skeptical, "I think I'm getting the picture."

Ian put his finger on the play button.

"Oh yeah," he said. "One more thing. I'm singing both parts on the tape, so it might not sound like a duet."

•   •   •

Something was wrong, Dave thought. Gretchen had been wild and athletic their first night together, grunting and yowling like Monica Seles in the throes of a tiebreaker, but now she seemed strangely subdued. She lay beneath him, limp and contemplative, watching him the way she might watch a television.

His own concentration was beginning to drift, too. Instead of attending to the here and now, he kept returning to that moment in Gretchen's poem when the woman opens the box and finds the liver inside. She pulls it out—''a slick slab of meat, dull and floppy''—and hugs it to her chest. ''This is the test,'' she thinks. ''To love even this sad gift, simply because it has been given.''

Dave couldn't pinpoint exactly what it was that bothered him about the poem. Was it just that it was disgusting to imagine someone hugging a liver? Or did it have something to do with the cryptic nature of those concluding lines, the idea that love could be some sort of test? Or was his uneasiness somehow related to his awareness of Gretchen's hands on his lower back, somewhere in the neighborhood of his own liver?

He closed his eyes and without any conscious effort, found himself thinking of Julie and the sudden turn his life had taken. Just a few weeks ago, they'd gone shopping for an engagement ring, and now here he was, in a bedroom in Brooklyn, making love to a woman who called herself Marlene Fragment and wrote poems he wouldn't be able to understand if he lived to be a hundred. Instead of guilt, he felt an electric surge of power hum through his body.

''Marlene,'' he whispered, opening his eyes.

''Yes,'' replied Gretchen. Her legs tightened around his waist.

''Marlene,'' he whispered again, moving with a new urgency. ''Marlene Fragment.''

''Yes,'' she repeated, again and again and again.

*   *   *

Ian considered the last song of *The Grassy Knoll* to be his masterpiece, potentially on a par with "The Impossible Dream" or "Tonight, Tonight." He imagined people streaming out of the theater, wiping tears from their eyes, yet feeling somehow enlightened and purified by their sadness.

He wanted it to be staged like the Zapruder-film sequences in *JFK,* a black convertible parked onstage against a grainy black-and-white freeze-frame of Dealey Plaza. A lone cello would introduce the song, repeating the main theme over and over in a frail, mournful tone as Jack and Jackie and the Connallys waved in slow motion from inside the car. The freeze-frame would advance every few seconds to provide the illusion of movement toward the Book Depository and the inevitable tragedy.

When the suspense had reached an almost unbearable level, the cello would fall silent. A blinding flash of light would paralyze Jackie and the Connallys in mid-wave. Only Jack would be spared. He would climb out of the car, walk up to the edge of the stage, and break into the final number.

When Ian first hit upon this device, he'd assumed that the song would have to be about JFK. The first version he wrote was called "I'm No Hero," a lackluster anthem in which the dead president acknowledged his faults and errors (ambition, lust, Bay of Pigs), and expressed disapproval of his elevation to the status of modern-day martyr:

> I'm no hero
> No saint carved out of wood
> Just a man who lived and loved and bled
> I did the best I could

The breakthrough came when Ian realized the song could move in an entirely different direction—instead of being about JFK, it could be about the audience. Once he had this insight, the lyrics pretty much wrote themselves. The song was called ''Where You Were,'' and Ian conceived of it as a kind of posthumous thank-you note from John F. Kennedy to the country that had mourned him:

> They say that you remember
> The moment when I died
> They say a cloud blocked out the sun
> And millions of you cried

He goes on to reflect upon the tragedies of the sixties (Vietnam, the other assassinations, cities on fire, parents at war with their children), as well as the triumphs (civil rights, Neil Armstrong's giant step), then loops back to the beginning of the song:

> Just know that I'll remember, too
> I know just where you are
> All of you
> —America—
> You're with me in the car
> All of you
> —America—
> You're with me in the car

When the music stops, the soon-to-be-murdered president turns around and walks back to the convertible. As soon as he takes his seat, his wife and the Connallys begin waving again. The freeze-frame advances. Then the lights go out. We hear gunshots. The picture of Dealey Plaza is replaced by a rapid series of images—the president's grieving widow, Oswald taking his own bullet, little John-John saluting the flag-draped coffin, the eternal flame at

Arlington Cemetery. Then the president himself, smiling that unforgettable smile.

Of course, Tammi had no way of knowing all this. All she knew of *The Grassy Knoll* were the songs themselves, a dozen of them, sung by Ian and recorded on his woefully inadequate eight-track system. But it seemed to be enough. When he turned to her, she was staring at him in openmouthed wonder.

"So," he said. "What do you think?"

"My God," she said. Her eyes were shining with admiration and disbelief. "You wrote that?"

Ian felt a hard-earned pride swell up behind his rib cage.

"Yeah," he said. "I guess I did."

Randy by Starlight

"So I hear it went pretty well," Julie told him over dinner at the Stock Exchange.

"Huh?" Dave tore his gaze away from the last slice of his pepperoni-and-roasted-pepper personal-size pizza, which he'd been eyeing with an emotion that verged on longing. He'd decided to start dieting the night before, a few seconds after Gretchen poked her finger into his spare tire and affectionately addressed him as *my little doughboy*. "What's that?"

"The big date. Ian and Tammi."

"Oh, right. They hit it off?"

"Apparently so." Julie grinned, the owner of good information. "Tammi called me at work. She didn't get home until four in the morning."

"Four in the morning? Does that mean what I think it means?"

"You'll have to draw your own conclusions. I'm sworn to secrecy."

"Unbelievable." Dave shook his head, registering the

quick pang of jealousy that accompanied the news of anyone else's sexual triumph. This reaction was completely
irrational, rooted in powerful feelings of early adolescent
deprivation. It made no difference that he'd been out until
two-thirty the same morning enjoying his own sexual ad-
venture.

"By the way," she said. "Did you know that Ian wrote
a musical?"

"Yeah. He told me the other night."

"Did he tell you what it was about?"

"We didn't get that far."

"The Kennedy assassination," she informed him. "Ian
wrote a musical about the Kennedy assassination."

"Come on." Dave laughed. "He did not."

"He did too. Tammi listened to the whole thing."

"You can't write a musical about that," he explained.
"It's not allowed."

"It sounds weird," Julie agreed, "but Tammi says it's
incredible. Good enough to be on Broadway."

Dave began humming "Springtime for Hitler," feeling
slightly guilty as he did so. It wasn't right to be making
fun of Ian behind his back. Maybe his musical was better
than it sounded. It was possible that Dave's contempt for
the genre was interfering with his judgment.

"All done?" the waitress inquired, swooping down on
them from out of nowhere. Like all the employees at the
Stock Exchange, she wore a white apron with dollar signs
on the front, a pink Oxford shirt with a black bow tie,
and a visor with a green eyeshade.

Feeling virtuous but ambivalent, Dave pushed the pizza
pan toward the edge of the table. Julie looked at him in
amazement. In all the years they'd known each other, he'd
never left a slice uneaten.

"So," said the waitress. "How about some dessert?"

"Not for me," Julie said.

The waitress turned her attention to Dave, the eyeshade
casting an eerie green glow on her forehead.

"I recommend the Death by Chocolate. It's my all-time absolute favorite."

Dave felt his willpower start to erode. He thought of the luscious chocolate mousse cake he and Gretchen had shared at the end of the Lambrusco wedding, the creamy morsel she'd fed him, like a bride, from the tip of her own plastic fork. His diet could wait another day.

"Bring it on," he said.

The waitress was delighted.

"Excellent," she said. "One Death by Chocolate."

"You can't," Julie cut in. "We don't have time."

"Why not? The movie doesn't start till nine."

"We have an eight o'clock appointment with that DJ."

"Excuse me?" This was the first Dave had heard about a DJ.

"I'm sure I told you. We're supposed to meet with that guy my father works with. Rockin' Randy."

"Rockin' Randy?" the waitress exclaimed. "He's the coolest."

Dave shot her an unencouraging look. Her face went blank; she slipped her pad and pencil into her apron pocket.

"I'll give you guys a few more minutes to decide," she said, retreating as she spoke.

"Sorry," Julie told him. "I can't believe I forgot to tell you. There's so much to keep track of these days."

Dave felt blindsided, but decided not to make too big a deal about it. Given his own transgressions, he figured he owed Julie a little slack. On the other hand, he thought he'd already cut her quite a bit of slack simply by agreeing to see *The Bridges of Madison County* instead of the new *Batman*.

"You know how I feel about DJs," he told her.

"I know," she said. "But he works with my father. And he's offering us a really good deal."

Dave closed his eyes and massaged the center of his forehead. The image of Rockin' Randy leading the conga

line through the lobby of the Westview lingered unpleas-
antly in his mind.

"Listen," he said, "that guy could shine my shoes and
give me a blow job and it still wouldn't be a good deal."

Julie stared at him, unamused. Although she had no
objection to oral sex as a practice, she disapproved of the
term *blow job*.

"Sometimes you have to say it," he explained, reaching out to rescue the last slice of pizza as the busboy lifted
the pan off the table. "Sometimes no other word will do."

Julie opted for the silent treatment in the car, gazing mo-
rosely out the window at the familiar landscape of houses
and drought-stricken lawns. Dave marveled at her ability
to seize the offensive when she was clearly in the wrong,
to sulk as though she were the one being dragged on a
disagreeable errand that had been sprung on her at the last
minute, an errand, moreover, that violated one of her most
deeply held principles.

"The thing about DJs," he said, "is that they're par-
asites. You might as well pay someone to come to your
house and change the channels on your TV."

"He'll give us four hours of music for five hundred
dollars. What would the Wishbones charge?"

"It's not the same thing. There are five of us. We actually *make* the music."

"That's not the point, Dave. My parents aren't rich. If
we can save a couple of thousand dollars by hiring a DJ,
then I can't see how we can afford not to do it."

Dave understood the math; there was no getting around
it. But there was also no getting around the fact that he
was not going to have a DJ at his wedding. No way in
hell.

"Maybe we can just make some dance tapes ourselves.
Save your parents the five hundred bucks."

"Oh, that's classy," she said. "And we can hold the

reception at a bowling alley. Ham sandwiches and Oreos for everyone.''

"Sounds good to me.''

She sighed in a way that reminded him of his mother. "You're not being very helpful. Planning a wedding is a lot of work. I don't have the energy to fight over every little detail.''

"This is not a little detail. This is like"—he groped for a metaphor—"like inviting Hitler to your wedding.''

"Hitler?" she said. "Are you out of your mind?''

"All right," he conceded. "So it wasn't the best comparison.''

She shook her head and turned back to the window. Dave caressed the steering wheel with his thumbnail, wondering where Gretchen was, what she was doing, wishing he could be there with her, far away from Rockin' Randy and *The Bridges of Madison County.* He thought of the subway turnstile, the thrilling *chunk* it made as you pushed your way through, into that musty, gum-paved underground world.

"Turn right at Cumberland Farms," Julie muttered.

Rockin' Randy lived in Chestnut Gardens, an old-fashioned apartment complex that consisted of six or seven squat brick buildings laid out along a cul-de-sac near Echo Lake. It was another beautiful night, planes blinking overhead, fireflies rising like dreamy sparks from the grass outside Randy's unit.

"2B," Julie told him as they approached the front door.

"Or not 2B," he added, more out of reflex than a desire to make a joke.

She shook her head. "Explain to me again why you didn't graduate from college.''

"That is the question," he declared, in his best Shakespearean baritone.

In spite of herself, Julie smiled.

"You're a real idiot," she informed him, as if this were something to be proud of.

"Thank you," he said, pressing the buzzer.

Dave almost didn't recognize Randy when he opened the door. Sleepy eyed, dressed in khaki shorts, a faded blue T-shirt with radio station call letters printed across the front, and rubber flip-flops, his hair untamed by lubricant, the DJ bore an uncanny resemblance to a normal human being who had just woken up from a nap. Dave felt bad about comparing him to Hitler. Randy scratched his head and blinked a few times, as though the twilight hurt his eyes.

"You must be Julie," he said, sticking out his hand. "Your dad's a cool guy."

"*Cool?*" Julie seemed genuinely astonished by this concept. "Are we talking about my biological father?"

Randy backtracked. "Not cool in the usual sense. He's just, I don't know, off in his own category."

"That's one way of putting it," Julie agreed.

Randy's eyes narrowed with concentration as he shifted his attention to Dave. He brought his thumb and index finger to his forehead and maneuvered them as though adjusting a knob.

"I know you," he said. "I just can't figure out from where."

"I'm a wedding musician. I play with a band called the Wishbones. I saw you at the Westview last month."

Randy tilted his head, framing Dave between his hands like a photographer. What he saw seemed to startle him. He glanced from Dave to Julie, then back to Dave again, as though something fishy were afoot.

"You look different without your tuxedo," he said.

"You look different, too," Dave told him.

"No shit." Randy clapped him on the shoulder, shaking his head in cosmic wonderment. "Small fuckin' planet, man. Small fuckin' planet."

Entering the DJ's living room, Dave experienced an immediate jolt of recognition, a funny feeling that if he'd had an apartment of his own, it would look a lot like this—simultaneously spartan and unkempt, a cool place to hang out and listen to music, if you weren't too particular about things like dust and crumbs and dirty socks draped over the lampshade like melted clocks. There was a big unframed poster of Miles Davis taped to the wall above the entertainment console; the other walls were occupied floor-to-ceiling by homemade cinder-block-and-pine-board shelves packed tight with CDs, tapes, albums, and 45s, all of them arranged by category and in alphabetical order.

"I'd offer you something to drink," Randy told them, "but I haven't been out to the store in a couple of weeks. I'm afraid to open the refrigerator and find out what's inside."

He pulled up a plastic milk crate and sat down on top of it, leaving the couch for his visitors. It was a green velour monster, balding in the high-traffic areas and mottled with uninviting stains. Dave sat down next to Julie and tried to ignore the elastic waistband of a pair of jockey shorts stuffed in the crevice between two cushions. The familiar blue and yellow stripes identified them as Fruit of the Loom, the brand Dave had been wearing since the day he graduated from diapers.

"The place is kind of a mess," Randy admitted. "I've got this insane schedule, you know? Full-time day job, plus the DJ gig on weekends, and then the radio show on top of everything else."

"Radio show?" said Dave.

Randy shook his head, apparently mystified by his own life. "In Bridgeport fuckin' Connecticut, if you can believe that. Every other Thursday from two to six in the morning. Randy by Starlight. It's a jazz show for insomniacs, truck drivers, and people who work graveyard.''

"Bridgeport?" said Dave. "That's like two hours away."

"More like an hour and a half. They got this great listener-supported station up there. Anyone can apply for a show. There's not a lot of competition for the 2 A.M. slots."

Julie seemed concerned. "So you drive up there at midnight, do your show, then drive back at six in the morning and put in a full day at Prudential?"

Randy nodded. "The Fridays after the show are brutal for me. I just drag myself around like a dead man for eight hours. That's why you caught me napping just now."

"It can't pay very well," Dave speculated.

"Doesn't pay at all."

"So why do you do it?"

"Because I'm the man," Randy replied, as though this were the most obvious reason in the world. "I spin the wax. I have no idea why you're driving through Connecticut at four in the morning, but that's my music jumping out of your radio, man. What could be cooler than that?"

"What kind of stuff?"

"Bebop mostly. Bird, Miles, Dizzy. The usual suspects. I'll feature lesser-known guys too, the sidemen who held their own with the greats. Or else I do birthday or death anniversary shows or just let the music reflect my mood. Last night was a tribute to Bill Evans."

"Wow," said Dave. "I wish I'd heard it. I'm not too familiar with his stuff, but what I've heard blows me away."

"I taped it," Randy said. "I'll make you a copy."

"Really?"

"No problem."

Julie glanced at her watch and pointedly cleared her throat.

"Boys," she said, "I hate to interrupt, but our movie starts at nine."

Randy's sales pitch for the wedding gig was low-key, almost perfunctory, centered on his complete lack of personal investment in the work. He declared himself open to just about anything.

"I'm totally flexible about this. If you want me to wear a tux and play dinner music all night, I'll wear a tux and play dinner music all night. If you want me to dress in a gorilla suit and bang on a tin can between songs, I'm happy to discuss that as well, though I generally charge extra for making an asshole of myself."

"We're not looking for an MC," Dave advised him. "DJs should be seen and not heard."

Randy didn't even blink. "No problem. I can do it either way, but I'm happy to just hang back and play the tunes."

"And no conga lines," Dave threw in for good measure.

"Why not?" Julie asked, a bit miffed by this instruction. "What's wrong with conga lines?"

"They're embarrassing."

"No, they're not." She turned to Randy for confirmation. "They can be a lot of fun."

Randy held up both hands, refusing to arbitrate. "It's up to you guys. Speaking from experience, I've found that conga lines are a good way to break the ice at the tenser receptions. The ones where the families aren't mingling. It's kind of hard to ignore someone who's been shaking their booty in your face for the past five minutes."

"That's a good point," said Julie. "I definitely don't want to rule out a conga line."

"As far as the music goes," Randy went on, "I'm happy to be as traditional or adventurous as you want. If it suits you, I can supply a whole night's worth of Sinatra and Madonna and Kenny Rogers. But if you want reggae or salsa or anything like that, just say the word.''

Instead of answering, Julie again consulted her watch. Her eyes widened with melodramatic alarm.

''Yikes,'' she said. ''I hate to cut this short—''

For the first time, Randy betrayed his eagerness.

''So, is it a deal?''

''Well?'' Julie turned to Dave, beaming her approval. ''What do you think?''

By that point, Dave had pretty much accepted the fact that Randy had the gig and would do a decent job of it. But cool as he was, Randy was still a DJ, and Dave couldn't imagine breaking the news to the Wishbones.

''Whatever,'' he said. ''Your dad's writing the check.''

Julie's smile slipped a little.

''You know what?'' she told Randy. ''I think we need to talk this over a little more. Can I get back to you in a couple of days?''

''Not a problem,'' Randy said, falling back on his earlier posture of complete indifference. ''Do what you have to do.''

Before they left, Julie asked to use the bathroom, which was located at the far end of the apartment, down a long hallway. She was barely out of earshot when Randy jumped up from the milk crate and beckoned to Dave with an urgent movement of his hand.

''C'mere,'' he whispered.

Groaning to himself, Dave rose from the couch and reluctantly approached the DJ, expecting to be the victim of some gentle man-to-man arm-twisting to close the deal. But Randy surprised him.

''I don't mean to pry,'' he said, keeping his voice low and confidential, ''but there's something I need to ask you.''

''Yeah?''

"That girl you were with at the Westview? The brides-maid with the glasses?"

Dave's brain snapped to attention; his body felt suddenly electrified, alert to danger.

"What about her?"

Randy cast a quick nervous glance in the direction of the hallway.

"It's an awkward question. I mean, people's lives are complicated. It's not my business to judge."

"I'm not following you."

Randy winced. "She kind of gave me the impression that you and her—"

Dave couldn't believe this was happening.

"You know Gretchen?"

"I bumped into her out by those Dumpsters on my break. We had a great conversation."

Dave shook his head. He felt Miles Davis peering down at him, not quite hostile, not quite amused.

"She didn't tell me," he said, more to himself than to Randy.

The toilet flushed, the explosive sucking sound of it audible down the length of the apartment.

"So I guess I misunderstood her," Randy said carefully.

"I guess you did."

The bathroom door creaked open. Julie's clogs smacked smartly on the wooden floor. Randy leaned in closer.

"There's only one problem," he confided. "I didn't catch her last name. You wouldn't happen to know it, would you?"

Dave's insides flooded with relief as Julie stepped back into the room, mouth bright with a new coat of lipstick, hair shining the way it always did after she'd brushed it. She was wearing old jeans and one of those tight ribbed shirts Dave was glad had come back in style. She looked good. She looked like her mother.

"Sorry." He laid his hand regretfully on the DJ's shoulder. "Wish I could help you out."

It was dark outside, oddly desolate. Dave's Metro was parked in the shadows, near a hulking green Dumpster bathed in the glow of a streetlamp. There was something almost purposeful about this tableau, as though it had been arranged to showcase the simple, bargelike beauty of the receptacle.

"What was that all about?" Julie asked him.

"What was what all about?"

"Your little conference with Randy."

"Just the usual chitchat."

"It looked like you guys were plotting to overthrow the government."

Dave unlocked the passenger door and walked around to the driver's side. Julie wasn't suspicious as far as he could tell, just curious. He could have let the matter drop, but for some reason he felt like talking.

"He was asking about a girl," he reported, slipping behind the wheel and yanking the seat belt across his chest. "He wants to find out the last name of this bridesmaid from the wedding we played the other night."

"How come?"

"He's got a crush on her. He wants to ask her out."

"Do you know her?"

Dave started the engine and clicked on the headlights. The beams landed on the side of an apartment building up ahead. A woman was framed in one bright window, washing dishes with an air of almost religious devotion.

"Nope," he said.

They bounced over four speed bumps on their way out of Chestnut Gardens, then turned right onto Springdale Avenue. The movie theater was only five minutes away, in the center of downtown West Plains.

"It can't be too hard to find out," Julie told him.

"Doesn't Artie keep a list of all the people in the wedding party?"

Dave hesitated, unsettled by this oddly practical turn in the conversation. He should have seen it coming, except that his brain had been overwhelmed by the simple, thrilling fact that he was discussing Gretchen with Julie and getting away with it.

"I don't know," he said. "Even if I knew her name, I'm not sure it would be ethical to share it with Randy."

"*Ethical?* What's ethical got to do with it?"

"Think about it. We don't know the first thing about this woman. Maybe she's married. Maybe she's got a boyfriend. Maybe she's not interested in Randy."

"If she's not interested, all she has to do is tell him."

"If she was interested, she probably would have told him her last name."

"Huh," Julie said, acknowledging his point. "All I'm saying is that if I were single, I'd be happy to get a call from a guy as cute and interesting as Randy."

"You think he's interesting?"

"Yeah," she said. "But not half as interesting as you do."

Dave didn't argue. He turned into the parking lot behind the theater, distracted by the question of why Gretchen hadn't mentioned meeting the DJ even in passing. An irrational feeling of jealousy seized him as he pondered the scene—Gretchen stoned and barefoot, Randy in his Hawaiian shirt, turning on the charm. The worst part of the feeling was that he had no right to it whatsoever. What claim could he have on her? For all he knew, she was off in some Village cafe at that very moment, drinking wine with the guy in the stovepipe hat, and that was none of his business either.

They bought their tickets and entered the theater with a couple of minutes to spare. The previews hadn't even begun yet.

"So was she pretty?" Julie asked as they settled into
their seats.

"Who?"

"The bridesmaid."

Gretchen's face appeared in Dave's mind with haunting
clarity, as vivid as if it had been projected onto the blank
screen looming in front of him. Her wary eyes and sexy
haircut, her downturned mouth and odd, pointy nose. He
thought about the way her breast fit his hand, and how
close he'd come the previous night to staying in bed with
her, not coming home at all.

"She was okay," he said. "A skinny girl with big eyeglasses. Nothing to write home about."

Two hours later they emerged from the theater as if in
mourning, Julie dabbing at her eyes with a crumpled yellow Kleenex, Dave rubber-legged, emotionally frazzled.

The Bridges of Madison County had been an unexpectedly difficult experience for him. It wasn't so much
that he saw any direct parallels with his own life: Meryl
Streep didn't remind him of Gretchen—or of Julie for that
matter—nor did he see himself as some kind of vagabond
romantic figure like Clint Eastwood, a cowboy with a
camera. The landscape and lifestyle of rural Iowa made
him wonder if suburban New Jersey was such a dull place
to live after all.

Despite its sluggish pace and disappointingly tepid sex
scenes, the movie simply made him ache for Gretchen in
such a hungry and direct way that he almost couldn't bear
it. He just wanted her to be there with him, bathed in the
light from the screen, her knee touching his through two
layers of denim. He wanted to suck flat Coke through a
straw that had touched her lips only seconds earlier. And
he wanted to watch her expression as she watched the
movie, to explore the fresh mystery of this woman who
seemed to have turned his life upside down in a matter of

weeks. The need to connect with her grew so strong that he got up in the middle of the movie, supposedly to use the rest room, and tried to call her from a pay phone in the lobby. Her line was busy, a circumstance that, though frustrating, had the effect of calming him down a little. At least she was home, and probably alone. But who was she talking to? A friend? An old lover? Some guy she'd just met? It pained him to consider how little he knew of her life, her romantic history, what kind of future she envisioned for herself.

Luckily for Dave, Julie was in no condition to notice the state he was in. A big fan of the book, she began sniffling a half hour into the movie, long before anything sad had actually occurred, and worked herself into a state of out-and-out weeping by the time the credits rolled. They were halfway home by the time she finally felt composed enough to pocket the Kleenex and make a stab at conversation.

"So what do you think? Did she do the right thing?"

"Who?"

"Francesca."

Dave kept his eyes on the road and shrugged like a disinterested party.

"Depends how you look at it, I guess."

Julie seemed disappointed by this answer. "Depends on what? It seems pretty straightforward to me. The woman gives up her one and only chance at true love because she can't bring herself to abandon her husband and family. Happiness or duty? Which do you choose?"

"It's not that simple. If you hate yourself you can't be happy. And she would've hated herself for leaving her family. So happiness wasn't in the cards for her either way. It's a false choice."

"No it's not," she said, annoyed by his logic. "They loved each other. I mean, what would you do five years from now if you met someone and fell madly in love with her? Would you stay with me just because it was your duty?''

Dave pretended to consider this scenario, but his mind was pretty much empty except for a growing sense of dread. This was not a conversation that could do anyone any good.

''It's too hypothetical,'' he said. ''I need to know the details. Do we have kids? Are we getting along?''

''I can't believe you're so wishy-washy.''

''Well, what about you?'' he shot back. ''What would you do if you fell in love with someone five years from now?''

''Me?'' She laughed triumphantly. ''I'd dump you in a minute.''

''Thanks,'' he said, not quite sure if she was teasing him or not. ''It's good to know these things in advance.''

''In a heartbeat,'' she continued, in a needlessly emphatic tone. ''Robert Kincaid shows up and I'm out of here in a heartbeat.''

''Great. And I'm left alone to change the diapers and slop the hogs.''

''You know it, buddy. And in a couple of weeks, those hogs are gonna be lookin' mighty good to you.''

As soon as they began kissing in the rec room, Dave experienced for the first time the full force of his infidelity, the sadness and shame generated by the act of touching one woman while desperately wanting to be touching another. It was a low-down, hollow feeling, complicated by a powerful surge of tenderness for Julie, a desire to protect her from the humiliating reality of the situation.

It occurred to him, while worming his hand under her tight shirt to massage her full, almost watery, breasts—so different from Gretchen's, so utterly different—that this deception would have been easier to live with if he'd resented Julie or felt somehow betrayed by her. But that wasn't the case at all. He *loved* Julie. That was an indisputable fact. The problem was, he *wanted* Gretchen, and that, at least at the moment, was more than a fact—it was a low-grade fever, a physical truth, the news his blood kept bringing him as it sloshed through his body.

Still he plowed on, stroking Julie's hair, kissing her mouth and neck, grinding against her in a halfhearted simulation of urgency. It was disheartening to notice how ritualized their lovemaking had become, how easy it was to coax her along the worn path from sitting to lying down, from fast breathing to slow purring to suddenly squirming out from under him with a move that would have made any Olympic wrestler proud and landing with a thud on the floor—

"Wait!" she gasped. "We need to talk."

"Huh?" He peeled his face off of the couch and sat up, trying to look puzzled instead of alarmed. "Did I do something wrong?"

She arranged herself in lotus position on the floor. Her face and neck were flushed a deep pink, the color of desire and embarrassment.

"It's not you," she said, still breathing hard. "It's us."

"What about us?" He spoke carefully, keeping his voice calm and neutral.

She brushed her hair out of her face and looked up at him. Her expression grew shy and hopeful.

"It's just—I've been thinking about something for a while now. A kind of experiment."

"Yeah?"

She shifted her gaze to her right knee, causing her hair to fall back in her face. She looked sexy like that, he'd always thought so.

"I want our wedding night to be special," she said.

"Me too." He made a conscious effort to look open-minded and agreeable. "Are you worried it won't be?"

"I'm not talking about the ceremony," she said. "I'm talking about afterward, when it's just the two of us in the hotel room. That's what I'm worried about."

"We'll manage. That's the one part we've never had any trouble with."

She peered at him through the curtain of hair, twisting her engagement ring around and around her finger. She toyed with it constantly these days, often staring at it for long intervals, sometimes rubbing the tiny diamond back and forth across her lips.

"Remember how it used to be? When nothing even came close?"

In spite of himself, Dave thought not of Julie but of Gretchen, the ecstatic look on her face as she'd sucked his toes the night before.

"Yeah," he said. "So what's the big experiment?"

Julie took a deep breath. Her expression turned skeptical, as though she harbored grave doubts about the proposition she was about to make.

"I don't think we should have sex again until our wedding night. Let's be virgins for a while."

She paused, waiting for him to protest. For the second time that night, Dave felt as though life had granted him a reprieve. Out of courtesy, though, he forced himself to seem less than enthusiastic.

"I'm not sure I can last that long."

"Me neither," she confessed. "But I'd really like to try."

"Okay." They smiled at each other for a few seconds. When it got awkward, Dave glanced at the door. "I guess I better go then."

"I guess so," she said, working her bottom lip into a pouty expression, as though she were already having second thoughts about the experiment.

Dave stood up and drummed a little nonsense rhythm on his thighs. The tune of "Like a Virgin" echoed in his head; Phil Hart collapsed again on the stage. Julie's ankles cracked as she rose from the floor. She kissed him good night, as chastely as possible, and led him upstairs with an air of cheerful regret.

When he got home, Dave found a manila envelope with his name on it resting on the welcome mat outside the front door. As soon as he saw it, his heart began to speed. Without even thinking, he knew it was from Gretchen. There was no other possibility. Somehow she'd made the trip in from Brooklyn, found his house, and dropped off the envelope.

The house was dark when he stepped inside. Curious as he was, Dave knew better than to open it downstairs. His mother had ambushed him too many times over the years, springing like a ghost from the shadows of the front hall, for him to be so careless.

He tiptoed to the bathroom, locked the door, and tore open the flap, his mind swarming with possibilities. Nude pictures? Poems? Airplane tickets?

What would he do then?

It was a false alarm, though. The envelope turned out to contain only a cassette tape, marked *Bill Evans Tribute/ Randy by Starlight,* and a brief note scrawled on a piece of Rockin' Randy letterhead.

"Dave," it said. "Enjoy."

Shiny Angels

For about the fifth time, Zelack brought the cheese-burger to his mouth, then pulled it away at the last second. He just held it there in front of his chin, a perfect circle, like some kind of oversized communion wafer. Sunlight streamed through the window behind him, igniting a blond aura around his head.

"I know what you're thinking," he said, "and I can't say I blame you. It's exactly what I was thinking when Mitch presented the idea to me."

Dave speared a forkful of crinkle-cut fries and shoveled them into his mouth. There was only one bite left of his hamburger, and he didn't want to scarf the whole thing down before Zelack had even begun eating. He wondered if this was how women lived all the time, keeping score at the table, trying not to look too hungry.

"What you need to understand," Zelack continued, "is that we're talking about the ground floor here, a real growth industry. This is the time to get on board. It's like I'm offering you stock in this new soft drink nobody's ever heard of—something called Coca-Cola.''

''I wish,'' Dave muttered, bending forward to take a sip of his Coke.

Zelack watched him intently, eyes like pool water.

''I'm telling you, Dave, Christian rock is the next hot thing. Amy Grant is just the tip of the iceberg. She's Bill Haley and the Comets. The Christian Elvis and Chuck Berry and Little Richard haven't even happened yet. Think about it. We could be the Christian Beatles.''

If anyone else had made this pronouncement, Dave would have had to stop himself from laughing out loud, but Zelack was different—he had a track record. The Misty Mountain Revue had toured up and down the East Coast for years, drawing big crowds wherever they went. Sparkle was offered more jobs than they could handle, and their asking price was almost double that of the Wishbones. For a long time now, Dave had harbored the resentful suspicion that Zelack was going places, and now, out of the blue, he was being asked to come along for the ride. The destination could have been more appealing, but he was flattered nonetheless.

''Tell me a little more about your concept,'' he said.

''Right now it's just a name. Shiny Angels.''

''Hmm.'' Dave tried it out in his mind as he swallowed the last of his burger. ''Shiny Angels. Not bad.''

''Angels are hot right now,'' Zelack assured him. ''Mitch thinks we should try to ride every wave we possibly can. He's envisioning a kind of Bon Jovi arena-type thing. Power ballads. Tight pants. Extended guitar solos. The whole mid-seventies rock star trip. He says these Christian kids eat it up.''

Mitch was a lawyer/talent agent from Nashville, the brother-in-law of Zelack's hot new girlfriend. He'd seen Sparkle play at a wedding and had instantly pegged Zelack as potential star material for the rapidly expanding Christian market.

"So what do you think?" Zelack asked. "Are you with us?"

Shiny Angels, Dave thought. He imagined sidling up to a beautiful woman, offering his hand. *Hi, I'm Dave. Lead guitarist for Shiny Angels.*

"Is it *the* Shiny Angels? Or just Shiny Angels?"

"Just Shiny. It's better that way. Punchier."

The booths at the Bayway Diner had individual juke-boxes built into the wall, an amenity that Dave had thought extremely cool as a teenager, but that recently had begun to strike him, for reasons he couldn't quite identify, as old-fashioned, vaguely embarrassing. Idly, he twisted the selection knob. Page after page of hit songs floated by, four decades of popular music indiscriminately jumbled on pale pink paper.

"So why me?" he asked, unable to suppress the question any longer. "There must be lots of younger, better-looking guys you could ask. Guys who look like rock stars."

If Zelack heard the faint undertone of bitterness in Dave's voice, or remembered the incident that had produced it, he did a good job of seeming not to.

"That's the great thing, Dave. Image doesn't count as much with the Christian audience. We're just looking for the best players we can find." Zelack looked away, frowning in the direction of the lunch counter. "I mean, you could always start going to the gym or something."

Zelack's cheeseburger languished on his plate, apparently forgotten, soaking in a puddle of its own greasy perspiration. Dave pondered it for a few seconds, trying to imagine himself as a Shiny Angel.

"There's only one problem," he said. "I'm not religious."

"Why's that a problem?"

"I don't know. I just figure if you're in a Christian band—"

"Mitch and I talked about this," Zelack assured him.

"We don't think it matters. Neither one of us is particularly religious either."

"But aren't people gonna ask? The minute you say you're in a band like this, it'll be, 'Hey, when did you get religion?' What are we supposed to say then? That we're just in it for the money?"

Zelack smiled. "Just say you're born-again. Who's to say you're not, right? Think of it as your professional identity. I mean, do you really think those heavy-metal guys are Satan worshipers?"

"Some of them."

"Right. And everyone in Aerosmith has a ten-inch cock."

"It's not just that. We still have to play the music. You can't do it right if your heart's not in it."

"What? You think my heart's in 'Stairway to Heaven'?" Zelack scoffed. "I must have sung that thing six thousand times and I still don't have a clue what the fuck it means."

"But that's a cover. I assume we'd have to write new material for Shiny Angels."

"That's the cool thing about Christian rock," Zelack explained. "You write a regular love song and let people think it's about Jesus. Just toss in a couple of lines like 'You're my guiding light' or 'my helping hand' or some crap like that. Mitch's been sending me some tapes. A lot of this stuff, if somebody didn't tell you it was Christian, you wouldn't even know. I've got about twenty songs sitting in my drawer right now. With a little tinkering, they'll do just fine."

Dave couldn't say he wasn't intrigued. It had been a long time since he'd allowed himself to seriously fantasize about being a rock star, standing onstage in a leather vest and no shirt underneath, gazing out on a sea of rapt faces and pumping fists as he performed his guitar heroics.

"It's kinda sad, though," he mused. "I can't imagine these Christian girls are deep into the groupie scene."

Zelack rolled his eyes. "Dave, Dave, Dave. Aren't you getting married in a couple of months?"

"I keep forgetting and people keep reminding me."

All at once, reality washed over him. The image of himself soloing on his knees in front of a stadium full of squeaky-clean teenagers lingered in his mind, but now he just looked foolish, like one of the guys in Spinal Tap.

"So what do you think?" Zelack asked again. "Mitch and I are hot to get this thing up and running."

"I'll have to talk to Julie. I don't think she'll be too crazy about the idea."

"The Christian Beatles," Zelack reminded him. "Coca-Cola."

"I'll let you know."

Later that afternoon, after making three deliveries in lower Manhattan, Dave lay beside Gretchen atop her folded-out futon, their damp skin cooling in the breeze from an oscillating fan. It was such a luxury, being naked in the daylight, having the opportunity to admire her body for as long as he wanted without fear of interruption. She was like a whole new world, slopes and angles and hollows unknown in his native land. Her smell was different too—spicier, less cloudlike and engulfing.

"You know what happened to me today?" he asked, watching the top joint of his index finger disappear into the void of her navel. "I got asked to join a Christian rock band."

She rolled lazily onto her side, parts of her chest and neck still flushed from sex. The splotches were large and oddly formed, pink continents floating on a pale ocean.

"Christian rock," she said. "Now there's an oxymoron for you."

Dave felt an impulse to defend the genre, but no plausible defenses occurred to him. The fan breeze swept across the bed, momentarily displacing his thoughts along with the humid air. Gretchen poked him in the sternum.

"You're not a Christian, are you?"

"Not really. I was raised Catholic, but it never really took. All I ever wanted to do on Sunday morning was eat donuts and read the funnies."

"Christian rock is big business these days," she informed him, absentmindedly plucking at her pubic hair, which was dark and silky, disconcertingly similar to the hair on her head. "I read an article about it in the *Times*. It was so depressing. All these kids taking pledges of chastity and blabbing about their personal relationship with Jesus. Teenagers! I mean, whatever happened to sex, drugs, and rock 'n roll?"

Dave couldn't say; it was something he often wondered about himself. The question hung in the air above them until the fan blew it away. He considered telling her about his and Julie's vow of short-term chastity, but then thought better of it.

"The guy who asked me is one of the best singers around. I have a feeling this band of his could really go somewhere."

She propped her head in her hand and peered down at him with a certain amount of interest. With her glasses off, her face had a vague, unfinished quality he found strangely endearing.

"You really gonna do it?"

He sighed. "I don't think so. It's a good opportunity, but I don't think I'm that much of a hypocrite."

Gretchen scooted herself into sitting position. She withdrew the scrunched-up pillow from behind her back and spread it out carefully in her lap. Dave watched from below, delighted by his new angle on her body as she ran her hand over the pillowcase, as though making a serious effort to iron out the wrinkles. Her small, sweetly up-curved breasts quivered in sympathy with the motion, somehow enhancing the effect of deep concentration.

"You're not?" she asked.

"Not what?"

"That much of a hypocrite." There was a flatness in her voice, all the teasing squeezed out.

"What's that supposed to mean?"

"It's pretty obvious," she said, not looking up, still doggedly petting the pillow. "You're here, aren't you?"

Dave groaned to himself, struggling to raise himself up to her level. His arms felt like jelly.

"I am here," he conceded, gazing around the tiny, suddenly unfamiliar room, the fog of post-orgasmic well-being lifting inside his head. "I thought you invited me."

"Invited you?" She made a face. "You called at two o'clock and said you'd be here at four."

"I asked if you were busy," he reminded her. "I thought you were happy to see me."

She looked up at the ceiling and exhaled like a smoker trying to be polite.

"I was. I am. This is just really hard for me. I mean, you get to breeze in and breeze out of here whenever you please, and I'm the one left holding the bag."

"The bag?" He spoke gently, placing a hand on her clammy, girlish shoulder. "What bag is that?"

Her voice was small, a little sheepish. "The bag of feelings."

"The bag of feelings?" He couldn't help smiling. "That sounds like one of your poems."

"Fuck you, Dave." She turned sharply, wrenching her shoulder out of his grasp. "Don't patronize me. I hate it when men do that."

"I was just making an observation."

He tried to put his hand back, but she brushed it away like an insect. She drew her knees up to her chest, and wrapped her arms around them. She sat that way for a long time, gazing straight ahead, through the window to the brownstone across the street.

"You think this is easy for me?" she said finally. "Being involved with a guy who's getting married in a month?''

"Seven weeks," he corrected.

"Excuse me. I must have misplaced my invitation."

"It isn't easy for me either," he said, neglecting to tell her that the invitations hadn't gone out yet. "If I'd met you a few months earlier, I might not be engaged at all."

She seemed to soften a little. She turned her head, revealing to him her stricken face. He hadn't realized she'd been crying.

"This is just a really vulnerable time for me, Dave. I've been lonely for too long. My defenses are really low."

"I tried to be honest with you. Right from the start."

"Well, you sure waited long enough," she said, laughing in spite of herself. "Your pants were around your ankles when you finally broke the news."

"It all happened so fast. I'm not used to having that kind of effect on women."

"It's been a long time since I've lost my head like that. I hadn't met a decent guy for so long, I'd forgotten what it felt like."

Dave wanted to ask her about Rockin' Randy, but knew that the moment was all wrong. He put his hand back on her shoulder. This time she let it stay there.

"I'd forgotten, too," he told her.

"So what are we supposed to do now?" she asked, her voice breaking with emotion.

She fixed him with a wild, nearsighted stare. They sat motionless for what felt like minutes as the fan swept back and forth across the room like a searchlight. It seemed to him that she really wanted an answer.

August

War Pigs

Ian picked an unfortunate moment to quit the band. He did it at Wednesday-night rehearsal, a few minutes after Artie had made what he called a major announcement: he'd gotten the Wishbones booked as house band on *The Genial Jim Show,* a cable-access program none of the other guys had heard of.

"Genial Jim?" said Buzzy. He was reclining on the wicker love seat that was the only piece of real furniture in Artie's basement. "Who the fuck is that?"

"Just a middle-aged guy with a talk show," Artie explained, perched atop his computerized exercise bike, lazily pedaling. "He's a shipping clerk over at Merck."

"What is it?" Stan wanted to know. "Some kind of *Wayne's World*–type thing?"

"Probably." Artie pedaled harder, raising his voice to compete with the hissing of the flywheel. "He's supposed to send me a videotape."

"So what kind of commitment is this for us?" Dave inquired.

"Minimal. One night a month. The show's taped in the back room of a restaurant in Union Village. All we have to do is play during the opening and closing credits, fill in between guests, and back Genial Jim for a song or two. This is not a difficult gig."

"Whaddaya mean?" said Buzzy. "Back Genial Jim for a song or two?"

"The guy likes to sing," Artie replied with a shrug.

"Fuckin' amateur hour," Buzzy muttered.

"What's it pay?" Stan asked. He was sitting on the stool behind his drum kit, curling twenty-pound dumbbells, the veins in his forearms bulging like drinking straws.

Artie stared at him like he was an imbecile. Stan stopped curling and looked to the other guys for support.

"What? All I asked was what does it pay."

Artie spoke slowly and carefully, as if for the benefit of someone with an imperfect grasp of English.

"This is a cable-access show, Stanley. It's not Jay Friggin' Leno."

"Exactly," said Buzzy. "So what's in it for us?"

"What's in it for us?" Artie's face took on the weary, headachy expression he adopted whenever someone questioned his business decisions. "Are you kidding me? What's in it for us is sixty minutes of free TV time a month, plus a promotional announcement at the end of every show with our phone number included. Do you have any idea what advertising like that would cost if we had to pay for it?"

"What advertising?" scoffed Buzzy. "Probably ten people are watching the show and five of them are the guy's immediate family."

"That's where you're wrong," Artie informed him in a superior tone. "From what I understand, Genial Jim has a real cult following. There's gotta be at least a thousand people tuning in for every show. I guarantee you we'll be seeing jobs as a result of this exposure. You guys gotta trust me on this.''

Finally Ian spoke up. He was sitting against the wall on an old weight-lifting bench bandaged with duct tape. Dave had been surprised by his silence on an issue of this magnitude. Usually he'd argue with Artie about what day of the week it was just to get his two cents in.

''When does this start?''

''Next Thursday.''

Ian's lips disappeared inside his mouth. He looked at the floor.

''I won't be there,'' he said. ''I'm giving my notice. I can't do this anymore.''

Artie stopped pedaling. ''Do what anymore?'' he demanded with a nervous laugh. ''We haven't even done it once.''

''I'm not talking about that.'' Ian's voice was gentle, apologetic. He looked around the room. ''I'm talking about this.''

For half an hour they went around in circles, trying to get him to change his mind. Artie got more and more worked up as time went on, unable to accept the fact that Ian's decision was final, and not just some cagey negotiating ploy.

''What is it?'' He had climbed off his bike and stationed himself in front of the weight bench. ''You want more money?''

''This isn't about money, Artie. You know me better than that.''

''What's it about then? Recognition? You want top billing? Ian Mickiewicz and the Wishbones? I'm willing to consider something like that. I'm sure the other guys wouldn't object.''

Artie looked pleadingly around the basement. One by one the other Wishbones nodded their assent. Sitting atop

his TV-sized amp, Dave was touched by Artie's desperation on behalf of the band, even though he could see it
was useless.

Ian smiled sadly. "Believe me, guys. That's the last
thing I'm looking for."

"Is it the ceremonial Wishbone thing?" Artie asked,
grasping at straws. "Say the word and it's gone. You
won't ever have to do it again."

Ian combed his fingers through his pretty hair, keeping
his gaze fixed on the wall above the love seat. There was
a Heineken mirror up there, along with an old travel
poster for Jamaica, featuring a woman with huge breasts
standing in waist-high crystal blue water, nipples erect
beneath her skimpy bathing suit.

"You're not listening to me. This part of my life is
over. I'm moving in a whole new direction."

"What direction is that?" Buzzy asked, generating a
surprising amount of bitterness for someone who was flat
on his back, feet elevated on a pillow.

"I'm gonna miss you guys," Ian went on. "I mean
that. I loved being part of this band."

"So what's the problem?" asked Stan. "You like us,
we like you. Let's just keep going."

Ian winced. "I don't mean to sound like a dick, but
I'm not really a lounge singer. I'm an artist. I've been
denying that side of me for too long. I feel like I owe it
to myself to start nurturing it for a while."

"What about us?" Artie asked in a plaintive voice.
"Don't you owe anything to us?"

Ian thought about it for a few seconds.

"No," he said. "I don't see that I do."

Ian left a few minutes later. Artie followed him outside,
still begging him to reconsider. Dave, Buzzy, and Stan
remained in the basement, exchanging uneasy looks.

Dave was surprised by how guilty he felt. Hard as he

tried, he couldn't shake the conclusion that he was some-how responsible for this mess. He was the one who had fixed Ian up with Tammi, and he knew, without Ian's so much as mentioning her name, that she was the real cat-alyst for his decision. People got brave new ideas about themselves when they fell in love. Tammi had told Ian he was a genius, and Ian had decided to start believing her. And now it was the Wishbones who were going to have to pick up the pieces.

Dave's guilt on this front was only compounded by his lingering sense of good fortune on another. Three weeks after their lunch at the Bayway, he still hadn't formally accepted or declined Zelack's offer to join Shiny Angels. Despite his distaste for religious rock, some sixth sense—not to mention a deep-seated fear of becoming the Pete Best of the Christian Beatles—had warned him that the smart strategy was to string things along for a while, to keep his options open and see what developed. And now that something *had* developed, the smart strategy was looking even smarter, especially since Zelack had de-parted for a week-long camping trip in the Smokies, giv-ing Dave that much more time to figure out his next move.

"Well, how do you like that?" Buzzy said, sitting up straight on the love seat. He took off his Yankees cap and scratched so vigorously at his bald spot it looked like he was trying to file his nails on his scalp. "I'd forgotten what it feels like to watch a good thing go down the toilet."

"Not me," said Stan. "It feels pretty fucking famil-iar."

"He's been restless for a while," Dave pointed out. "I guess we should've seen it coming."

"Everybody's restless," Buzzy told him. "But you've got to be pretty fucking stupid to jump ship on a mon-eymaking operation like this. The guy doesn't even have a day job."

"Maybe he'll change his mind," Stan suggested.

"Maybe he's just depressed or something."

"I doubt it," said Dave. "He sounded pretty definite."

Buzzy stood up and grabbed his crotch in the manner of Michael Jackson.

"I'm an artist," he said, shaking his head in sorry amazement. "Good luck, buddy."

He walked over to his amp and strapped on his bass. He turned the volume up as high as it would go and began thumping out a slow angry riff that Dave heard through the soles of his feet as much as he did with his ears. The music seemed vaguely familiar, like the face of a kid he'd known in high school but hadn't thought about since graduation. Buzzy repeated the riff eight or ten times, then stopped and looked around, a gleam of challenge in his dark eyes.

"What's the matter?" he said. "Don't you assholes know any Sabbath?"

Dave plugged into his ancient fuzz pedal and did his best to keep up. Buzzy had not only the music, but also—amazingly—the lyrics of "War Pigs" committed to memory. He did a decent job with the vocals—it was the first time Dave had ever heard him sing lead—and his bass made the foundation of Artie's house shake and rumble as though in the grip of a minor earthquake. Stan complemented him with a malicious assault on the drums.

It had been so long since he'd played at this volume that Dave had forgotten what it felt like. When the din reached a certain level you lost the sense that you were actually creating it and entered this space where the noise just seemed to exist, surrounding you, independent of the movement of your fingers on the frets and knobs. You were inside it, your bones and teeth humming, your body pumped full of voltage and adrenaline. It was a giddy, grinding, out-of-control feeling, like driving through an avalanche on a rickety old school bus.

They segued into "Iron Man" and were halfway through "Sabbath Bloody Sabbath" when Artie finally returned. As soon as they saw him, they slammed on the brakes. Silence crashed down, almost as loud as the music it replaced.

"Jesus," said Buzzy. "What happened to you?"

Artie stood in front of them for a few seconds, hunched over, hands on his thighs, trying to catch his breath. His pink polo shirt was torn and stretched at the neck and his usually manicured hair hung in a shock over his forehead. There were grass stains on both knees of his off-white Dockers.

"Did you guys have a fight?" Dave asked in disbelief, his voice echoing weirdly over the ringing in his ears.

Artie stood up and shook his head. A trickle of blood ran from his left nostril down into his mouth.

"Not a fight per se. More like a heated discussion."

"Who won?" asked Stan.

Artie wiped the back of his hand across his mouth, smearing the blood. "He's gonna sing with us for the rest of the month. That'll at least give us a little leeway to try and find someone new."

Buzzy and Stan decided to grab a beer after practice, to sit around and mourn the passing of Ian. As much as he wanted to be part of the wake, Dave had to take a rain check. He'd promised Julie he'd come over around nine to help her address the invitations, and he didn't want to upset her by changing plans at the last minute.

Keeping two women happy—or at least not seriously unhappy—was harder work than he'd expected, and Dave had found himself feeling unusually frazzled of late. His whole life seemed to have reduced itself to pure logistics—planning the wedding, working, stealing a few hours to see Gretchen, getting to gigs on time, keeping straight the various lies he'd told to different people. He'd developed a sudden sympathy for Stan, an understanding of how it might happen that you showed up at the wrong banquet hall or got stuck in traffic when you least could afford it. One fire was always flaring up while you were busy extinguishing another one. Everywhere you went, there was someone you needed to apologize to. The only upside to this hectic balancing act was that it didn't leave a lot of time left over for thinking about why the hell you were doing it in the first place.

Right now his main worry was Gretchen. She'd seemed distracted and unhappy for the past couple of weeks, and Dave had the feeling he needed to do something drastic to get their relationship back on track. One of her main complaints was that they never got to spend the night together—or any other quality time for that matter—so he had made arrangements to spend Friday night and Saturday morning in Brooklyn to help celebrate her birthday. It was a risky gesture, but he wanted her to know that he was doing the best he could to take her happiness into account.

On his last visit, she'd refused to go to bed with him and had instead taken him for a walk in Prospect Park. Dave had been surprised by the number of people with free time in the middle of a hazy Tuesday afternoon, not just kids but lots of adults too, biking, running, Rollerblading, flying kites, drinking, reading, sunbathing, as though it were some sort of holiday only celebrated in New York City. Even the cops seemed to be enjoying themselves, patrolling that green and bustling world on horseback, on expensive-looking mountain bikes, and in these weird little roofed-in electric carts. Gretchen sat him down on a bench near the road that encircled the park and spoke to him at length about her unhappiness with their situation, her loneliness at night, her jealousy of Julie's claim on him.

"Don't be jealous of her," he said, patting her bony, rectangular kneecap. She was wearing a baggy tank top over skintight biker shorts, and he would rather have been touching her in a less brotherly way. "She's the one being cheated on, not you."

"She's the one getting married," Gretchen said bitterly. "Not me."

"Is that what you want?"

She looked away. Two lanky black guys with dreadlocks and identical teardrop helmets whooshed by on Rollerblades, swinging their right arms in perfect unison, like Olympic speed skaters.

"Eventually," she said. "Maybe not right this minute."

"Huh," said Dave.

He understood exactly why Julie wanted to get married. It was part of the natural course of her life. She was tired of living with her parents, bored by her job, eager to move on to the next phase of adulthood. But Gretchen was independent, a poet, a single woman in the city. Her life looked pretty great to Dave. It hadn't occurred to him that she'd be in any kind of a hurry to trade it in for a different one.

"I'm not getting any younger," she reminded him, as a Muslim woman jogged by in a baggy sweatsuit, panting beneath her veil. "I'll be thirty next week."

By the time Dave showed up, Julie and her mother were almost done with the invitations. Two neat stacks of sealed, addressed envelopes rested on the dining-room table, along with a bottle of wine, two glasses, a checklist, and several books of stamps.

"Anything I can do?" he asked.

"Not really," said Julie. "All we have to do is lick a few stamps and we're finished."

"I've got a tongue," he said, doing his best Gene Simmons imitation to prove it.

Mrs. Muller averted her eyes from this display, as if

reliving her traumatic glimpse of another of Dave's protuberant organs. How many years would he be required to walk on eggshells, he wondered, just because his mother-in-law had once laid eyes on his hot pink manhood?

"Why don't you go downstairs and relax," Julie told him. "I'm sure my father could use a little company."

"It's true," said Mrs. Muller, risking another glance in Dave's direction. "He's been alone since suppertime."

Entering the rec room, he was greeted by the sound of explosions and the triumphant voice-over of a World War II documentary: *The mighty Allied war machine rolled on toward Berlin, encountering only sporadic resistance from the demoralized Nazi forces.* Dave recognized the narrator from football highlight films he'd watched as a kid.

"Hey," he said, crossing between Mr. Muller and the TV to take his inevitable seat on the couch.

Mr. Muller muted the set. He was still wearing his jacket, tie, and tasseled loafers, as if he'd just come home from work five minutes ago. In all the years he'd known his prospective father-in-law, Dave had never seen him in shorts, or shirtless, or barefoot, or unshaven. Julie claimed to have no memory of her father that involved a bathing suit, or even pajamas. Except for a small strip of shin that poked out from between the top of his socks and the bottom of his pants, his legs were purely theoretical.

"Good to see you," he said, swirling the scotch around the inside of his glass with a practiced motion. He nodded toward the TV. "You been watching this?"

Dave shook his head. On the screen, a ragged band of German soldiers exited a bombed-out building, hands on top of their heads. Many of them were adolescent boys and gray-haired men. All of them looked bewildered.

"Quality stuff," Mr. Muller declared. "Not like the

garbage you see on the other channels." He pronounced "garbage" as though it were a French word.

"My father's a big World War II buff," said Dave. "He can't get over the fact that fifty years have gone by. He says it feels like yesterday."

Mr. Muller nodded, still swirling his drink. "Half a century. Water under the bridge."

They watched from the air as a load of bombs plummeted earthward, blossoming in a swath of destruction. The perspective shifted to the ground, where German women in winter clothing combed through the smoking rubble, glancing anxiously at the sky.

"So how's the wedding coming?" asked Mr. Muller.

"Okay. Getting there."

It was, too. Most of the major decisions had been made. They'd booked a room at the Westview and hired Rockin' Randy to handle the entertainment (Dave still hadn't told the Wishbones). Chicken cordon bleu and poached salmon had been selected as entrees. The invitations had been printed on off-white paper in gold lettering and would be mailed tomorrow. Julie had found a gown she was happy with; Dave would take the plunge in his Wishbones tux. Suitably hideous dresses were on order for the bridesmaids. All that remained to be nailed down was the honeymoon plan. They were debating whether to postpone the trip to Hawaii for a year or so, sparing their limited funds for the more practical purpose of furnishing their new apartment, the top half of a small two-family on Pine Avenue.

Mr. Muller chuckled. "It's all we ever talk about around here. Wedding, wedding, wedding. You'd think we were planning the Normandy invasion."

"No kidding," laughed Dave. "It's a lotta work."

"I'll be glad when it's over."

"Me too."

"You nervous?"

"A little," Dave admitted. "Were you?"

"When?"

"Your own wedding."

Frowning, Mr. Muller consulted the ceiling.

"I can't remember. Probably not, though. I didn't have the brains to be nervous."

"What do you mean?"

"Those were different times," he explained with a shrug. "People didn't think so much about what they were doing. You had a few good dates with a girl, and the next thing you knew you were standing at the altar with a flower stuck in your coat. Dolores was a beautiful bride. That much I remember."

Their attention returned to the screen. The documentary had arrived at the liberation of the concentration camps. As many times as he'd seen the pictures, Dave still wasn't prepared for them. The barbed wire and watchtowers. The gas chambers and ovens. The piles of confiscated shoes and eyeglasses, the trenches filled with broken, naked bodies. The half-dead faces of the survivors, many of them too weak and hungry to move.

"Man," said Dave.

"Jesus H. Christ," muttered Mr. Muller.

Abruptly, the subject shifted to the Pacific theater. A kamikaze airplane came spiraling out of the sky, crashing in a fireball on the deck of an American destroyer.

"So how are the folks?" Mr. Muller inquired. "Everybody healthy?"

Julie came downstairs shortly before ten o'clock, just in time to watch the atomic bomb fall on Hiroshima, the slow-spreading cloud seeming oddly familiar on the small screen, almost beautiful. It reminded Dave of the feeling he had watching the *Challenger* disaster over and over again, how he'd forgotten about the people involved and allowed himself to appreciate the strange, arcing beauty of the explosion itself.

Mr. Muller yawned and said it was time for him to turn in. Julie kissed him good night, taking possession of the remote as she did so. The TV snapped off before her father had even reached the base of the stairs. Dave and Julie remained frozen until Mr. Muller had completed his ascent.

"Sorry to leave you stranded," she whispered, as soon as her father was safely upstairs. "My mother felt like talking."

"No problem."

She lay down on the couch, resting her head on his lap, peering up at him with a dreamy half smile. Even if he hadn't smelled her breath, he would have known from her expression that she'd been drinking.

"We polished off that whole bottle," she said cheerfully. "That's a first for my mother and me."

Dave moved his fingers through her thick, outspread hair. She'd worn it short for a couple of years, thinking she might look more like a teacher when she went on job interviews, but recently had decided to let it grow again. He loved the mass and sheen of it, the way it was always getting caught in their mouths when they kissed. He loved Gretchen's short hair too, which was right for her the way long hair was right for Julie. Somehow the contrasts made each of them more interesting, though that was the kind of secret he had to keep to himself.

"So what were you talking about?"

"Their marriage."

"What about it?"

Julie's mouth puckered. A deep, horizontal groove appeared in her forehead.

"It's sad," she said.

"What?"

"She says he never touches her anymore. Not for a long time now. It's like that part of him just disappeared."

"Does she want him to?"

"She cried when she told me."

Dave didn't know what to say. He stared at the blank TV, mindlessly stroking her cheek. He didn't know much about his own parents' sex life, and preferred it that way. Julie rolled onto her side, her face resting lightly and intriguingly against his crotch.

"That's not going to happen to us, is it?"

"I hope not."

"Don't let it."

"I won't," he said, understanding even as he spoke that his words meant nothing. There was no way of knowing what your life would look like thirty years down the road, no way of controlling your feelings.

"Don't let it," she repeated, nuzzling him through his jeans. "I don't want it to turn out like that."

"Okay," he said, his eyes widening with surprise as she undid his pants and tugged gently on his zipper.

"We can do this for the rest of our lives," she whispered, pulling down the waistband of his underpants. "Until the day we die."

"Sounds good to me," he agreed.

He was about to remind her of their chastity agreement, but decided not to. Everybody backslid now and then. There was no sense being a jerk about it. He closed his eyes and concentrated on the warmth of her mouth, the slow tugging, the thrilling sensation of his own growth. In the whole pantheon of sex, almost nothing beat a blow job when you least expected it. She paused midway, looking up at him with an oddly serious expression.

"I'm drunk," she explained. "This doesn't really count."

Afterward they lay tangled together on the couch, Dave's mind and body humming with a pleasant, low-frequency buzz. He felt himself drifting toward sleep and didn't bother to fight it. Julie lifted her head off his chest.

"I hear Ian quit the band," she said.

"What?" Dave blinked a few times, struggling back toward alertness. "Who told you that?"

"Tammi. She called me this afternoon. Was it a bad scene?"

Dave thought back on the rehearsal, wondering at the speed with which he'd put the evening's events out of his mind. Part of it was distraction, he thought, and part of it was denial, but most of it was simple disbelief: on some level, he simply couldn't accept the fact that his days of making music with Ian were over. The Wishbones weren't just another throwaway band. Something about them felt real and permanent, like a family. Ian just couldn't walk away from it.

"I'm not sure he's really leaving," he said.

"Tammi said he's fed up with it."

Dave didn't respond. All at once, everything seemed wrong. He concentrated on controlling a momentary surge of panic that made him want to leap up from the couch and shout "No!" He didn't want to get married. He didn't want to join Shiny Angels. He didn't want the Wishbones to fall apart.

"Maybe this is a good time for you to quit too," Julie suggested.

The bad feeling passed. Slowly, his breath returned to normal.

"I've been in bands ever since you've known me," he explained. "I wouldn't know what to do with myself."

"You'd be fine," she said, tracing her finger lightly over his collarbone. "There are other things in life besides playing music."

She must be right, he told himself. Other people seemed perfectly happy living normal lives, working and raising families. It didn't seem to matter to them that they were never going to be rock stars, weren't even going to get the thrill of playing covers at a wedding, making people dance until they glowed. Other people seemed perfectly happy.

"I'd be lost," he told her.

Karma House

Dave generally liked spicy food and was often disappointed by what passed for Mexican or Indian or Chinese food in the suburbs. But this Karma House vindaloo was way out of his league: moments after he swallowed the first bite, it ignited like a blowtorch in his throat.

He snatched up his water glass, only to discover it empty. Gretchen's glass was empty too, as were the two twenty-two-ounce bottles of Taj Mahal they'd polished off waiting for their food to arrive. Dave grinned to conceal his anguish. A small, strangled cry escaped from his lips. His mouth was a seething cave of fire.

"Are you okay?" Gretchen asked. Her face seemed warped and blurry, as though viewed through a pair of bad eyeglasses.

"Water," he gasped, abandoning all pretense of composure. "Water."

Gretchen waved, and a tuxedo-clad waiter came charging down the narrow aisle, metal pitcher in hand. He poured the water, then stood by without expression as Dave downed the whole glass in a single gulp.

"A bit spicy?" the waiter inquired. He was a trim young man with delicate features and a haughty posture.

"A bit," Dave conceded. His vision had returned to normal, and he saw the people at nearby tables watching him, some with compassion, some with amusement, others with that peculiar New York look of bland curiosity that probably wouldn't have changed if he'd keeled over and died right in front of them.

He tossed the second glass down the hatch, but the fire still wasn't extinguished. When he requested a third, the waiter set the pitcher down on the table.

"Anything else?" he asked.

"More poori bread," Gretchen instructed him. "And another Taj Mahal."

Generously, she offered to swap entrees. Hers was lamb curry; she said it was a little on the bland side.

"No thanks," he said. "I couldn't do that to you. I'll just fill up on bread and rice."

"But I *like* hot food."

"This isn't hot. It's satanic."

She ignored the warning, stubbornly pushing her own plate across the crowded table.

"I'm not going to sit here and watch you starve on my birthday."

"In that case, I'll order another entree."

"Don't be ridiculous. Hand it over."

With grave reluctance, Dave surrendered the fearsome vindaloo. He gritted his teeth in sympathetic dread as she took a cautious first bite, tilting her head thoughtfully as she chewed. Her second bite was larger, without fear.

"It's a little hot," she said without conviction, obviously humoring him.

"A little? It's like eating napalm."

"It's good," she said with a shrug. "Much better than the curry."

Now that his mouth was pacified, Dave picked up where he'd left off, admiring her from across the table, her glossy dark hair, long neck, and slender arms, all bathed in the strange pink light of the Karma House, a festive glow produced by crisscrossing chains of red Christmas bulbs strung across the ceiling. The restaurant was tiny, narrow as a bowling lane, the cramped feeling only intensified by piped-in sitar music and mirrored walls that multiplied the dozen or so tables into a dizzying wilderness of diners.

Aware of his scrutiny, Gretchen looked up, her expression at once shy and oddly direct. Dave smiled back. It felt good to be alone in public with her, on a legitimate date. He took a moment to reflect on the care with which he'd planned the evening, and how well it was panning out. Julie and his parents were under the impression that he'd traveled into the city with Alan Zelack to check out a marathon Battle of the Bands at CBGB's, an event that wouldn't start until midnight and probably wouldn't conclude until four in the morning, and that they would spend the remainder of the night in Zelack's cousin's apartment in the meat-packing district. The alibi, as far as Dave could determine, was airtight—neither his parents nor Julie knew Zelack except by reputation—and the resulting sense of freedom had left him exhilarated all day, a feeling that had reached its pinnacle when Gretchen appeared at the door of her apartment in that simple, dusty blue sleeveless dress, her arms elegantly unencumbered by their usual platoons of bracelets. He still couldn't get over how great she looked.

"You're amazing," he said.

"Excuse me?"

"I said you're amazing."

"Why?"

"You just are." Dave surprised himself with his enthusiasm; he felt stupid and happy and full of conviction,

drunk on beer and pink light. "You're just so perfect tonight."

She didn't respond quite the way he'd hoped. Instead
of blushing or thanking him, she turned away. Her face
in the Karma House mirror looked wounded, almost
stricken.

"Please don't talk to me like that," she said, addressing
her reflection instead of Dave.

"Why not?" he said. "It's true."

"It just makes it worse."

Dave knew better than to ask her to clarify her pro-
nouns. They'd been down this road before; he just hadn't
expected to be back on it tonight. Her birthday was supposed to have been a reprieve, an antidote to the sadness
that had been dogging them. He felt the bottom falling
out of the entire night, all because he'd told her she was
amazing.

"It's the dress," he explained. "It's perfect on you."

"*Please,*" she said. "Don't make me cry in public."

Just then the waiter arrived with their poori bread. He
set it down on the edge of the table, a round, steaming
envelope of air, balanced precariously on a small wooden
board. Dave and Gretchen paused to study the puffy loaf
for an improbable length of time, waiting for its inevitable
collapse. Miraculously, the bread held its shape. Dave
wondered why it didn't just float up to the pink ceiling
like a tiny dirigible.

"I really don't think I can see you anymore," she told
him.

She said it would be one thing if she had even the vaguest
idea of what was going on in his head. But she didn't
have a clue what he thought about any of it—her, Julie,
his impending marriage, his entire life.

"If I were you I'd be going crazy. But you just keep

drifting along like all this makes perfect sense. Well, I've got news for you, Dave. It doesn't.''

He had to admit she had a point. There really wasn't a reasonable explanation for his behavior, at least not one he'd feel comfortable speaking out loud to another person. If someone had told him a story about a guy who got involved in a torrid affair a couple of months before his wedding, Dave would've assumed, at the very least, that the guy was an asshole, and he had no doubt that that was what other people would think of him if they got wind of what he was up to with Gretchen. But the truth was, Dave didn't actually *feel* like an asshole. It seemed to him, though he knew better than to try to persuade anyone else that this was the case, that he was doing what was possible to save himself from being a complete asshole—to Gretchen, to Julie, and also to himself. He mopped some curry off his plate with a piece of bread.

"It was a case of bad timing."

"Spare me," she said. "I'm sick of hearing about our bad timing."

"But it's true."

"So what? What good does it do to keep repeating it? The question is, what do we do now?"

"Try to be happy," he said. "It's all you can ever do."

"Try to be happy?" Her eyes grew wide and miserable. "How am I supposed to do that?"

"We're here together now," he pointed out, trying to ignore the strains of Bob Seger's "We've Got Tonight" that had suddenly flared up in his head. "Can't that be enough?"

Her expression seemed to soften as she considered this possibility. With a little imagination, he thought, the cryptic look on her face might even be taken for a smile.

"You're the one who's amazing," she told him.

"How so?"

"I thought I was a master of denial, but you're incredible."

"What am I denying?" he asked, honestly surprised by the charge.

"Nothing important." She brushed away the question with a breezy flick of the wrist. "Just that you're getting married in a couple of weeks."

Dave almost laughed. "I'm not denying *that,* believe me. I couldn't if I wanted to. People don't realize what a big job it is to plan a wedding."

"I wouldn't know."

He ignored the bitterness in her tone. "So what else am I supposedly denying?"

"See?" she said. "You even deny that you're in denial."

"Isn't that the whole point? I mean, you can't be in denial and know about it. That defeats the whole purpose."

He knew he'd scored a point, but it came at the price of Gretchen's interest in the conversation.

"Forget it," she said, sounding more bored than irritated. "I'm sorry I brought it up."

Dave knew he was screwing up. All he'd wanted was to give her one great night, a birthday celebration they'd both be able to remember no matter what happened in the future. And yet here they were, despite all his good intentions, mired in a nitpicky debate about the meaning of denial.

He found himself thinking, for some reason, about a news item he'd followed a while back, the story of a young woman from Long Island who disappeared shortly before her wedding. She'd gone out to the mall on a Tuesday night and simply vanished. Sick with worry, her family and fiancé pleaded for her safety on the eleven-o'clock news. One of her sisters talked about how excited the missing woman was about her upcoming wedding.

"It was her dream," the sister said, smiling through her tears. "A June wedding to the man she loved."

"She's a level-headed girl," her fiancé told a reporter.

He was an ordinary-looking guy with glasses and a mustache, doing his best to be brave. "She never went anywhere without telling someone."

A few days later, long after it seemed certain that something terrible had happened, the cops reported that the missing woman had been located alive and well in Canada, where she'd fled to escape a marriage she couldn't face. Her family seemed stunned by this turn of events, perhaps more stunned than they would have been if her partially clothed body had been discovered in a shallow grave in a wooded area behind the mall. Dave remembered watching a second interview with the shattered fiancé standing in the doorway of his parents' house, choking out a barely intelligible apology to the "level-headed girl" who'd left the country to get away from him.

"I'm sorry if I pressured you," he sobbed. "You could have said something. You didn't have to go scaring us all to death."

At the time, Dave hadn't given the story a lot of thought. It was just one of those incidents you shake your head over and then shove to the back of your mind. But now he found himself wondering. Did the woman have a lover in Canada? Had she been planning her escape for a long time, or had the idea just come to her in a desperate flash as she walked through the mall parking lot? Where was she now? Had her family forgiven her? What about the fiancé? There were so many loose ends to consider, he didn't even realize Gretchen was speaking until her words had shot right past him.

"Excuse me?" he said.

"The curry," she told him, enunciating as though he were hard of hearing. "I asked if you liked the curry."

As if she hadn't just broken up with him inside the Karma House, Gretchen let Dave hold her hand as they made their way downtown toward the Brooklyn Bridge.

The fresh air seemed to have cheered her up, and she'd decided that she couldn't stomach the thought of descending into the subway on such a beautiful night.

"Why don't we just walk?" she suggested. "It's only a couple of miles."

A couple of miles didn't sound like "only" to Dave, but he had no desire to argue. It was her birthday; by definition, whatever made her happy was okay with him. Besides, a long walk would give him that much more time to work his way back into her good graces before they got to her place and had to face the inevitable question of whether he was going or staying. The hand-holding seemed like a step in the right direction, a step away from the gloomy alternative of a lonely drive back to New Jersey, where no one expected him anyway.

Their path took them west and then south, onto a familiar stretch of the Bowery. Dave experienced a peculiar, almost teenaged sense of vindication as they walked past CBGB's, as though the very sight of it negated the lies he'd told earlier in the day. *See, Mom, I told you.* A cluster of spiky-haired punks stood in ripped T-shirts and combat boots outside the door, passing a cigarette in a circle and halfheartedly scowling at the people who passed. They looked sad and defiant at the same time, as though they understood as well as anyone that they'd missed their moment by twenty years and had no one left to shock.

The streets grew more deserted as they approached Canal. Gretchen seemed unconcerned, but Dave's urban danger monitor went on red alert. He felt deeply vulnerable, a short, slightly out-of-shape white guy dressed for a night out, holding hands with a taller woman in a pretty dress. There might as well have been a "Mug Me" sign taped to his back. He didn't allow himself to relax until they'd crossed safely into Chinatown, where the pedestrian traffic was thicker and it wasn't unusual, even at this time of night, to see an old woman walking alone, multiple plastic bags suspended from each hand.

"I love this city," he said. "It's incredible. You cross the street or turn a corner and the next thing you know, you're in another world."

"Why don't you move here then?"

"I always wanted to."

"So do it."

There was nothing flip about this suggestion. Her voice was soft, almost fearful; she understood the magnitude of what she was asking him to consider. Dave thought about the place he and Julie had rented on Pine Avenue, a nondescript house on a sleepy street, the quietly predictable life it seemed to embody.

"I missed my moment. I should have come here ten years ago."

"Why didn't you?"

"Chicken," he said, humbled by his own adjective. "I wasn't up to it."

They walked past a Chinese video store, the front windows plastered over with posters of scantily clad women and ferocious martial artists, bare-chested warriors confronting a hostile world with nothing but their hands, their feet, and their expressions of furious, almost insane determination. Gretchen squeezed his hand.

"It's never too late to get some courage," she told him.

Dave had known for some time that there was a pedestrian walkway on the Brooklyn Bridge, but he'd never set foot on it until that night. The effect was breathtaking, nothing at all like driving across: there you were, Brooklyn ahead, skyline behind, moon above, lights all around, traffic and water below. Swooping, strung with cables, the bridge reminded him of a gigantic harp, humming a single, soothing note. The walkway wasn't crowded, but it wasn't deserted either. Hand-in-hand, Dave and Gretchen wove their way through the complex pattern of late-night joggers and bike riders, strolling couples, briefcase-toting professionals, packs of teenagers, and one spectacularly unconvincing platinum-wigged transvestite wobbling his way toward Manhattan atop three-inch stiletto heels.

"So I'm thirty," Gretchen said, shaking her head in what appeared to be genuine dismay. "Is this possible?"

"Oh, it's definitely possible," he assured her.

"I don't feel different," she complained. "I expected to feel different."

"Different from what?"

"From the way I felt all through my twenties."

"What way was that?"

She laughed. It wasn't a happy sound.

"Like a bad poet with a lousy job, no boyfriend, and barely enough money to pay the rent."

"You're not a bad poet."

"I'm not a good one," she said, shooting him a sharp sidelong glance. "Believe me, I stopped kidding myself on that score a long time ago."

"Well, you do have a boyfriend," he ventured, after a few uncomfortable seconds had gone by.

"In a manner of speaking."

Dave could feel the unhappiness radiating from her like heat from a bad sunburn, and realized that he had to do something fast. He stopped short and pulled her against him, right there on the walkway, and kissed her. She responded with way more enthusiasm than he expected or deserved. The kiss went on and on; a couple of teenaged guys whistled at them and some others offered obscene shouts of encouragement, but not even that was enough to unseal their spicy mouths. He felt the world falling away, until it seemed as though there were nothing anywhere but that small patch of bridge, the two of them suspended, almost in the air, high above the East River, sharing a desperate kiss halfway between one place and another.

They were both exhausted by the time they got back to her place. The walk was longer than she remembered, ending with a laborious twenty-minute climb to the top of Park Slope.

"Come to think of it," she said, "I've only done this going *into* Manhattan. It goes a lot faster when you're heading downhill."

"There's a concept for you." Dave didn't mean to snipe, but his feet were killing him. He was wearing black dress shoes that he'd bought the previous year but had never properly broken in. A raw spot had opened at the top of his right heel that screamed out in protest every time he lifted his foot. He thought sympathetically of the transvestite on the bridge. "If I'd known we were going on a hike, I would've worn sensible shoes."

"Poor baby," she laughed. "Come upstairs and I'll make it better."

This invitation came more easily than Dave had expected, despite the passion generated by the kiss on the bridge, but he was in no position to savor his victory until he'd mounted the three flights of stairs to her apartment, yanked his shoes off in the living room, and propped his aching, sweaty feet on top of the coffee table. Even then, his first thought was less of romance than of how good it would feel, after a cold drink or two, to collapse on her futon and simply go to sleep.

She brought him some ice water from the kitchen and sat down across the room, sprawling carelessly on the beat-up armchair. Her dress hiked up as she did so, knees splayed wide enough to reveal a glimpse of her silky black panties. Dave was normally a sucker for this sort of foreplay, but at the moment it commanded less of his attention than the incipient blister on his heel.

"I'll be limping for the rest of the summer," he informed her, gingerly probing the sore spot, which he figured to be the approximate size and shape of an eyeball.

Gretchen didn't bother to stifle a yawn.

"Sorry," she said. "It's not that I'm not interested in your foot. Eleven o'clock just feels a lot later than it used to."

Dave nodded. "Especially after a few beers and a forced march. It's nature's way of telling you you're over thirty."

"Please," she said. "Don't remind me."

"Sorry."

They sipped their water and traded tired smiles. Gretchen sat up straight, smoothing the front of her dress down over her thighs, then cast a skeptical glance in the direction of the bedroom.

"Shall we?"

"Sure," he said. "If I can manage to stand up."

The sight of her undressing revived him. A burnt mouth, a blister, and a few harmless lies seemed like a small price to pay for the privilege of watching her drop her bra on the floor and turn to him, wearing nothing but her glasses. *Remember this,* he instructed himself. *You have to remember this.*

Setting her glasses on the bedside table, on top of *The Collected Poems of Emily Dickinson,* she turned out the light and climbed in beside him. A peculiar calm settled over him, a concentrated feeling of alertness he only experienced playing music and making love, and even then, only when he was lucky and beyond distraction.

She began with her foot, rubbing her heel up and down the length of his shin for a minute or more, setting a thoughtful, unhurried pace. She didn't kiss him or touch him with her hands, and he seemed to understand, without her saying a word, that his job was to lie there and let it happen. Her hand slipped into his mouth, four dry fingers at once, tasting of salt, skin, and curry. After exploring his mouth for a while, she removed her hand and pulled him to her breast.

"Suck on it," she whispered. "Don't be afraid."

Her voice was patient, almost instructional, and he did as he was told, not bothering to inform her that this activity was not one that frightened him in the least. He had the feeling she was trying to teach him something, but he didn't know what—a lesson about her body, perhaps, or maybe just something about following directions. In any case, he had a long time to think about it.

"Now the other one."

He noticed a slight tremor in her voice, as if she were finally allowing herself to surrender control of the proceedings. She leaned forward, resting her head on top of his, her breath quick and fluttery in his ear. Time stretched out; he hoped he wasn't hurting her nipple. Then, without warning, she pulled herself away from him, falling backwards on the bed.

"Lower," she said, wriggling out from under him, guiding his head in that direction.

She came the moment he tasted her, with a sharp cry and a quick shudder. The next thing Dave knew, she was on top of him, pressing on his chest as if performing CPR, and he was thrusting up into her, babbling a crazy flood of praise and gratitude.

"Does this mean we're not broken up?" he asked, when he'd finally recovered the power of articulate speech.

She took a while to answer; the pause gave him hope. But when she did there was sadness in her voice and a calm sense of finality.

"I can't do this anymore. I have to protect myself."

"From what?"

"From what?" she repeated in disbelief. "From I don't want to be sitting here a month from now, eating popcorn in front of some stupid rented movie while you're out getting yourself married. I'm thirty years old, Dave. I can't afford to be that pathetic anymore."

"Why don't you make plans with a friend?" he suggested. "Go out to a nice restaurant or something."

"That's just as bad. There's no way to behave on the night of your boyfriend's wedding that isn't pathetic. You're just pathetic by definition. And it'll get worse after that. Like what am I supposed to do when you tell me Julie's pregnant? Break out the champagne?"

"Babies are a long way off."

"Not as long you think. Julie's the same age as you, right?"

"Yeah."

"She's ready," Gretchen said firmly. "I know she is."

Dave didn't reply. The fatigue that had lifted during their lovemaking had returned with a vengeance. His body felt like a bag of cement. His thoughts were coming in like a bad radio station.

"Does this really mean it's over for us?"

"It was over before it started," she told him. "We were just too stubborn to admit it."

Wursthaus

The *Genial Jim Show* was taped at Larry's Wursthaus in downtown Union Village. Buzzy worked a couple of miles away at Prostho-Tek ("World's Largest Supplier of Quality Artificial Limbs"), so instead of heading home after work, he'd made arrangements for Dave to meet him at the Beer Barrel Inn, a quiet neighborhood bar across the street from the Wursthaus.

Losing his license had turned every simple thing in Buzzy's life into a humongous pain in the ass. When JoAnn dropped him off at Prostho-Tek that morning, he'd had no choice but to lug his bass and garment bag into the factory with him, thereby guaranteeing that he'd spend a good part of the day listening to stupid comments from his co-workers.

"What's in there? A machine gun?"

"Goin' on a trip?"

" 'Free Bird'!"

On top of pretending to be amused by this crap, he had to approach four different people before he found someone willing to give him a ride downtown at the end of the day. And now here he was, entering a bar where no one knew him, facing the prospect of asking someone to keep an eye on his instrument while he changed clothes in the rest room. (He could've changed at work, but the idea of punching out in a tux was beyond consideration.) It was all so fucking humiliating. The only upside to the situation was knowing he could drink as much as he wanted without having to worry about getting home.

Luckily, the place was empty except for the bartender, a pudgy guy sitting on the wrong side of the bar, sipping ice water and watching *Oprah* on the wall-mounted TV. He didn't look too thrilled about the idea of getting off his ass to serve Buzzy, but both of them knew he didn't really have a choice.

"Double Early Times straight up," Buzzy said, when the bartender had finally manned his battle station. He was an older guy, probably close to retirement age, with a thick broomlike mustache that reminded Buzzy of the guy in the Quaker Oats commercials.

The drink appeared and for a few minutes they watched the show in companionable silence. It featured a bunch of good-looking women in revealing clothes talking earnestly about the need to pay the rent.

"These are mother-and-daughter prostitute teams," the bartender explained. "Some country, huh?"

"It's those father-and-son teams that are the really sick ones," Buzzy replied, shaking his head as if deeply troubled.

The bartender studied him for a few seconds, then chuckled uncertainly.

"Good one," he said, turning back to the screen.

The bathroom was small, but still relatively clean at that time of day. Buzzy was surprised to see that it boasted both a condom machine and a coin-operated cologne dispenser, amenities that seemed beside the point at a no-nonsense gin mill like the Beer Barrel.

Getting dressed in a public rest room, particularly one as cramped as this, was a little like using a changing room in a clothing store, only more complicated. First there was the issue of whether or not you were willing to remove your shoes; then you had to deal with where to put the stuff you took off, and how to minimize the time spent standing around in your underwear. In the end, the process took twice as long as it did at home, and seemed even longer while it was happening.

The bartender didn't bother to hide his amusement when Buzzy emerged. He stroked his bristly mustache, nodding with exaggerated approval.

"Hey," he quipped. "Into a nearby phone booth."

"That was no phone booth," Buzzy told him, climbing back onto his stool and polishing off the dregs of his bourbon.

The bartender smirked. "Formal wear becomes you."

"I'm a musician. My band's playing across the street in a couple hours."

"Across the street?"

"The Wursthaus. Some cable-access show."

"You mean Genial Jim?"

"That's the guy."

The bartender's eyes darted toward the door.

"You a fan of his?"

Buzzy shrugged. "Don't know the first thing about him." He lifted his empty glass. "How about another?"

"Genial Jim's something else," the bartender told him, pouring a generous double.

"How so?"

"Pretty hard-line."

"Hard-line what?"

"See for yourself. He draws a pretty unusual crowd."

Fuckin' Artie. It was bad enough the band was stooping to this two-bit cable-access crap without Genial Jim turn-

ing out to be some sort of crackpot. Buzzy found himself
wondering if Ian didn't have the right idea, if it wasn't
time to get out while the going was still good. But as
quickly as the thought appeared, he shoved it out of his
mind. He didn't even want to think about what his life
would look like without the band, an endless cycle of
work and home, work and home, work and home, prosthetic devices and cheesy sitcoms as far as the eye could
see. Now he knew why his father belonged to three bowling leagues for most of his adult life.

"Jesus," the bartender moaned. "Listen to this."

One of the mother prostitutes was talking about the
disappointment she had initially felt when her daughter
had opted to follow her into the profession. "My dream
was for her to go to college," the mother explained,
sounding sad and proud at the same time. "I wanted her
to have the opportunities I never did. But she was just
like me—too stubborn for her own good." The camera
pulled back to show the daughter dabbing at her eyes with
a Kleenex, obviously touched by her mother's public
show of support. Buzzy waited for the next commercial
break before speaking.

"Hey, chief," he said, "you wouldn't have any free
pretzels or anything like that back there, would you?"

•   •   •

Dave spotted him right away, the combination of ponytail
and tuxedo a dead giveaway even in the murky light of
the lounge. He was sitting way at the other end of the
long bar, as far as he could get from the raucous crowd
of grass-stained landscapers gathered around the pool table by the front window.

Buzzy seemed unusually subdued, almost pensive. He
nodded to acknowledge Dave's arrival, then turned his
attention back to the TV above the bar. Hootie and the
Blowfish were on, the sound turned all the way down so

as not to interfere with the Doors' "Soul Kitchen" blasting out of the jukebox.

"Been here long?" Dave asked.

"Couple hours."

"Couple *hours?* What time'd you get off work?"

"Four."

It was six-fifteen now. Dave considered the shot glass
on the bar in front of Buzzy, the messy pile of bills and
change, the bowl lined with salt and pretzel crumbs.

"Did you eat any supper?"

"I'll grab a bratwurst at Larry's."

Buzzy didn't sound drunk, exactly, just a little stiff, like
a politician reading off a TelePrompTer. He tapped his
glass on the bar to get the attention of the barmaid, a
flashy blonde who understood the relationship between
cleavage and tips.

"Hey, Sally," he said. "How about a refill?"

"You sure?" she asked.

"As regards this small matter," Buzzy assured her, "I
have achieved a high degree of certitude."

Sally selected a bottle from the shelf by the register.

"I hope you're not driving," she said.

"Nope." Buzzy watched carefully as she filled his
glass, then jerked his thumb in Dave's direction. "My
buddy here's the designated drunk driver."

Stone-faced, Sally subtracted some money from the pile
and marched it over to the till. Buzzy dispatched the double in a businesslike manner, squinting at the television.
An MTV veejay was opening and closing her mouth, the
pretty one with the stupid name. Dave slapped Buzzy on
the back.

"Come on," he said. "Time to head across the street."

Buzzy turned slowly, his smile vague and distant.

"You know what I've always wanted to do?"

"What?"

"Toss a TV off a hotel balcony." He paused, savoring

the fantasy. "Be cool to watch it explode from about thirty floors up, don't you think?"

"Come on," Dave said again. "Time to go."

Buzzy didn't move.

"You ever want to do that?"

"Sure." Dave smiled in spite of himself. "I wanted mine to land in a pool."

Buzzy seemed pleased by this information. He gathered up the remaining bills on the bar, leaving only the coins for Sally.

"Good," he said. "I was starting to think I was the only asshole left in the whole fuckin' country."

Dave hadn't given *The Genial Jim Show* a lot of thought in the past few days. He'd been too absorbed in his private life, the effort of acting like everything was fine around Julie while his heart and brain were screaming Gretchen's name.

He still couldn't accept the idea that things were over for them. Even after she'd broken up with him, supposedly for good, her behavior toward him hadn't changed. They woke up in each other's arms the morning after her birthday and made love with such heartbroken abandon that she'd wept, and it had taken all the self-control he could muster not to do the same.

Then he kissed her good-bye, drove home, and hadn't found a moment's peace ever since. He called her twice from pay phones during courier runs into the city, but she hadn't picked up either time, even though he was pretty sure she was home, screening her calls. He had no idea what his next move would be, but he knew he had to do something and do it fast. He couldn't afford to just let her fade out of his life—not now, when he was just getting to know her.

If he'd given tonight's gig any thought at all, it was only to wonder how things would go with Ian, if there would be any tension between him and the rest of the band, or if he had possibly begun to reconsider his decision to quit the Wishbones. Genial Jim hadn't entered Dave's mind at all. He simply hadn't had the time or energy to worry about who the guy was, or where he'd dug up such a stupid name, or what a shipping clerk was doing with a talk show.

As soon as he and Buzzy entered the Wursthaus Banquet Room, though, Dave started to wonder what Artie had gotten them into. At first it was just a vague sense of being out of his element, nothing he could put his finger on. The Banquet Room was gloomy and forbidding, all dark wood and red Naugahyde. The waitresses wore dirndls; the air reeked of sauerkraut.

His misgivings intensified as they threaded their way through the tables toward the stage at the opposite end of the room. Most of the patrons were men, and a fair number of them, regardless of age, were decked out in camouflage fatigues and combat boots. One booth was occupied solely by pumped-up, angry-looking teenage skinheads. Buzzy grabbed hold of Dave's arm and whispered excitedly in his ear, "Wow, did you see the size of those beer steins?"

Stan had already arrived and was busily assembling his drum kit. On their way to the bandstand, Dave and Buzzy were accosted by Lenny, the wedding videographer, who was squatting by his equipment at the foot of the stage. Despite the fact that he was busy inhaling a heaping plate of liver and onions, he insisted on leaping to his feet and greeting them both with one-armed bear hugs.

"Welcome," he said, balancing the plate waiter-style in the palm of his free hand. "Welcome to the family."

"What family is that?" Dave wanted to know.

Lenny's gesture encompassed the whole room. Dressed in jeans and an army-surplus shirt, he seemed like a different person, way more relaxed and expansive than he was in his wedding garb.

"We're a family here. Have you guys seen the show before?"

Dave shook his head.

"You're in for a treat," Lenny promised. "Genial Jim speaks the truth."

Dave started to feel a bit queasy. He looked past Lenny and spied Artie standing beside a PA column, chatting with two burly, cheerful-looking guys, one of whom wore a green Tyrolean hat, the other a rumpled brown suit.

"Is that him over there?"

"Yup," said Lenny. "Jim's the one with the hat. The bald guy's his sidekick, Cookie. He used to be a cop in Newark. Come on, I'll introduce you."

"Wait." Buzzy leaned forward, sniffing at Lenny's plate as though it were a bouquet of flowers. "First tell me how I can get hold of some of that."

Lenny led Buzzy off toward the kitchen, and Dave made his way over to the bandstand, trading a swift look of dread with Stan as he undid the clasps on his case. He didn't even have time to tune up before Artie summoned him to meet their hosts.

"Jim Baumeister."

"Cookie Dockery."

"Dave Raymond."

Genial Jim greeted Dave with a handshake and a wary look of appraisal. He was about fifty, with an oddly boy-ish face and gray muttonchop sideburns. A black T-shirt pulled tight over his bulging belly bore the challenge, *Go Ahead, Try to Take My Gun Away.*

"You're not Jewish, are you?" he asked.

"Who, me?" said Dave, startled by the question.

"He's just pulling your chain," Cookie chortled, faking a punch to Dave's midsection. "He does it to everyone."

"Some people are," Genial Jim noted. "I like to know who I'm dealing with."

Dave shot a quick look at Artie, whose only response

was a helpless shrug. Genial Jim rubbed his hands together with brisk enthusiasm.

"Great show tonight," he said. "Quality theme, quality guests."

"What's the theme?" Dave asked.

"Big-time stuff," Cookie chimed in. "One-world government and why it can't happen here."

Just then a bunch of guys in softball uniforms piled into the room. Genial Jim and Cookie excused themselves to say hello to the newcomers, leaving Dave to glare at Artie in speechless bewilderment.

"Don't start with me," Artie warned him.

"Do you know what these people *are?*"

"I do now."

"You didn't before?"

Artie shook his head. "It was that douche bag Lenny. He called and said his friend was looking for a band for his TV show. We didn't get too deep into the politics. I mean, shit, Dave, the guy calls himself Genial fucking Jim. I figured he was a comedian or something."

"He's a riot all right."

They watched Buzzy emerge from the kitchen, smiling ecstatically, a beer stein in one hand and a plate in the other. The plate held a single enormous sausage, pinkish-gray in color, and nothing else. Lenny trailed behind him, carrying the bass and garment bag like a roadie.

"By the way," Artie reported. "Ian canceled on me."

"Oh, great."

"It's not really a problem. We're only slated for two numbers, and Jim wants to sing both of them himself."

Lenny gave the signal to begin taping a few minutes after seven. The Wishbones struck up an improvised *Tonight Show*–style intro while Cookie did his best Ed McMahon voice-over through Ian's microphone.

"From Larry's Wursthaus in the heart of the New

World Order, it's *The Genial Jim Show,* with your host, Genial Jim, and Jim's guests, Al from Pennsylvania and Otto from New Hampshire. Rest assured, friends, *The Genial Jim Show* is *not* brought to you by the United Nations, the Bureau of Alcohol, Tobacco, and Firearms, the Trilateral Commission, the O.J. Simpson Defense Team, or anyone named Goldberg. And now heeeere's . . . Jimmy!''

The Banquet Room burst into hearty applause as Genial Jim bounded onto the stage, still wearing his Tyrolean hat, and took a seat behind a green metal desk. A narrow glass vase containing a single red rose decorated one corner of the otherwise bare desktop.

''All right,'' he said with a big smile, pushing his palms against the air to suppress the ovation. ''Good crowd tonight. We've got a great show coming up. Two friends from the great states of Pennsylvania and New Hampshire are here, and they're gonna tell us about plans they're making to resist the coming one-world government, so you won't want to miss that. But before we bring them out, I'd like to do one of my Top Five Lists.'' The room erupted with shouts of approval; Genial Jim's lists were apparently a popular feature of the show. ''I know, I know, one of these days I'm going to have to kick David Letterman's butt for ripping off my idea.''

Cookie climbed onto the stage with an armful of posters, which he laid facedown on the desk. He cleared his throat, signaling his readiness to proceed.

''All right,'' said Genial Jim. ''Without further ado, here are the top five reasons why gays *should* be allowed in the U.S. military.''

Cookie lifted the top poster of the stack and showed it to the crowd.

''It's upside down,'' someone called out.

Cookie flipped it over.

''Reason Five,'' said Genial Jim. ''They need something to do when they retire from the ATF.''

The crowd hooted; Cookie tossed the poster over his shoulder and reached for the next one.

"Reason Four: Bill Clinton would finally have a good reason to serve his country."

Cookie presented the third card, but Genial Jim was laughing so hard he couldn't read it. He had to signal for a time-out.

"You want me to take over?" Cookie asked him.

Genial Jim shook his head. "That's okay. I'm better now." He wiped the grin off his face like a schoolkid. "Reason Three: *Hillary* Clinton would finally have a good reason to serve *her* country."

Dave had played a lot of weird gigs in his time—sad weddings, dances where nobody danced, a graduation party at which his amp exploded—but this was, without a doubt, the low point of his career, the nadir, the crawl space below the basement. He should have just packed up his guitar and left—they all should have—but some inexplicable sense of obligation kept him standing there, frozen by a paralysis familiar from bad dreams. *I'm just a musician,* he reminded himself. *This has nothing to do with me.*

"Reason Two: Janet Reno looks good in green."

By now the audience had reached a fever pitch of enjoyment. Genial Jim turned toward the bandstand.

"Drumroll, maestro."

Stan looked at Artie. Artie nodded. With an obvious lack of enthusiasm, Stan produced a drumroll.

"And now, the Number One Reason why gays *should* be allowed in the U.S. military—"

Cookie flipped the poster, his shoulders already heaving with unsuccessfully suppressed mirth.

"Blacks are allowed, so what the heck's the difference!"

The crowd roared; Cookie dispatched the last poster and sat down in a folding chair set up next to the desk.

"You know what?" he told his boss. "That may have been your best list yet."

"You say that every show," Genial Jim reminded him.

"I always mean it," Cookie insisted.

"It's possible," Genial Jim conceded. "I just keep getting better."

"I see we have a new addition tonight," Cookie said, pointing his finger at the Wishbones.

"That's right. These handsome fellows are our new house band."

Dave saw Lenny's camera swing in his direction and quickly bent down to tie his shoe.

"Why don't you sing a song with them?" Cookie suggested.

"Oh, I couldn't do that," said Genial Jim, suddenly the picture of shyness and humility.

"Sure you could. Why don't you sing that John Denver song, 'Country Roads.' I know you've always wanted to do that on the show."

"It's true. He writes pretty good songs for a tree-hugging, granola-sucking pansy." Genial Jim appealed directly to the crowd. "What do you think? Is a song in order?"

Cookie waved his arms, inciting applause. Genial Jim didn't seem to notice. He seemed as surprised and touched as he would have been by a spontaneous ovation.

"What the heck!" he said, leaping up from his desk. "It's my show. I can sing if I want to."

• • •

Al from Pennsylvania and Otto from New Hampshire both wore paper bags over their heads, a ploy Buzzy found hysterical despite the fact that he had to take a wicked piss. He didn't know how long he'd be able to last before laughing out loud, the way he had during Genial Jim's embarrassingly terrible rendition of that pathetic

John Denver tune. As it was, he kept snickering under his breath, despite Artie's repeated attempts to glare him into submission.

"I've got a dozen AK47s in my basement, a rocket launcher in the trunk of my car, and personal access to an armored personnel carrier in the event of an invasion by the Blue Helmets," Al from Pennsylvania boasted through his mouth hole. He was a rangy guy in camouflage pants and a khaki T-shirt; his right leg bounced up and down as he spoke, which only made Buzzy that much more aware of the fact that his own bladder was on the verge of exploding.

"An armored personnel carrier?" Genial Jim's voice hovered somewhere between admiration and disbelief. "How do you get hold of one of those?"

Al grinned inside the bag. "Let's just say I have some good friends down at the armory."

"Same goes for New Hampshire," Otto added in his laryngytic wheeze. "The armed forces of this country are crawling with white Christian warriors who are not about to lay down and die when Boutros Boutros-Ghali decides it's time to impose his globalist tyranny on American soil."

The need to laugh was an itch that demanded scratching, but Buzzy wasn't so drunk that he didn't know that laughing at Nazis—even Nazis with bags on their heads— was probably a bad idea, at least in present company. As quietly as he could, he unhooked the strap on his bass and set the instrument carefully against his amp. Ignoring the question on Dave's face, he stepped off the bandstand and tiptoed through the obstacle course of tables, chairs, and combat boots in the Banquet Room, smirking as he went. He was conscious of drawing a few dirty looks, but the hostility of these armchair storm troopers wasn't a major concern of his at the moment. He burst through the swinging doors and broke into a full-scale trot down the hallway, laughing all the way to the bathroom.

Unzipping his fly, he groaned with a relief so intense it was indistinguishable from pleasure. It occurred to him that he'd been drinking steadily for close to four hours and hadn't taken a piss since he'd started. It had to be some kind of record.

Pissing is an underrated pleasure, he thought, listening to the satisfying hiss of urine colliding with porcelain. *I feel like a fucking fire hose.*

He had barely gotten started when the skinhead with the bad complexion pushed open the door and entered the bathroom. Buzzy nodded over his shoulder to acknowledge the new arrival, but the kid responded with a sixteen-year-old's idea of an icy stare.

Buzzy returned to the business at hand, mildly perplexed by the presence of the kid so close to his back. There were, after all, two unoccupied urinals at his disposal.

"You think something's funny?" the kid snarled.

Buzzy ignored the question. His stream had begun to abate, but he wasn't anywhere near finished. A lot of piss can build up in three and a half hours.

"You hear me, dickhead? I asked you a question."

"I heard you," Buzzy sighed.

Buzzy was forty-one years old, and he'd spent much of the past quarter century in biker bars and at metal shows. He'd slam-danced, rumbled, and gotten into his share of drunken altercations. He was retired from all that, but his old instincts remained intact. His body filled with a strange sense of calm.

"I saw that smartass look on your face," the kid told him, his voice tight with fury. "Believe me, cocksucker, nobody comes here and disrespects Genial Jim like that. Especially not a faggot like you."

"What look?" Buzzy replied, still buying time. He

couldn't believe how long it was taking for him to empty out. "I don't know what look you mean."

The kid shoved him hard in the back. Buzzy stumbled forward, only keeping his balance by slapping his free hand against the wall in front of him.

"During the song. I fucking *saw* it."

Buzzy heard the hysterical edge in the kid's voice. Whatever was going to happen was going to happen soon, probably before he was ready. He didn't see much choice but to engage in a preemptive strike.

"What can I tell you, Spike?" He turned around and calmly pissed on the kid's leg, waggling his dick for maximum coverage. "Genial Jim sucks dog shit."

Despite his shaved head and weight-lifter's physique, the kid was just a kid; he couldn't get over the fact that he'd just been pissed on. He stared down at his splattered pants in amazement, as though time had stopped. Buzzy almost felt sorry for him. He'd had a bad complexion as a teenager and knew how much it hurt.

"You're guh—" the kid began, but the rest of his sentence collided with Buzzy's fist.

The impact was like nothing Buzzy had ever experienced before. He felt everything crumple at once—his hand, the kid's face. The poor kid stumbled backwards, his head slamming into the paper towel dispenser. He didn't actually collapse; he just sat down on the floor, put one hand over his mouth and nose, and started to cry like a baby.

Something terrible had happened to his right hand— Buzzy knew it right away. He had to put his dick away and zip up with his left, and it was harder than he expected. When he was finished he looked down at the bawling skinhead and shook his head.

"You're lucky," he said. "Twenty years ago I would've kicked your teeth down your throat."

At the door he turned around. Blood was oozing from between the kid's fingers.

"And do yourself a favor," he added. "Get some fucking Clearasil."

·   ·   ·

By the time they got to the hospital, Buzzy's hand bore a faint but unmistakable resemblance to a baseball glove. It was too painful for him to let the injured arm hang at his side, so he held it in front of him, cradled against his chest.

"Overlook Hospital," he muttered, as the glass doors parted to admit them to the emergency room. "Hardly a name that inspires your confidence."

Dave filled out the admission forms on Buzzy's behalf and they took their seats in the waiting area, exchanging sad smiles with relatives of the two other people in need of urgent medical attention. A fiftyish guy in a gray suit rocked back and forth in his chair, gritting his teeth and pressing on his stomach, while his wife sat beside him, doggedly paging through a *People* magazine. An Indian woman with a gold ring in her nose and a red dot on her forehead hummed softly to the beautiful little girl whose head rested on her shoulder, eyes wide open. Buzzy lifted the ice pack the nurse had given him and inspected his mutant hand.

"I hope Artie and Stan make it out of there okay. Those skinheads are not gonna be happy campers."

Dave still couldn't quite get his mind around the story Buzzy had told with such pride and relish on the way to the hospital. He'd seen the kid leap up from his table and follow Buzzy out of the Banquet Room, a scary teenage bundle of rage and acne and muscles, and a small part of his mind had registered the possibility of violence. (An even smaller part blamed Buzzy for bringing it down on himself by acting like an asshole in such obviously dicey circumstances.) He'd felt a deep sense of relief when Buzzy reappeared a few minutes later, alive and apparently well. It wasn't until he'd returned to the bandstand that Dave became aware of his injury.

"I need to go to a hospital," Buzzy told him. "I broke my hand on someone's face."

"You what?"

Buzzy grinned, a little crazily, Dave thought.

"A skinhead. I pissed on him too."

A furious round of whispering ensued as Dave and Buzzy tried to explain the situation to Artie. Buzzy thought they should all leave together ASAP, but Artie refused to abandon the equipment. At one point the discussion got so heated that one of the softball players found it necessary to make his way over to the bandstand and tell them all to "pipe the fuck down." In the end, Artie and Stan opted to stay behind.

The guy with the monster stomachache's name was called, and he and his wife were led off to an examining room. The Indian woman kept humming the same sinuous, almost hypnotic melody to her little girl, who still hadn't moved. Dave was starting to worry about her.

"This is the worst fucking thing I could have done to myself," Buzzy said. "I guess you guys are gonna have to find yourselves a new bass player on top of a new singer."

"Maybe even a new guitarist," Dave said, surprising himself with this declaration.

"Excuse me?"

Dave felt a strange pressure gathering inside his head, as if something were about to come to a boil. He reached up and massaged his temples.

"My life's a total fucking mess. I don't know what I'm doing about anything anymore."

"I'm not following you," Buzzy told him.

"I'm in love," he explained. "Her name's Gretchen. I'm a total fucking mess."

•   •   •

It was after eleven when Buzzy finally got home. He trudged upstairs, crouched down by the bedroom window, and tried to do what he had to do in the dark, with one hand. It wasn't long before JoAnn stirred.

"Buzz," she whispered. "That you?"

"Yeah."

She turned on the lamp and sat up in bed, blinking like a mole in broad daylight.

"What are you doing? What happened to your hand?"

Buzzy stood up. He put one finger to his lips.

"Don't ask questions," he told her. "There's something I have to do. You have to trust me on this."

She stared at him for a few seconds, taking stock of the cast on his hand and the sling around his neck. Buzzy knew she'd do what he asked her to. She was a good woman, the best thing that had ever happened to him. If it hadn't been for JoAnn, he'd probably be dead by now.

"Can you get this window open for me?"

"It is open."

"The screen. Pull open the screen. As high as it will go."

JoAnn climbed out of bed, wearing an old Slayer T-shirt and a pair of Buzzy's boxer shorts, white with little blue stars on them.

"I don't like the sound of this," she said.

"Trust me," he said again, brushing past her as she made her way over to the window. "I need to do this."

She lifted the screen. With his good hand, Buzzy unplugged the sixteen-inch portable TV they kept on top of his dresser for occasional bedtime viewing. The set was fairly light; he found he could lift it with one hand and carry it the short distance to the window. He set it down on the sill and looked at his wife.

"Buzzy," she said softly. "What happened to your hand?"

"No questions," he told her.

The toss he'd imagined was a dramatic two-handed overhead release, something like an inbounds pass in soccer. He'd imagined the TV falling from a great height, shattering on the concrete patio of some California luxury hotel, shards of glass sparkling like little ground stars. This was nothing like that. This was just a quick one-handed shove, followed almost immediately by a soft thud, and then a neighbor's dog barking, less in alarm than in confusion. He stuck his head out the window and saw the little white Samsung—they'd paid thirty-five dollars for it at a garage sale—lying facedown on the grass.

"There," he said, stepping back from the window, doing his best to smile. "I feel better now."

You Still Here?

Dave had already pulled up in front of his house and shut off the engine by the time he realized that he would not be going home. The confession in the emergency room had jolted him: it was the first time he'd found the courage to admit, even to himself—*especially to himself*—that love was the issue between him and Gretchen. From the moment they'd met, he'd trained himself to couch his attraction to her in safer, more tentative terms. But now the real word was out, unpremeditated, with all its unpredictable power.

He was in love, and love required drastic action. *It's been a long time,* he thought. *A long time since I've been in love.*

He had barely turned onto South Avenue when another, more radical thought entered his mind: *Was I ever in love with Julie?* He'd never doubted it before. They'd said the words thousands of times, in all kinds of tones and inflections—with awe, with sadness, playfully, matter-of-factly, angrily, in all sincerity, uncertainly, over and over.

Julie had written it on her jeans in Magic Marker, on her school notebooks, under her picture in their yearbook. Once she'd even scrawled it on his butt in red ink. He'd said it in song lyrics, whispered it in her ear, proclaimed it in letters, carved it into picnic tables and trees.

But what did it mean? They were just kids, drunk on sex and dreams, playing at something they didn't really understand. She figured he was going to be a rock star: *I love you, Dave.* He'd never gotten over the sight of her breasts: *I love you, Julie.* That was all it was. And once you start saying it, it's easier to keep saying it than it is to stop. Say it enough and you start to think it's true.

But maybe it isn't, he thought, speeding through Roselle into Elizabeth, heading for the Goethals Bridge.

Maybe it never was.

He wasn't precisely sure what he meant to do when he got to Gretchen's apartment, beyond telling her that he loved her. That was his mission, and on that small, but hardly insignificant matter, his mind was clear and resolved. Everything after it was a big scary blur.

At least he'd stopped kidding himself, though. No matter how he looked at it, he saw that he was making a dramatic break with the only life he'd ever known. At some point in the next couple of days he'd have to drive back to New Jersey and clear up the mess he'd made. The wedding would have to be canceled. Julie would hate him forever. His parents would never forgive him. They'd probably throw him out of the house.

If he was lucky, Gretchen would offer to let him move into her place, even though it was still too early for such a big step in their relationship. There they'd be in that little nothing apartment with pictures of bicycles all over the walls, trying to create a life for themselves in a swamp of bad circumstances, guilt, and next-to-no money. That was the best scenario he could imagine; lots of other ones came to mind as well.

Even so, he felt freer than he had in years, shooting down the Staten Island Expressway, listening to an old Fleshtones' tape, moving closer to his hard new life with every tick of the odometer. They could eat croissants for breakfast, take long walks in the park, maybe even get a puppy. In time he would find a New York band to play with—not a wedding band or a Christian band, but a real band, a cutting-edge garage combo that would play the small clubs downtown, the ones the people from the record labels were known to drop in on from time to time. He and Gretchen would wear berets and secondhand overcoats in the winter; they'd stay out late and have lots of friends. He'd take her best poems and set them to music. He'd been playing it safe for too long, clinging to his high-school girlfriend, sleeping in his little twin bed down the hall from Mommy and Daddy. The time had come to risk it all, to roll the dice, to finally let go and jump off the fucking cliff.

He found a parking space right in front of her building, an unheard-of stroke of luck that he couldn't help but interpret as a good omen. Parking was going to be a bitch if he moved here; he was already dreading it. But maybe he wouldn't need a car. Maybe he could quit the courier business, find something steadier, a little more challenging, maybe in a big midtown office tower, use public transportation like everyone else.

Peering up through the dense leaves of a curbside sycamore, he saw the light shining in her bedroom window, the only light on in the entire building, almost as though she were waiting up for him. He'd never imagined a street anywhere in New York City could be this quiet, even at midnight, even on a Wednesday.

His legs felt hollow and wobbly as he climbed the front

steps and entered her vestibule. For the first time, he allowed himself to wonder if he should have called first, if he was going to frighten her by ringing her doorbell unexpectedly at this time of night. But even as he raised the question he understood that this was the way it needed to be done. He put his finger on the buzzer and held it down for a long time, an interval that would have been obnoxious under any other circumstances.

He waited.

Nothing happened.

He buzzed again, this time less theatrically. Her voice crackled through the intercom, staticky and suspicious.

"Who is it?"

Dave had to hunch over, almost to waist level, to use the intercom on his end. He wondered if it had been placed that low so kids could use it, or if the builder was just an idiot.

"It's me. Dave."

Heart racing, he put his sweaty hand on the knob of the inner door, expecting to be buzzed in as usual.

He waited.

He waited some more, his courage evaporating by the second.

Finally, he buzzed again.

"Go away," she told him. "It's over."

He put his lips against the warm metal of the intercom, hating to have to do it like this. He wanted to say it in her apartment, to watch her face, to take her in his arms and repeat it a second, third, and fourth time. This was no good, overenunciating in a darkened vestibule, not even sure if his words were coming through on the other end. But there didn't seem to be any choice.

"I love you," he told her.

"Go away. You had your chance."

"Can't you hear me? I'm saying I love you."

Again he waited for her to buzz him in, unable to believe that his magic words had failed to do the trick. He rang the buzzer again, this time as uninsistently as possible.

"Go away," she said again. "Don't make me call the police."

She sounded frail and ragged through the muddled speaker, but nonetheless strangely determined. He saw no recourse but to do as she said. *Let her sleep on it,* he thought. *This is just a misunderstanding. I'll try again in the morning.*

He retreated backwards down the steps, craning his neck for a glimpse of her face in the yellow window.

But she wouldn't even give him that.

He wasn't sure how long he'd been sitting in the car, reminding himself of the necessity of starting the engine and beginning the long journey home, when he sensed some activity on the stoop of her building. Straining across the front seat, trying to ignore the gearshift jabbing into his ribs, he pressed his face against the partly opened window and saw two shadowy figures embracing in the vestibule, one of them propping open the outer door with a sneaker-clad foot.

Moments later, a man started down the steps, an overnight bag slung over his shoulder. Almost simultaneously, the outer door cracked open behind him, revealing Gretchen's head and shoulders, her glasses catching the streetlight and giving it back in two sharp glints. Furiously, Dave cranked the window all the way down.

"Good night," she called out, her voice clearly audible on the silent street. "I'll call you tomorrow."

Then she was gone. Before Dave could process this sudden glimpse and her equally sudden disappearance, the man had pushed open the wrought-iron gate and stepped onto the sidewalk, just a few feet away. With obvious annoyance, he patted the pockets of his jeans—front, then back, then front again.

"Fuck," he said, turning around to peer up at Gretchen's window.

Dave leaned further across the car, his mouth opening in disbelief.

"Randy?"

The DJ whirled on the sidewalk, startled by the sound of his own name. He squatted, bringing his face almost level with Dave's.

"Jesus," he said, squinting into the car. "You still here?"

Before Dave could manage a reply, Randy changed the subject, hitting him for a loan of twenty dollars for train fare. He'd left his wallet up at Gretchen's, he explained, and preferred not to disturb her if he could avoid it.

"She's upset. You caught her off guard with that love stuff. She wants to be alone for a while."

"I—I don't get it," Dave spluttered. "What are you even doing here?"

Tired of squatting, Randy straightened up with a grimace, supporting his lower back with both hands. There was a weariness in his voice that Dave understood he was meant to take as an accusation.

"I was *supposed* to be spending the night." Randy patted his luggage as if to supply proof for this distressing assertion. "Now I'm trying to catch the late train."

Dave's right arm had begun to quiver from the strain of supporting his awkward lean across the front seat.

"How long have you been—?"

"A couple of days. Just since Sunday."

"How'd you get her number?"

"I didn't. She called me."

"She called *you?*"

Randy shrugged. "I'm in the Yellow Pages." He glanced impatiently at his watch. "I'd love to hang out and chat, but I'm fucked if I miss this train."

Now that the initial shock had worn off, Dave had a clearer picture of his options. Gretchen was upstairs, alone in her apartment. He could give Randy the twenty bucks, send him on his way, and try her buzzer again. Maybe that was what she wanted. Maybe she'd asked Randy to leave for just that reason. Even if she didn't buzz him, he could still call her from a pay phone or leave a note in her mail slot, figure out some way to reinforce the message he'd been forced to deliver via intercom.

But all at once, with a certainty that washed over him like a wave of fatigue, he discovered that he wasn't going to do any of these things. It was late; the day had been full of nasty surprises. He had some thinking to do, but his brain felt muddled, no longer up to the task. He popped open the passenger door, sweeping some cassette boxes off the seat to clear a space for Randy.

They took the Manhattan Bridge instead of the Verrazano, cutting across Canal to the Holland Tunnel. Dave had been stuck inside the tunnel so often on his courier runs that he couldn't help but feel his spirits lift a little as they passed through the sickly yellow tube at sixty miles an hour. Randy must have sensed the change in his mood. He hadn't said much since climbing into the car, but now he wanted to explain himself.

"I couldn't believe it when she called," he said, tracing one finger over the zipper on his overnight bag. "I'd kinda forgotten about her, to tell the truth. She said she'd been thinking about calling for a while, but didn't because she was involved with someone else. But now the other thing was over, so she was wondering if we could get together sometime."

He looked up, checking to see how Dave was taking this.

"Go ahead," Dave told him. "I'm listening."

"It didn't occur to me that you—"

"I know." Dave nodded, accepting his share of the blame for Randy's confusion. "Sorry about that."

Randy made a vague gesture of absolution. "So anyway, I went into the city that night. She was even better than I remembered. We've got this chemistry, right?" He paused, in what appeared to be silent tribute to their chemistry. "Do you know she writes poetry?"

Dave nodded, smiling in spite of himself at Randy's enthusiasm.

"She mentioned it," he said.

"It's incredible stuff," Randy assured him. "Blew me away. Anyway, it wasn't until afterward . . . you know . . . that I found out that you—"

They emerged from the tunnel on the brightly lit Jersey side. Randy didn't seem to know how to finish his sentence, and Dave couldn't see much point in helping him out. The situation was painfully clear without having to dot all the *i*s.

"It's a real fucking soap opera, isn't it?"

Randy chuckled nervously, granting him that much. He waited for Dave to elaborate, but Dave had nothing to add. For a moment, all he could think about was the awful, embarrassing fact that Randy worked all day with Julie's father. It seemed like a miserable secret for Randy to have to drag around the office, the knowledge that he had listened to Jack's prospective son-in-law tell another woman that he loved her through an intercom in Brooklyn. On reflection, though, Dave couldn't imagine Randy telling Jack, or Jack believing him if he did. It hardly seemed possible, even to Dave, even this close to the actual event.

Finally, Randy couldn't stand the silence or the uncertainty any longer.

"Is it over between you and Julie?"

Dave considered the question as they followed the highway through the swampy wastelands outside Newark Airport. A tangy industrial odor flavored the air rushing through the open windows. He understood that Randy was really asking if he was going to keep fighting for

Gretchen. And it wasn't until that moment that Dave realized he wasn't.

The clear strong feelings that had launched him into the city that night already seemed like a memory. The effort it had taken simply to begin imagining a new life with Gretchen had drained him; the actual task of making that life a reality seemed way beyond his strength, too daunting even to contemplate, especially with Randy's sudden appearance in the picture. He was wiped out, like one of those underdog football teams that gives everything it has just to win the conference championship and has nothing left for the Super Bowl. This realization saddened him, but the sadness was sweetened by a faint undertone of pride. He had been defeated in some way, but not for lack of trying. He hadn't just laid down and died.

"It's never over between Julie and me," he said. "I keep thinking it is, and I keep finding out I'm wrong."

The last fifteen minutes of the ride passed in awkward patches of silence interrupted by equally awkward stabs at small talk. Dave felt a deep sense of relief when he finally pulled up in front of Randy's building in Chestnut Gardens.

"Here we are," he said.

Randy undid his seat belt, but seemed reluctant to leave the car.

"Listen," he said. "I won't hold it against you if you decide you need another DJ."

Dave couldn't help laughing. "Yeah, right. I'll explain it all to Julie. I'm sure she'll agree."

Randy nodded, conceding the point. "Maybe I'll catch a cold or something," he decided. "I know a few people who could fill in at the last minute."

"Whatever," Dave told him. The wedding felt unreal, a million miles away.

Randy slid one leg out the door, but the rest of his body

didn't follow. His face tightened with concentration.

"I'm probably gonna see Gretchen tomorrow night. I'm supposed to, anyway. Anything you want me to tell her?"

Dave shut his eyes. There were still hundreds of things he had to say to Gretchen. But she was already slipping away from him, into another orbit. It hurt to see that, to know she was lost, along with some version of himself that she'd helped to keep alive. His world seemed smaller already.

"Tell her to send me some poems."

"I'll do that," Randy assured him.

An air of finality had been hanging over the conversation for some time now, but Randy didn't seem to notice. He gnawed worriedly at his thumbnail for a few seconds, then filed the ragged edges down on the leg of his jeans.

"I know it's none of my business," he said, "but a guy could do a helluva lot worse than Julie Muller."

September

Fifteen Years in Fifteen Minutes

The rehearsal dinner makes it official in a way that none of the other preliminaries in this final hectic week have—not picking up the wedding rings and the engraved key chains at Gold Star jewelers, not spray-painting the rust spots on his Metro at the strong urging of Julie's father, not submitting, against his own better judgment, to a last-minute trim and sideburn adjustment at Hair Down Below, not renting a tropical-motif bow tie and cummer-bund at Rod's Formals to add a little zest to his otherwise plain—Julie called it ''drab''—Wishbones tuxedo. An ex-cruciating forty-five-minute discussion on ''the joys and obligations of marriage'' with Julie's minister, a burly, New Age Presbyterian who insisted on the three of them holding hands in a circle as though conducting a séance hadn't done the trick, nor had the somewhat dispiriting bachelor party at Glenn's house, which Dave had spent shuttling between a basement jam session, a kitchen-table poker game, and a seemingly endless living-room video—on loan from Artie's private collection—that featured one "amateur" couple after another engaging in anal sex, close-up and in real time.

But now, surveying the single long table in the lavender-walled "Function Room" in the basement of Aldo's Ristorante, occupied end-to-end by smiling, well-dressed people, some of whom have traveled impressive distances to be here, he feels an unfamiliar sense of shyness and solemnity settle over him, and he freezes in the doorway, his mouth dropping open as though this is a surprise party in his honor, rather than an event he's known about for several months and, in fact, helped to plan.

The obvious people are here—his parents, brother and sister-in-law, Julie's parents, her two sisters and their respective spouses, her great-aunt Bertha, the wedding party, a handful of out-of-town guests, and a couple of stragglers. This last category includes Ian, who's tagging along with Tammi; as Maid of Honor, she apparently managed to finagle a last-minute addition to the guest list. Dave's happy to see him, his lingering resentment temporarily eclipsed by pleasure that another one of his bandmates could make it. His eyes settle next on his brother Chuck—Dave can't help thinking of him as "Chick," his now-renounced boyhood nickname—just in from North Carolina with his hugely pregnant wife, both of them basking in the attention that her condition can't fail to evoke at a gathering such as this, especially since Linda's packing twins, fruit of the best fertility technology two large corporate salaries can buy. Chuck and Linda met in business school and happily describe themselves as "bean counters" to anyone who inquires about their line of work, though the beans they count belong to a gigantic poultry-processing empire. Dave has only met Linda a few times, and her main effect is to remind him of how far apart he and his brother have drifted since the days when Chick shared the room that Dave now considers his own, back when they engaged in elaborate Nerf basketball

tournaments, played each other their new records, and
gawked in undisguised wonderment at Carly Simon's nipples on the cover of *No Secrets*. It's less that Dave dislikes
Linda than that they simply miss each other, like cars
traveling at high speed in opposite directions. She wrinkles her forehead at his jokes and asks lots of complicated
questions about the courier business, as though he were
the owner of the company, rather than a thirty-two-year-
old schmuck without a real job. This visit already feels
different, though. His marriage and her pregnancy have
saved them; small talk is simple, her happiness both radiant and infectious. She even seems to have acquired a
North Carolina accent over the past couple of years, a
surprising development considering that the first three decades of her life were spent in Minnesota and Chicago.

Julie studies him from her seat at one end of the table,
head tilted at an angle that seems to convey flirtation and
suspicion at the same time. She's been looking especially
good to him now that they've stopped having sex, and
tonight she's glowing. Her hair looks different, flowing
over her shoulders in a loosely kinked perm he finds as
alluring as it is unexpected. After all these years, his
straight-haired girlfriend has suddenly turned into one of
those wavy-haired women he sees all the time on the
streets of New York and can't help fantasizing about.
She's wearing a new dress, a sleeveless, mustard-colored
sheath similar to the one Gretchen wore on her birthday,
but the effect is entirely different—warmer, less elegant,
more overtly sexual. Less Gretchen and more Julie.

He's been thinking a lot about Gretchen these past few
weeks, sometimes with a piercing sense of loss, sometimes with a quieter sadness, as though she were someone
he'd loved a long time ago and had somehow learned to
live without. They've had no contact at all since his last
visit except for a spiral-bound book of her poems that
arrived in the mail about a week ago, with no note attached. He reads them almost daily with the concentration

he'd devoted as a teenager to lyrics by Patti Smith and Blue Öyster Cult, teasing out the implications of every single line, hoping for a flash of mental lightning. He's given up trying to understand them, searching only for a glimpse of her in the language, or a possible secret message for himself. He's looking forward to hearing more about her tomorrow from Rockin' Randy, who called yesterday to report that he'd been unable to find a substitute DJ and would, in fact, be providing the entertainment as planned, if Dave didn't mind. Dave said he didn't.

By now, he's been standing in the doorway a little too long, and the Function Room has grown appreciably quieter. Almost everyone at the table is staring at him, their smiles beginning to fade. His mother's giving him that squinty look, the one that means *Grow up, already!*, and Julie's jabbing her finger to indicate that the empty seat between her father and her sister Melanie belongs to him, and Dave finally understands that the moment has arrived, and that he really is going to do this.

• • •

Artie's aware of the risks, but the band's in bad enough shape that it almost doesn't matter. The inspiration came to him a couple of weeks ago, shortly after the Genial Jim fiasco, and since then he's put the plan into operation with such speed and conviction that it's starting to feel eerie, almost as if he's the tool of some higher power. He canceled a scheduled gig—an unheard-of act in the annals of the Wishbones—and found top-notch replacements for Buzzy and Ian and Dave. All that remains is this one last obstacle, minor but potentially treacherous.

At quarter to nine sharp, he pulls up in front of Stan's house and beeps twice. *You better be home,* he mutters to himself. *Don't fuck up on me now.* The words are barely out when Stan's shadowy form comes lumbering down the steps. He's not mean-looking, but he is big—football-player big—with meaty biceps and a vaguely Neanderthal dangle to his arms. Considering that he was able to face down three angry skinheads who wanted revenge for their buddy's broken nose, Artie figures he'll do just fine on tonight's more placid mission.

Stan slides into the passenger seat, dressed exactly as Artie instructed him—black jeans, black T-shirt, the same scuffed-up work boots he'd worn to the showcase the night Phil Hart collapsed, the boots Artie almost fired him over. It's disconcerting to admit it, but in a matter of a few months, Stan's gone from being the least reliable Wishbone to the one guy Artie knows he can count on. Sure, Buzzy cares about the band, but a bass player with a broken hand, no driver's license, and a serious drinking problem hardly rates as a model employee. Even Dave— rock-solid Dave, the guy he'd always considered his pillar of strength—has been faltering lately, fucking up at practice, going through the motions at gigs. Artie hopes like hell it's just the temporary distraction of his marriage, but he's seen these signs before and they're not encouraging. And Ian—Artie can't even think about Ian without having to pop a Motrin and wash it down with a mouthful of Mylanta. He still wakes up in a cold sweat a couple of nights a week, wondering what the hell they're supposed to do without him, how they're going to scrounge up someone even remotely qualified to fill his shoes. Artie's not stupid; he knows what's out there. It's scary, a frigging horror show of no-talent crooners whose egos somehow haven't gotten the message. The thought of auditioning a parade of these clowns paralyzes him with dread; this, he knows, is when the enormity of the band's loss will finally become apparent. And avoiding this moment is the real, if unlikely, objective of Artie's plan. As much as he wants to celebrate Dave's wedding in the proper style, what he really wants to do is make Ian jealous, to remind him, as vividly as possible, of the good thing he's turned his back on.

"So tell me," Stan says, ostentatiously cracking his knuckles as Artie pulls away from the curb, "how are we going to work this?"

"We're just gonna talk to the guy," Artie explains. "Show him what's in his best interest. I don't expect any trouble."

"But what am I supposed to say?"

"Nothing. I'll do all the talking. You just stand there and look interested. I've got it all figured out."

"How do we even know he's gonna be home?"

"We've got an appointment," Artie informs him. "We're the search committee for our company Christmas party."

Stan seems pleased by this ruse, but also a bit concerned. "What's the name of our company?"

"Who the fuck cares? It's just some bullshit I fed him to make the appointment."

"What if he asks?"

"Trust me, Stan. It's not important."

Stan shrugs. "I just like to be prepared."

"Okay," Artie tells him. "Fine. Just make something up. Dickhead Industries, Cocksucker, Incorporated, whatever you want. Fuckwad Technologies."

"Pussyco," Stan adds, after a moment's consideration.

"Prick, Wang, and Peter."

"Sphincter Brothers."

"Turd-Tek."

"Dildo and Son."

"Cunnilingus Farms."

Stan pauses, momentarily stumped. Then he smiles with satisfaction.

"Testicle Laboratories."

"Scrotum World."

"Scrotum World." Stan shakes his head, choking with laughter. "I like that." He mimes a handshake. "Hi, there. We're from Scrotum World. Damn glad to meet you."

They fall silent for a minute or two, unable to continue. A new one occurs to Artie, and he can't stop himself from laughing.

"What?" says Stan.

"Nothing."

"Come on."

"You won't get it."

"Sure I will."

"You won't. I'm telling you."

"Try me anyway."

"Okay." Artie clears his throat, smirking with barely suppressed hilarity. "The Merkin King."

Stan's eyes narrow. "The Merkin King?"

Artie slaps his leg, celebrating his own cleverness.

"Yup," he says. "The Merkin King."

"What the fuck's a merkin?"

"Look it up," Artie tells him. "You're in for a treat."

• • •

Dave's always liked Julie's sister Mel, but something seems to have happened to her in the past year or so. She hasn't worked for a long time now, not since the birth of her first child, but now that both girls are in school she clearly has too much time on her hands. All through dinner she talks obsessively about the O.J. Simpson trial, which she's been watching pretty much in its entirety, almost as though she considers herself some kind of alternate, out-of-state juror.

"But what about the Vannatter testimony?" she asks Paul, the annoying guy who's hogging the spot in the wedding party Dave had hoped to reserve for Ian. (Paul had inexplicably asked Dave to usher at his wedding, and Dave felt he had no choice but to reciprocate.) "You've got to admit, some of his behavior was pretty suspicious."

Paul doesn't want to hear it.

"The guy's guilty," he says, offering the table a candid

glimpse of the chewed-up mouthful of chicken parmigiana he seems curiously reluctant to swallow. "His DNA's all over the place."

Paul shifts his glance from Mel to Dave, hoping to bolster his case with some moral support from the groom-to-be. Dave hesitates, dreading the thought of becoming enmeshed in yet another conversation about O.J. Simpson. For months now, he's been doing his best to ignore the trial, but it's been an uphill battle, like pretending not to notice that it's Christmastime in December. He's also less than eager to cast his lot with Paul, whom he's had trouble talking to ever since Julie mentioned that he makes his wife have sex with him pretty much on a daily basis, whether she wants to or not. It's not that Dave thinks it's any of his business what Paul and Margaret do in bed, but it's hard to focus on anything else when he happens to find himself in their company. On the other hand, he's just spent fifteen minutes listening to Julie's father explain his elaborate theories about car washing and knows there's more where that came from, so it's not like he has anywhere else to turn.

"I haven't really been following it," he admits, "but I thought he was guilty right from the start. I mean, that suicide note, or whatever it was, didn't sound like it was written by an innocent man."

"Right." Paul turns back to Melanie, nodding triumphantly. "Exactly. What about that note?"

"It wasn't admitted into evidence," she tells him. "Besides, you're changing the subject. I was talking about the police."

"The guy's guilty," Paul insists. "He beat her, he threatened her, and then he sliced her throat."

"What about the glove?" Mel asks. "It didn't fit. There are just so many ways for a jury to find reasonable doubt."

"Bullshit," Paul declares. "No jury in their right mind could acquit."

"You never know," Dave points out. "Look at the Rodney King case. There you had the videotape and everything and they still acquitted."

Paul looks troubled, almost like Dave's betrayed him. He picks up his napkin and dabs at the corners of his mouth, buying time.

"That was different," he says finally.

"Why?" asks Mel.

"The cops were scared," Paul informs them. "The guy was going apeshit. He had to be restrained."

Dave takes another sip of wine and looks around the table, searching for a way out. Ian's locked in conversation with Tammi. Julie's chatting with Dave's mother and sister-in-law, and Buzzy's telling a story to Dave's father. Glenn's disappeared. Dave sighs and turns back to Mr. Muller, who's been eating his pasta with an air of deep reflection.

"So," he says. "What's that you were saying about Armor-All?"

In the middle of dessert, Dave's father begins tapping his butter knife against his water glass. He keeps this up longer than necessary, looking flushed and cheerful, necktie askew, and doesn't stop until Dave's mother takes hold of his wrist.

"Hear ye, hear ye," he says. "Before Julie makes her, uh . . . presentation, Jane and I would just like to say a couple of words."

He turns to Dave's mother, yielding the floor. Dave leans out over the table, trying to make eye contact with Julie, but she's looking the other way. No one's told him anything about a "presentation."

"This is a very happy night for all of us," his mother says, and he can see from her face that she means it. Her smile seems effortless, not strained and fake the way it sometimes gets during holiday gatherings, when she's been on her feet too long, cooking and cleaning with next-to-no-help from the men in the house. "There are so many people we'd like to thank, especially Jack and Dolores Muller, for their kindness to us and our son for all these"—she screws up her face, as if the math is too complicated to perform on the spot—"these many, many years."

Laughter ripples through the room. *Oh great,* Dave thinks, warm blood rising into his face as he spoons up a melted blob of ice cream, *here it comes.* His mother looks across the table, her eyes locking with his.

"I have to be honest," she continues, her smile morphing into a sadder, more thoughtful expression. "There were times when I didn't think I'd live long enough to see this day."

"Me neither," Julie's great-aunt Bertha chimes in emphatically. Bertha's eighty-seven and uses a walker, so it's not really a joke, but everyone laughs anyway.

"Thank you," his mother tells Julie, her voice wavering with emotion. "Thank you for waiting."

Almost as if it's prearranged, like some kind of reunion of long-lost relatives on Phil Donahue, both women rise simultaneously from their chairs. Dave's mother stands still while Julie loops around the head of the table to meet her. Then, with a passion that startles Dave, they embrace in front of everyone, the woman who is his mother and the one who's going to be his wife. As the room bursts into applause, it suddenly occurs to him that they are the exact same height and share the same basic build, sturdy and shapely—*womanly* is the word that comes to mind. It's strange that he's never noticed it before.

His mother sits down, smiling to fight off tears, while Julie makes her way back to her own seat, blushing fiercely. Dave tries to signal her, but she keeps her eyes down, unwilling to share the moment.

Some invisible baton seems to have been passed and his father takes the spotlight. He's got that scary look on his face, the pompous, slightly bemused expression Dave has come to associate with supper-time oratory.

"Maybe the other parents in the room see it differently," he begins, "but it's always seemed to me that the most mysterious people in the world are your own kids. You bring them into the world, you feed and clothe them and teach them as best you know how, and then one day you wake up and find these . . . these *strangers* living in your house. These teenagers. They listen to this horrible music, they wear these awful clothes, they mumble when they talk. They don't always smell so good. You know it's a phase, but sometimes it doesn't seem like that. Sometimes you can't help wondering what happened to that cute little kid you used to bounce on your knee, if you're ever going to see him again, or if you're going to have to get used to this alien who's invaded your kid's room and taken over his name."

Dave finally catches his mother's eye and wordlessly asks her what the hell his father is blathering on about. She responds with an indulgent shrug, still beaming from her moment in the sun.

"I went through this with both of my sons," his father continues, "but I have to admit, the whole thing was much more severe with Dave. Part of it was the music, I guess, the way he threw himself into it and couldn't seem to think about anything else. There were days when he didn't really seem to be living in the same world—let alone the same house—as the rest of us. We stopped talking and I almost came to dread those times when I had to take him somewhere, just the two of us in the car, because that meant we'd have to try to talk to each other. I mean, there was a year or two when I really did think he was lost. If he was taking drugs or whatever, or if he maybe just hated my guts. And then one day in . . . 1979 or '80, it must have been, he brought this girl home. She was pretty and smart and she looked you right in the eye and had the most wonderful laugh, and my son seemed like a different person around her, like the Dave I used to know, funny and attentive, and I remember looking at this girl and thinking, *Marry her, kid. Don't let this one get away,* and I've never stopped thinking it since. Not for a day." He pauses as the room releases a collective "aaah," then smiles across the table at Dave. "Congratulations, kid. You finally read my mind."

Dave's father raises his glass, his arm fully extended in front of him. Dave sees it all so clearly—his father's face, the pale yellow wine, his mother nodding and biting her lip as she reaches for her water glass, Buzzy in the foreground, stuffing a cannoli into his wide-open mouth.

"God bless you," his father says, his voice clear and strong. "God bless both of you."

• • •

No deception, persuasion, or arm-twisting is even remotely necessary. Randy recognizes them right away as members of the Wishbones, and invites them upstairs for a beer. He doesn't seem at all troubled by the fact that they aren't the search committee for Fuckwad Technologies.

The guy's apartment is a music lover's paradise, and for a minute or two Artie and Stan forget why they've come and just scan the shelves like kids in a toy store. An old Weather Report album's on, something Artie hasn't listened to for years. It sounds even better than he remembered.

"We need to talk to you about the wedding tomorrow," Artie begins, as soon as Randy returns from the kitchen with the beers.

Randy nods, as if he'd expected as much.

"I guess Dave sent you," he says.

"Excuse me?" Artie can't quite hide his confusion. "What makes you think that?"

"He didn't?" Now it's Randy's turn to look puzzled.

Artie shakes his head. "We're doing this on our own. How would you feel about letting us take the gig?"

Randy shrugs. "No problem."

Artie shoots a quick glance at Stan, who seems more concerned with the label on his beer bottle than he is with the conversation.

"Elm City?" he says.

"It's from Connecticut," Randy informs him. "It's not bad."

"Interesting." Stan takes a swig, swirling the beer around in his mouth like a wine taster. "What is it, one of those microbrews?"

"I think so," says Randy.

"Expensive?"

"Pretty reasonable, actually."

"You're okay about this?" Artie asks, trying to steer the conversation back to more relevant matters.

"No problem," Randy repeats. "You want it, it's yours."

"You'll still get paid," Artie assures him. "I'll work it out with Julie's father."

"Don't worry about it."

"I mean it," says Artie. "We're not trying to steal anything. This isn't about money. It's just our wedding present to Dave and Julie."

"It's cool," Randy says, waving him off. "I don't want the money. It's kind of a relief, actually. I've got this new girlfriend, and these weekend gigs are starting to interfere with our relationship. I'm happy just for the night off."

Artie's getting that weird feeling again, like everything's falling into place a little too easily. He turns to share his astonishment, but Stan's wandered away from the conversation, kneeling to examine the albums Randy's filed under the rubric of "Acid Rock."

"We appreciate it," Artie says. "It's really big of you."

"Dave's a good guy," Randy tells him. "Good taste in women."

"Damn," Stan calls out. He pulls an album out of the stack and waves it in the air. "Do you have everything Captain Beefheart ever did or what?"

"His stuff holds up," Randy says, nodding his approval. "You want me to put that on?"

•   •   •

Dave never expected to find himself home at eleven o'clock with no one to talk to on the night before his wedding, but here he is. He figured he'd be out getting drunk or watching some nearly naked woman hump a metal pole, doing *something* to mark the passing of the last night of the first phase of his life. But when the time came, no one was available. Ian and Tammi had another party to go to. Glenn was wiped out; he said his new medication was wreaking havoc with his sleep/wake cycle. Even Buzzy begged off. He was making an effort to cut down on his drinking and be a more responsible husband and father, and had promised JoAnn he'd be home as soon as the dinner ended.

His own family didn't have much more to offer in the way of company. Chuck and Linda disappeared upstairs as soon as they got into the house, both looking exhausted. (They're sleeping on the twin beds in Dave's room, leaving him to fend for himself on the furry couch in the TV room, hardly luxury quarters for his last night in the family home.) His parents stayed up for a brief, self-congratulatory postmortem on the dinner, then hightailed it up to bed, repeatedly reminding Dave and themselves of the fact that they all had "a big day coming up."

Dave gives some serious consideration to calling Julie, but resists the temptation, knowing how concerned she is about looking fresh and rested on her wedding day. He wants to tell her again how surprised and moved he was by her slide presentation, which she'd introduced to the dinner guests as *Dave and Julie: Fifteen Years in Fifteen Minutes.*

"Some of you might have been wondering what took us so long," she said. A few people giggled, even though Julie didn't seem to be making a joke. "It's a question I've asked myself more than once. This was the only answer I could come up with."

What followed was a blizzard of images, arranged in no particular order. Prom pictures, vacation snapshots, photographs from weddings, retirement parties, graduations, picnics, birthdays, Christmases, and countless forgotten occasions. Julie making a human pyramid with some college friends. Dave singing with the Tragics, his short-lived New Wave band, wearing his trademark dinner jacket and ascot. Julie in a pink bikini and sunglasses, sitting atop a tall lifeguard chair, whistle around her neck. Dave with his shirt off, posing beneath his father's prize sunflower. Dave and Julie mugging in a photo booth, looking impossibly young and happy. The boys from Löckjaw. A chorus line of Julie and her sisters, all three wearing identical flannel nightgowns and kneesocks, kicking for the camera. The Wishbones rehearsing in street clothes. Julie as a bridesmaid. Dave in an ugly suit. Julie acting in a college play Dave never saw, due to the fact that she was living with Brendan at the time. Four of the five members of Lost Cause standing in front of a kiddie airplane ride on the boardwalk at Asbury Park, looking like contestants in a Bruce Springsteen wannabe contest. Julie and her young-looking father carrying boxes into a dorm. Sensitive Dave singing at an open mike, during an abortive attempt to reinvent himself as a folkie. Julie glamorous in a black leather jacket, cigarette planted between bright red lips. Five-year-old Dave, wearing an Indian warbonnet, blowing on a toy trumpet. Five-year-old Julie, dressed like a bride for Halloween.

It wasn't just the pictures, though. Julie had put together a sound track of songs performed by bands Dave had played in over the past decade and a half. Exit 36 doing a credible rendition of ''Angie.'' Lost Cause covering ''Should I Stay or Should I Go?'' The Tragics playing ''Scared of the Light,'' probably the best song Dave had ever written. And finally, the Wishbones' exuberant version of ''Brown-Eyed Girl,'' from a promo tape they'd put together about a year ago.

The show ended with a rapid-fire series of Dave and Julie kissing. Some of them were little pecks obviously staged for the camera, but others were candid shots. They kissed in a pool. In a photo booth. At someone's wedding. On Christmas morning. Passionately. On a couch. Under a tree. As sixteen-year-olds. Just the other day. Dave sat there laughing as the memories rolled by, and for a minute or two, his life seemed to have consisted of nothing but love and music, and it seemed to him as good a life as he ever could have wished for.

Sometime after midnight he looks up and sees his brother standing in the doorway of the TV room, a bulky, balding guy with incongruously trendy eyeglasses, wearing a V-neck T-shirt and red flannel boxers with blue cowboy hats and yellow lassos printed on them.

''Hey,'' says Dave. ''Cool shorts.''

Chuck ponders his racy underwear for a few seconds, shaking his head as if at a loss to explain the presence of such an item of clothing on his body.

''Doctor's orders,'' he reports. ''Boxers are better for the blood flow.''

''After those twins are born you might want to go back to briefs, just to be on the safe side. Maybe get them a size or two too small.''

Chuck lifts the front of his T-shirt to display an impressive roll of flab drooping over the puckered waistband of his shorts. "These days everything is a size or two too small. I think I'm having a sympathetic pregnancy or something. I have more cravings than Linda does." He says this in a tone that expresses wonder rather than regret, and Dave understands for the first time just how happy his brother is at the prospect of fatherhood. Ever since adolescence, Chuck's been fighting a weight problem with a near-religious regimen of jogging and weight lifting and pickup basketball. It was his only vanity, and he seems to have surrendered it without a second thought. "Twenty pounds in seven months," he laughs. "It's kind of amazing."

Dave clicks off the TV to signify his availability for a more serious conversation, and his brother accepts the invitation, abandoning the doorway for a seat on the worn velveteen recliner.

"I thought you were asleep," Dave tells him.

Chuck shakes his head. "I got a second wind."

"Linda looks great."

"Doesn't she?" His brother grins. "I never realized how sexy pregnant women could be."

Dave doesn't reply. Linda looks happy, all right, but "sexy" isn't a word he'd use to describe her in her present state. Her face is bright red and she needs help just to get out of a chair. She wears sneakers all the time because her shoes no longer fit her swollen feet. Dave can't even begin to imagine how big she's going to be in another eight weeks.

"That was a terrific slide show," Chuck tells him. "I guess you two have a lot of pictures to choose from."

"Julie did the whole thing. I didn't even know she was putting it together."

"Mom and Pop really enjoyed it." Chuck glances up at the ceiling, as if he can see right into their bedroom. "I haven't seen them so happy in a long time."

"Listen," Dave says. "About the Best Man thing. I hope—"

Chuck waves him off. "No problem. It's a hundred percent okay with me."

"You sure?"

"Absolutely."

"It's just—I don't know, I thought it would be good for Glenn. He's so cut off from the world most of the time. I just hope he's not too nervous tomorrow."

"He'll be fine," Chuck says, and for some reason Dave knows that his brother's right. Glenn will be fine. For the moment, it seems like they all will.

The conversation appears to have run its course. Chuck yawns and a pleasant feeling of drowsiness settles over Dave, the first inkling he's had that he might actually be able to fall asleep tonight. He puts his feet up on the couch and leans back against the armrest.

"I can't believe I'm getting married tomorrow," he says.

"Believe it," Chuck tells him, getting up from the chair.

Brothers in another family might have chosen this moment to hug each other, but Dave and Chuck say good night the Raymond way, trading casual, almost imperceptible nods, like distant acquaintances passing on the street. In the doorway, Chuck stops and turns around.

"By the way," he says, "who's Marlene Fragment?"

"What?" Dave says, a little too loudly.

"Marlene Fragment," Chuck says again. "The poet."

Dave can't quite believe what he's hearing.

"How do you know Marlene Fragment?"

"There's a book of hers up in the bedroom. I'm thinking about using one of the poems for my reading tomorrow."

"I thought you were doing that thing from *Four Weddings and a Funeral.*"

"I was. But I talked to Paul, and he said he was doing the same thing."

Dave's shock has begun to wear off. He tries to think

of a good reason why Chuck shouldn't read one of Gretchen's poems at the ceremony, but can't come up with any. In fact, he kind of likes the idea.

"Which poem?"

"I'm not sure yet. There are a couple that look like they might work."

"It's your call," he tells his brother.

It's a warm night, and Dave likes sleeping with the window open. At first, he thinks it's a raccoon outside making the scratching noise and tries to ignore it. But then he hears the whisper, just inches from his head.

"Hey," she says. "It's me. Open the window."

Dream of a Lifetime

Despite the fact that it's held in a church rather than on a football field, the wedding ceremony reminds him of nothing so much as high-school graduation. There's that same feeling of anonymous ritual, the same need to walk more slowly than usual, the same illusion that the audience consists of his family and a bunch of extras. Taking his place next to Glenn at the front of the church—there's no altar in the Catholic sense, just a raised stage and a podium surrounded by flowers—Dave wonders if the bridesmaids and ushers flanking him on both sides share this feeling of déjà vu, or if it's somehow a product of his own arrested development, if the day will ever come when the world stops reminding him of high school.

The minister, Godfrey Tucker, greets him with a toothy smile and an unsolicited full-body hug that Dave has no choice but to submit to, like a child set upon by an adoring grandparent. Glenn, less demonstrative by nature, settles for delivering a kindly, somewhat tentative pat on the shoulder. He looks bug-eyed and a little sweaty, and Dave can see the effort it's costing him to stand up here in full view of the hundred or so assembled guests. Further down the line, his brother, Buzzy, and Paul flash a synchronized thumbs-up that would have made the Temptations proud. To his left, the Maid of Honor and the three brides- maids—Julie has repeatedly instructed him to use the term *attendants* but he can't bring himself to do it—are all peering at him with the kind of unqualified approval that life so rarely offers, at least in Dave's experience.

The minister clears his throat, and Dave turns just in time to see Julie and her father move into view at the far end of the church. At almost the same moment, the au- dience rises as one, turning to face the center aisle. A strange hush overtakes the church. Then, for a few sec- onds, nothing happens. Clothes rustle, voices murmur. Heads peer up in the direction of the choir loft. The min- ister clears his throat again, this time more loudly, and suddenly the watery strains of an organ fill the air, the inevitable fanfare signaling that the star is here, the show's ready to begin.

And this too is like commencement: the stupid music gets to him. An instantaneous lump forms in his throat, squeezing upward, and before he has a chance to defend himself, his eyes are crinkled and dangerously moist, and his bottom lip is sliding around so much he has to bite it to keep it in place. His shoulders start to heave. By any- one's definition, he's crying. "Pomp and Circumstance" did the same thing to him, but at least then he was lost in a crowd, and only had to worry about the snickering sidelong glances of Mark Rizzotti, the asshole to his right, who kept elbowing him and saying, "Don't cry, honey. It'll be okay." But now he's standing in full view of a churchful of Mark Rizzottis, gulping for air as his bride approaches.

The bridal march, or whatever the hell it's called, seems to take forever. Flashbulbs are popping, Julie's smiling and mouthing hellos to people on both sides of the aisle, her father's looking dead ahead, his eyes wide open and oddly unfocused. Dave usually hates that description of someone looking like "a deer caught in the headlights"—he, for one, has never seen such a thing—but that's the phrase that comes into his mind as he watches Mr. Muller approach, moving as stiffly as a toy soldier, his lovely daughter welded to his arm.

Julie looks radiant, not tired at all, despite the fact that they'd stayed up until three in the morning, making up for weeks of voluntary prenuptial celibacy. (After he helped pull her through the window—a task greatly facilitated by the picnic bench she'd dragged up against the house—she confessed that she'd always wanted to sneak out of her parents' house in the middle of the night for a wild sexual encounter, and figured that she'd never have the chance again.) And it was wild, in an unexpected sort of way. For the first time since her abortion five years earlier, they made love without protection—Dave's novelty condom assortment was upstairs, hidden in his bedroom closet—and he understood without her having to tell him that it was for real now, that they were summoning forces beyond their control. And it felt different to him, more adult and consequential than any sex he'd ever had before. He's still terrified by the thought of becoming a father, but the fear seems less theoretical now, more intimate and potentially manageable, something he might even learn to live with or move beyond. Julie must have felt something new as well, because she'd given herself up to the act with a passion Dave had almost forgotten she was capable of, crying out like she wanted to wake up his parents and show them the spectacle her own parents had stumbled upon such a short time ago, in what already felt like another era.

But the events of the previous night are just one of the many secrets they share—among the many others they don't—as Mr. Muller unlocks his arm from Julie's at the front of the church and offers Dave a clammy handshake.

"Take good care of her," he mutters. There's a weary resignation in his voice, as though he doesn't quite believe this is possible, but has no choice but to take his chances.

"I will," Dave promises.

Mr. Muller extracts his hand from Dave's. He kisses Julie on the cheek and retreats to his front-row seat. Julie passes her bouquet to Tammi and takes her place next to Dave, interlacing the fingers of her right hand with the fingers of his left. Except for this odd little fairy godmother tiara her mother insisted upon her wearing—they've been squabbling about it for weeks—she looks stunning in her gown, which is both simple and traditional, and also happens to reveal what strikes Dave as a daring amount of cleavage. She glances at him quickly, but then does a double take, her face lighting up with pleasure.

"Are you crying?" she whispers.

He doesn't have time to answer, though, because the minister chooses just that moment to tap on the microphone and ask if everyone can hear him in the back.

All through the readings Julie keeps sneaking delighted looks at him, as if he's won her heart forever by crying at their wedding. Dave's composed now, slightly sheepish, but also a bit irritated; he has a feeling he's never going to hear the end of it for as long as he lives. He imagines her telling it to their kids—*I was such a beautiful bride, your father wept when he saw me walking down the aisle*—the story becoming one of those family legends passed down for generations, like the one about his mother's parents meeting at Ellis Island or the one about his father getting a flat tire on the way to his wedding, then opening the trunk only to discover that his spare was flat as well. He and Julie aren't even married yet and already he feels himself being transformed into a historical figure, frozen into anecdote by his unborn children and grandchildren.

Julie's sister Claire is reading that passage from the Bible about love being patient and kind; Dave's heard it a hundred times, and the words drift past him like Muzak, pleasant and forgettable. The two previous readings affected him in the same way—Margaret led off with "the marriage of true minds," and Paul followed with that poem from *Four Weddings and a Funeral*—the sentiments so airy and pure they seemed to have about as much to do with him and Julie as a commencement speech does with the average graduate. It's a formality, something you have to sit through before the diplomas get handed out.

But maybe he's just distracted. His brother's last on the list of readers, and Dave finds himself unexpectedly jittery at the approach of Gretchen's poem (he still doesn't know which one his brother has chosen). Now that he's here, trying to focus on the moment at hand, he senses clearly the danger of her presence, even in verse form. She might as well be sitting in the front row, right between his mother and his pregnant sister-in-law, wearing a short dress and the pained expression he always found—and would still find, if he were lucky or unlucky enough to see her—inexplicably attractive and challenging. He remembers her telling him that there's no way not to be pathetic on the day of your boyfriend's wedding and wonders what she's doing to mark or ignore the occasion. At least he knows she's not with Randy, and for some reason—not that he's proud of it—this gives him a certain amount of satisfaction.

Claire steps down from the podium, a forty-one-year-old hospital administrator trying gamely to uphold her dignity in a shiny peach-colored dress with puffy sleeves, a plunging neckline, and an orange sash tied around her waist. Chuck brushes past her on his way up, looking mature and substantial in his tux, every inch the prosperous bean counter that he is. Once installed behind the lectern, he fishes a pair of reading glasses out of his pocket and makes a bit of a production out of affixing them to his face. Dave wonders if he learned to do this at some sort of public-speaking seminar.

"On the occasion of Dave and Julie's wedding," he says, pausing to make eye contact with his audience, "I'd like to read a poem by Marlene Fragment."

With a subtle flourish, he withdraws a folded sheet of paper from his jacket pocket and smooths it out on the lectern. Dave glances at Julie, but she's busy whispering something to Tammi. As soon as his brother begins to read, Dave recognizes the poem. It's a new one, entitled "my FINAL offer," and not a favorite of his, though it is one of the few poems in her collection even remotely suitable for a wedding:

> You were a gift, I think
> And now I offer one in return
> If I could
> I'd take my beating heart
> And place it in a box
> Tie it shut with a pretty pink ribbon
> And deliver it to your doorstep
> Urgent overnight
>
> But that's no longer possible
> So here's the next best thing
> A little brown bag
> Full of hopes, dreams, and feelings
> My earthly treasure
>
> Take it, my love
> Treat it well, and carry it with you
> Always
> The red pulsing heart of everything I am.

Chuck looks around for a few seconds after he's finished, as if he's willing to entertain questions from the audience. When it's clear that none are forthcoming, he carefully refolds the paper and tucks it back in his pocket. Then he removes the glasses with a slow, deliberate air, stretching out his time in the limelight. When Dave finally works up the courage to check Julie's reaction, it's clear she's been smirking at him for some time.

"Jeez," she whispers. "Where'd he dig that up?"

Once the vows begin, the world shrinks down and time speeds up. The most crucial phase of the ceremony vanishes in a blur of repeated words, more like a memory test than a pledge of lifelong commitment. Rings are exchanged; a blessing is spoken. A kiss follows—a nice one, sexy but not ostentatious—but it's over before it starts, and the next thing he knows the organ's playing again, and people are clapping.

"Come on," Julie says, tugging at his arm. "Time to go."

Dave looks around in disbelief. Flashbulbs pop. Every face he sees is smiling. *That's it?* he wants to say. *That's what all the fuss is about?*

By contrast, the receiving line seems to take forever. It's a little like drowning, your life passing before you in the form of aunts, uncles, neighbors, friends, co-workers (with a few strangers thrown in to keep you guessing), kissing your cheek, shaking your hand, telling you you're a lucky man, demanding to know what took you so long, saying, "Ha ha, welcome to the club," and making not-so-discreet inquiries about the possibility of a little Dave or Julie on the horizon.

When the line finally dwindles down to nothing, the newlyweds step out of the church into the sunlight—it's a glorious September day, warm and golden, as if summer hasn't yet heard the news that it's history—and hustle through a hailstorm of rice into a waiting limo that will whisk them off to Nomahegan Park for a photo session by the lake.

Someone shuts the door behind them and the limo pulls away. Dave and Julie wave out the back window until the well-wishers recede into specks, then turn around and look at each other, disoriented for a few seconds by the sudden silence and privacy.

"You okay?" she asks, reaching out to knock a few grains of Uncle Ben's out of his hair. She's still clutching her bouquet, wearing so much makeup it reminds him of seeing her backstage at one of the high-school musicals she used to perform in. For some reason, he hadn't noticed this in the church.

"I think so. How about you?"

She looks down at her lap, smoothing one hand over the billowy fabric of her skirt, and gives a soft laugh.

"I can't believe you're my *husband*," she says, grimacing at the strangeness of the word.

"Scary, huh?"

"It's not that. It's just that you've been my boyfriend for so long, it's hard to think of you as anything else."

"I'll consider it a promotion."

The limo follows the same route their school bus used to take to Harding High. Dave gazes out the tinted window at the modest houses lining the road, the small, well-tended lawns. Except for a couple of older guys washing their cars, the world seems deserted. Now it's Dave's turn to laugh.

"What?" she says.

He shakes his head. "I'm finally doing it."

"Doing what?"

"My teenage fantasy," he explains. "Riding through town in a limousine."

"See that?" she tells him. "You should have married me a long time ago."

The photographer's a moonlighting high-school English teacher with perfectionist tendencies. He seems flummoxed by the late-afternoon light, and keeps herding his subjects from one lakeside location to another to reshoot the entire series of group portraits.

Until now, Dave has never stopped to consider the number of possible combinations and permutations hidden inside the average wedding party, but it turns out to be way more than he ever could have imagined. They've allotted forty-five minutes for the session, but an hour and fifteen minutes into it, the end is nowhere in sight. Dave's face hurts from smiling so much, and he can't help envying the less important guests, already trickling into the Westview, enjoying the open bar and whatever music Rockin' Randy is providing for their listening pleasure. He watches as the photographer's assistant poses Julie, her sisters, and her parents for yet another Muller family portrait.

"Come on!" the photographer cajoles, studying them through his viewfinder. "This is a happy occasion, right?"

All five of them show their teeth at once. Claire and Melanie peel off, and the assistant rearranges Julie, Jack, and Dolores into a suitable Bride and Her Parents tableau. Dave turns away from the picture to stare vacantly at a softball game in the distance. The batter strokes a single up the middle, and the whole field explodes into motion. Just then Glenn detaches himself from the cluster of ushers nearby and taps him on the shoulder. His face is ominously pale, a bit panicky. It's a look Dave remembers well from the Talent Show fiasco so many years ago.

"Uh, listen," he mumbles. "I kind of have to split."

"How come?"

Glenn shifts his gaze from Dave's face to the ground.

"I'm not quite done with my toast. I need some quiet time to polish it up."

Dave lays his hand on his Best Man's shoulder. "You're not gonna disappear on me, are you?"

Glenn looks up, neither surprised nor offended by the question, and shakes his head.

"Not tonight," he says, forcing a smile to signal his resolve. "I'm in this till the bitter end."

"I'm counting on you."

"Don't worry. I'll catch you at the reception."

Glenn starts off for the parking lot, walking a little too fast, like a criminal trying to make an inconspicuous getaway. Dave's wondering if he's going to have to deputize another Best Man when the photographer's assistant calls out for him.

"Groom," she says.

He turns around and sees Mr. and Mrs. Muller waiting for him in the grassy clearing by the lake. They look dazed in their pretty clothes, a bit wilted; Dolores's cotton-candy bouffant appears to be in the early stages of a collapse. Dutifully, Dave takes his place between them, waiting for Julie to step in and complete the picture. Instead she hangs back, off to one side with her sisters and the rest of the bridal party, as the assistant adjusts his chin and straightens his boutonniere.

"What about the bride?" he asks.

"It's just us," Mr. Muller informs him.

Surprised by this information, Dave reluctantly snakes an arm around each of his in-laws. Mrs. Muller tenses beneath his touch, and all at once, Dave knows that the three of them are all thinking about the same thing. *They've seen my penis!* Before he can stop himself, he finds himself wondering if Dolores was impressed or if she somehow found him lacking. The photographer looks up, clearly dissatisfied.

"Yo, people," he says, "can we at least pretend?"

They're so late for the reception, Dave barely has time
to pause in front of the black velvet directory sign in the
lobby of the Westview—*Muller-Raymond, Black Forest
Room, 2nd Floor.* The wedding party has assembled in
double file at the top of the stairway, under the supervi-
sion of the tall maitre d' whose name Dave doesn't actually know, despite the fact that they've worked together
any number of times.

The introductions begin almost immediately, Margaret
and Paul breaking off from the larger group and entering
the banquet room to a smattering of polite applause.
Buzzy and Melanie go next, followed by Chuck and
Claire. The ritual feels both familiar and weird; Dave's
used to experiencing it from the other side of the door,
strumming the chords to the same bouncy Spyro Gyra
instrumental that's playing right now . . . *Wait a minute,*
he thinks. Something peculiar is afoot. The music he's
hearing is live, and the MC is most definitely not Rockin'
Randy. It's Artie, speaking in the unctuous School-of-
Broadcasting-tone that never fails to grate on Dave's
nerves no matter how many times he hears it: "And how
about a warm Westview welcome for our lovely Maid of
Honor, Miss Tammi Cullen, and our *outstanding* Best
Man, Misss-ter Glenn Stella!"

For a second or two, Dave feels like he's dreaming,
like he's going to walk through the door and see himself
onstage with the Wishbones, working his own wedding
from both sides of the fence, when it occurs to him that
Artie has somehow managed to assemble a full-fledged
band, despite the unavailability of himself, Buzzy, and
possibly Ian. Unable to suppress his curiosity on this
score, he extricates his hand from Julie's and attempts to
poke his head into the banquet room, only to be restrained
by the maitre d'.

"Come on," the guy tells him. "You know better than that."

Defeated, Dave retreats to the back of the line and listens to the loud ovation that follows the announcement of his parents.

"What happened to Randy?" he whispers.

"He's got the flu," Julie informs him, as her own parents' names are called. "It was really great of Artie to fill in on such short notice. He's not charging anything, so we're actually going to save five hundred dollars."

"How come no one told me?"

"And NOW," Artie continues, "the couple you've all been waiting for—"

"You're on," the maitre d' says, pushing them toward the doorway.

"Here we go," Julie tells him, squeezing his hand as they step forward.

"Mr. and Mrs. Dave Raymond!"

Dave's first impression, as they make their way through a tunnel of photographers toward a clear spot in the middle of the dance floor, is of pure chaos. Flashbulbs explode like fireworks at the edges of his vision. Heads appear and disappear. Hands wave and clap. Except for his mother crying and his father looking lost in thought, he can't really make out individual faces, just a welcoming blur of smiles everywhere he looks.

Behind and above the throng, he sees the band. They're the Wishbones and not the Wishbones: Artie faking it on guitar, Stan holding the fort on drums, Alan Zelack, of all people, manning the bass, and eighty-two-year-old Walter, formerly of the Heartstring Orchestra, banging on the keyboard. They sound exactly like what they are, a bunch of good musicians who aren't used to playing with one another. The overall effect is sloppy but exuberant, and Dave can't help feeling a little jealous. He has to fight off a powerful impulse to break free of Julie, jump onstage, and join them.

Dave's always been self-conscious about his dancing, but he and Julie manage to kick off the festivities with a respectable senior prom shuffle to "Stand By Me," which Zelack delivers with enough grimacing, clench-fisted, Michael Bolton–style passion to propel him to the final round of *Star Search*.

"He's good," Julie whispers.

"You think so?"

Dave's not so sure. Despite Zelack's obvious gifts, Dave's always been a little put off by his flashy, egotistical style. Watching him in action makes Dave more certain than ever that he did the right thing by finally declining to join Shiny Angels, a decision Zelack accepted with gracious regret. Nonetheless, Dave's flattered by his presence, which adds an unmistakable touch of star quality to the proceedings, and curious as to how Artie finagled him into doing it.

He and Julie separate for the second song, each linking up with their opposite-sex parents for the Bride-and-Her-Father dance. Whether at Julie's request or the inspiration of someone in the band, "Daddy's Little Girl" has been scrapped in favor of the still-sappy, but definitely preferable, "Turn Around."

"You're not very good at this," his mother informs him as they stumble over each other's feet. "You'd think a musician would have a better sense of rhythm."

"Thanks for the support, Mom."

"Julie's a good dancer," she continues, thinking out loud. "I guess it's just something you're born with."

A great sense of relief descends upon him when the song ends and he can finally take his seat at the head table, his dancing dues paid. His butt's barely made contact with the chair, though, when dozens of people begin tapping forks and knives against glasses, expressing a collective demand for the bride and groom to kiss. Julie looks at him and shrugs. They lean together and touch lips, holding the pose for a few seconds to appease the crowd.

"Where's the Best Man?" Artie asks through the microphone. "It's time for the champagne toast."

Heads turn in every direction, scouring the room, but Glenn is nowhere in sight. *Uh oh,* Dave thinks, but just at that moment, Glenn appears in the main doorway, looking pale but determined, and threads his way to the stage. The glass-clinking starts again before he gets there, and Julie responds to it before Dave does, grabbing hold of his head with both hands and planting a kiss on him that almost makes him forget where he is. She's doing something strange and marvelous with her tongue, a maneuver he's never experienced in a decade and a half of kissing her, as if to let him know that she's still got a few new tricks up her sleeve.

When she finally lets him up for air, something totally unexpected has occurred. Glenn's onstage all right, but he doesn't look like a Best Man preparing to deliver a toast. He appears to have been transformed into a member of the band, his pale blue Stratocaster riding high across his chest, an arrangement he swears by, though it looks both nerdy and unwieldy to Dave.

"I'm not really very good at public speaking," he says, "so if you don't mind, I'd like to toast Dave and Julie with a song."

Just like that, the band breaks into the opening of "Bell-Bottom Blues," Glenn picking out the arpeggios with studied casualness, like standing up in front of a roomful of people and playing his guitar is nothing new or frightening to him, like he hasn't just broken through the wall that's been holding him back for half of his life. The wedding guests listen politely, not quite sure what to make of the musical toast, but Dave is riveted. During Glenn's flawless solo, he feels the lump from church rising back into his throat. Under the table he grabs hold of Julie's hand.

"I can't believe this is happening," he tells her.

"I know," she says. "Thank God for Prozac."

When the song is over, Glenn raises a glass of champagne and wishes the happy couple a lifetime of health and happiness.

"Here's to you," he concludes. "Love's a precious thing."

All around the room, people touch glasses and drink to Dave and Julie as the band, still in a Clapton mode, roars into the power chord intro of "Cocaine." Glenn's inside it now, making faces and moving his head around like he's having problems with his neck, and a new kind of energy enters the room, as palpable as a cool breeze. Dave wants to watch, but Julie's already out of her chair and yanking on his arm.

"Come on," she says, glancing in the direction of the dance floor, which is suddenly the scene of frantic activity, not all of it pretty. "I love this song."

Dave's been to enough weddings to know the difference between a good one and a bad one, and this is a good one. You can tell from the dancing. Even when the food arrives, lots of people don't want to sit down. The floor doesn't clear until the band finally decides to take a break, after playing for well over an hour. Dave understands their reluctance to close the set: when it's happening like this, you just want to keep riding the wave.

He and Julie don't really get a chance to eat. Instead they drift from table to table, chatting up the guests and posing for one picture after another. Everywhere he goes, someone's tugging at his cuff, telling him he's a lucky man, he's looking sharp, Julie's beautiful, the food's great, does he want a drink? The maitre d' has a quick question. His mother wants to know if he remembers Mrs. Pollo, their landlady from the house on Franklin Street, which they moved out of in 1969. Ian tosses him a trivia

softball, the answer to which is "Pure Prairie League."
His cousin Lori's new boyfriend—a guy named Butchie
with a gleam in his eyes that makes you want to keep
your distance—keeps pestering him to set up an appointment to discuss his insurance options. ("You're married,
dude," is how Butchie likes to put it. "You've got some
heavy life issues to consider.") Everybody wants a piece
of him. It's exhausting and exciting at the same time, and
Dave thinks that this is how it must feel to run for president—like attending your own wedding night after night
after night.

He's happy to see that the musicians have been given
their own table in the main hall, and are being treated as
guests rather than employees. (This makes a lot of sense,
considering that Stan and Artie were invited anyway.)
With the exception of Zelack's fiancée, the occupants of
the table are all male, the original imbalance made all the
more conspicuous by the added presence of Buzzy and
Ian, both of whom have drifted over to hobnob with the
band. Artie's the first one out of his seat, grabbing Dave
with one arm and Julie with the other, pulling them
against his chest in a sweaty, three-way hug. His guard's
down and his cologne's working overtime; he seems happier than Dave's seen him in a long time.

"Were you surprised?" he asks excitedly, grabbing
hold of Dave's lapels and butting foreheads with him. "I
bet we surprised the shit out of you, right?"

"It's great of you to fill in like this," Julie tells him.
"I don't know what we would've done without you."

"This is not a job for a DJ," Artie explains, pinching
Dave's cheek with his thumb and forefinger. "This is a
job for your friends who love you."

"You sound good," Dave says, reaching up to separate
Artie's hand from his face. "It's quite a lineup you put
together."

"A fuckin' All-Star team," Artie tells him. "You
gonna sit in with us next set?"

Before Dave can answer, Zelack intervenes, wrapping him in an embrace that falls somewhere between a hug and a headlock.

"Congratulations!" he says. "Bet you didn't expect to see *me* tonight."

"I didn't," Dave says, his words disappearing into the crook of Zelack's arm. "But I'm glad you could make it."

"Wouldn't miss it," Zelack assures him, releasing Dave to perform a thorough, two-handed spot-check of his hairdo, flicking it into place like a professional. "I was touched when Artie asked me. I mean that."

"By the way," Dave tells him after an awkward pause, "I'm sorry about the Shiny Angels thing. This just doesn't seem like the right time for me. Especially if it's going to involve touring."

"I hear you." Zelack casts a quick glance over his shoulder at Monica, who's inspecting the splint on Buzzy's hand with a look of profound sympathy. "I'm going through a similar situation myself. The whole project's up in the air."

Dave nods. Zelack shrugs.

"You guys sound good up there," Dave tells him.

Zelack grins. "Not bad for two rehearsals, huh?" He leans closer, speaking in a conspiratorial tone. "Your friend Glenn, man—"

"I know," says Dave.

"The guy can play."

As if on cue, Glenn wanders over from the bar with Buzzy's wife, JoAnn, who's looking cranky but elegant in a little black dress and fishnet stockings. Both of them have their hands full of drinks, but Glenn stops on his way to the table for a word with Dave.

"Speak of the devil," says Zelack.

"You're kicking ass," Dave tells him.

Glenn's face colors with embarrassment.

"Really?" he asks.

"Really," Dave replies.

"How's it feel?" asks Zelack.

Glenn thinks it over for a few seconds, pondering the triangle of glasses pressed between his hands, each with a wedge of lime floating on top. Then he looks up, his face breaking into a broad, incredulous smile.

"I had no idea," he says. "How come nobody told me?"

Dave and Zelack watch as Glenn delivers the drinks to the table, placing one each in front of Walter and Stan, who seem to be locked in a tense discussion, and keeping the third for himself. He takes a long swig, smacks his lips in satisfaction, and surveys the room, grinning at nothing in particular.

"Now there's a happy man," Zelack observes.

"No kidding," says Dave. "Wait'll he hears about sex."

Ian sidles up to him at the bar and explains that the bouquet toss has been rigged in Tammi's favor. He asks Dave to send the garter his way, if it's not too much trouble.

"Don't worry," Dave tells him. "Just stand in front. Everyone else will run away."

"I bought her a ring last week," Ian confides. "As soon as I find a job I'm gonna pop the question."

"Wow. That was quick."

"She's the one. There's no sense trying to fight it."

Dave grins. "Now you tell me."

"I'm grateful," Ian says, placing a sincere hand on Dave's shoulder. "I hope this stuff with the band doesn't get in the way of our friendship."

"You gotta do what you gotta do," Dave says with a shrug. "Don't you miss it?"

Ian looks back at the stage. The guys are cooking now, cranking out a raucous version of "After Midnight." Buzzy's up there with them, singing background vocals and shaking a tambourine with his good hand. The floor's packed; even Dave's father is out there, doing a strange dance that consists of standing on one leg and wiggling his raised foot in the air. Dave's hands are itching for a guitar.

"Not really," Ian tells him.

After the bouquet and garter ritual runs its tedious course, Zelack invites Dave to join the band for a couple of numbers.

"If your lovely wife doesn't mind," he adds with a smirk.

Dave looks at Julie. Her tiara's gone and her hair is loose. Her shoes came off an hour ago, and her face is flushed from close-to-nonstop-dancing and several glasses of wine. Envelopes full of money litter the table in front of her. She wouldn't object if he said they were moving to Africa.

"Go ahead," she tells him. "Have your fun."

Something changes when Dave gets onstage. The band's been hot all night, but now something clicks and they rise to a whole new level. Everything tightens up at once; the ragged edges disappear. It's as if a puzzle has found its missing piece.

He can feel it as soon as they launch into "I Saw Her Standing There." Dave understands what's happening: he's a unifying force, the link between the Wishbones' nucleus of Artie and Stan and the new center of gravity occupied by Zelack and Glenn and Walter. The rest of the guys understand it too, and the knowledge is passed around in a series of surprised smiles and nods. Dave and Glenn trade solos with the telepathy of twin brothers; he and Zelack mesh on the harmonies like they've been singing together for years.

The audience seems to notice something as well. The conga line starts to form midway through the second number—a suitably festive take on "When the Volcano Blows"—and attracts new members like a magnet as it snakes through the room. Julie's leading the charge, followed by Tammi and Ian and Dave's own mother, who seems intimately familiar with the lyrics, even though Dave knows for a fact that she doesn't own any Jimmy Buffett records. His father's back toward the end of the line, hands around the waist of Buzzy's wife, the only person Dave has ever seen who can look morose on a conga line. Buzzy himself is bringing up the rear, holding onto Dolores Muller with his bad hand and waving a bottle of champagne around with his good one.

Not wanting to lose the momentum, the band segues right into Bob Marley's "Stir It Up." Dave's never really mastered the reggae rhythm, but Glenn has it down. After a few bars, Dave stops trying to keep up on guitar and concentrates instead on singing the low harmonies. Zelack's voice is so high and pure above his, Dave almost feels like he's levitating on the chorus.

Something's happening. Glenn and Dave and Zelack keep trading these quick glances of amazement and disbelief, the kind of glance that's as much a question as it is a confirmation. *What's this all about?* they seem to be asking one another. *Is this what I think it is?* Dave remembers sharing looks not so different with Gretchen in this very same room not so long ago, experiencing a similar suspicion that his life might be about to change in a very important way.

They've already shifted into "Havin' a Party" when the conga line stops short in front of the stage, like a train waiting in the station. This unexpected pause wreaks havoc with the back of the line, which begins to collapse in on itself like an accordion. Julie's smiling happily, waving at him to put down his guitar and come join the dancers, but all Dave can do is shake his head. He wants to tell her that something beautiful is happening up here, something he can't let go of, but as is the case with most of life's important matters, neither the time nor the place is right for saying what needs to be said. Julie's smile starts to melt into a more complicated expression, not quite a pout but something in that neighborhood. Dave doesn't want to upset her, so he makes his way to the edge of the stage, as far as his cord will stretch, and raises one finger in the air.

"One more song," he tells her, not quite sure if he's making a plea or a promise. "Give me one more song."

BEGIN TO EXIT

HERE

"Funny and touching."
—*New York Times Book Review*

A novel
of the
wayward
press

Kurt Clausen has worked as a salad girl, a porn salesman, and—perhaps most reluctantly—a journalist. In this "terminally irreverent" (*Richmond News-Leader*) novel, he finds himself taking on everyone from his editor and his girlfriend to the fundamentalists and vegetarians covered on his beat—and along the way, learns some surprising (and hilarious) lessons about life, love, and the press.

by John Welter

A Berkley Signature Edition __ 0-425-16262-1/$6.99